SHALOM SAP

Easily, Camellion ducked an assault rifle a command swung at his head and shot another Israeli coming at him with a double-edged fighting dagger, the blade painted black for night use. *This is almost as bad as going into a bar in Phoenix on a Saturday night!* Twice more the Auto Mags roared, the .357 137-grain projectiles almost lifting two commandos off their feet and killing them instantly, the big, brutal bullets stabbing into the midsections of the two men who had been trying to come in at Follmer to the CIA man's right.

Follmer's Astra barked and another commando, pulling a 9mm Browning from a shoulder holster, went down, his mouth slack, blood spreading from a burn hole in his chest, although the wine red on the camo desert fatigues could not be readily seen.

"Shalom, sap!" murmured the Death Merchant, jumping back and to the left to avoid a knife swipe and pulling the trigger of the left Auto Mag, the weapon jerking in his hand. The Israeli was so close that Camellion could see his young face, a face smudged with dark camo paint, a face that dissolved in a miniexplosion of flesh and muscle, bone and blood from the force of the .357 magnum projectile that broke apart his skull and brain.

THE DEATH MERCHANT SERIES:

53 in the incredible adventures of the

DEATH MERCHANT

THE JUDAS SCROLLS

by Joseph Rosenberger

PINNACLE BOOKS　　　　　　　**NEW YORK**

DEATH MERCHANT #53: THE JUDAS SCROLLS

Copyright © 1982 by Joseph Rosenberger

An original Pinnacle Books edition, published for the first time anywhere.

First printing, December 1982

ISBN: 0-523-41660-1

Cover illustration by Dean Cate

Printed in the United States of America

PINNACLE BOOKS, INC.
1430 Broadway
New York, New York 10018

Christmas Prayer—1960**

The final soldier with his
Finger on the ultimate button
For the new slaughter of the innocents
Is innocent.

Herod had the dignity of choice
And a worthy object.
What are a few innocent babes
When one might catch a God?

There is no God among us,
Perhaps not even a saint.
Slim pickings, button pusher.
Don't push!

From No Poem for Fritz
by Patrick O'Connor

**It's the same in 1982.

"There will be only two Popes to follow Pope Paul II. This will be the end of the reign of Popes.

There will be extreme persecution of the Roman Church. The last Pope, Peter the Roman, will lead his flock amid many tribulations. The City of the Seven Hills shall vanish, and the Great Judge will come to judge the people."

De Labore Solis
By Saint Malachy

Special Adviser
Colonel George Ellis
Le Mercenaire

THE
JUDAS SCROLLS

CHAPTER ONE

Strolling lazily along Al-Salt Street, one of the main thorough-fares of Amman, Richard Camellion was amazed at how the capital of Jordan had changed since his last visit many years before. The city was larger. There was more activity—*Even at night. But it's only eight-thirty.*—so much so that a first-time visitor from the States would wonder how such a modern, dynamic city could flourish in such a poor (by American standards) Arab state that was about the size of the United States's Indiana and had a population of less than 2 million, of which slightly more than 550,000 lived in Amman.[1]

Modern Amman was built partly in a narrow valley through which flowed the Zerqa River and partly on steep hills that enclosed it on two sides. A wonderful city for tourists, too, thought the Death Merchant. There was the Roman theater, seating 6,000 people, the Odeon, a smaller theater, and the Jordan Archaeological Museum on Citadel Hill. The museum had a rare collection of Nabataean pottery, relics of the wars between the Moslems and Crusaders, and local artifacts dating back to 180,000 B.C.—*Which is a lot of mileage!* On Jebel Hussein were the ruins of a Temple of Hercules, built by the Romans in the center of the Citadel, which was already an antiquity in their time. And a pretty city, most of its buildings of

---

[1] Arabic: Àmmān—one of the oldest cities in the world. In biblical Hebrew: Rabbah, or Rabbat Bene Ammon, meaning "the Great"— or "Capital"—"City of the Sons of Ammon." Amman was the "royal city" taken by King David's general Joab—2 Sam. 12:26— about 1000 B.C.

Ptolemy Philadelphus of Egypt, who rebuilt the city in 265–63 B.C., named it Philadelphia.

Amman is the capital of the present-day Hashemite Kingdom of Jordan and of al-Asimah muhafazah (governorate). The Arab name for Jordan is Al Mamlaka al Urduniya al Hashemiyah.

gleaming white limestone. Nearby quarries furnished beautiful colored marble for floors and decorative touches.

In spite of all the lights from cars and neon signs on the wide street the Death Merchant could see the full moon to the west, a large white yellow orb—*Waiting! It's a stalking moon!*

Only a fool lies to himself. A realist always knows who he is and lives with what he is. Camellion didn't like to admit it, he was superstitious. Full moons always meant trouble of the worst kind.

"I thought it was only in motion pictures that intelligence agents met in parks?" murmured Kelly Dillard, who was walking next to Camellion and was between him and the road. "I would have chosen a restaurant, anyplace that has a crowd. Anywhere but a park!"

"Maybe our contact has been reading too many James Bond paperbacks," Camellion said, giving Dillard a quick sideways glance. Dillard, a clandestine specialist, was very broad in the chest; although he was not quite five feet eight inches tall, his lack of stature made him seem even wider. Dillard had thinning brown hair, a deeply trenched, tanned face, and an unmistakable cast of authority, while his air of total competence was, at times, disquieting, even annoying.

The Death Merchant still had to see how good Dillard was at the merciless business of deceiving, deception, and Death, even if Courtland Grojean had reassured Camellion that "Dillard can think of almost as many ways to kill a man as you can. He is highly experienced. He won't let you down."

"I prefer Lestern Vernon Cole," Camellion had insisted.

The suave chief of the CIA's covert section—always more slippery than a greased pig, but always diplomatic—had readily agreed. "So would I, were I you. I can't give you Cole. He's busy in Central America." Grojean had then taken another tack, speaking the way a father would speak to a son. "Really, Camellion, you needn't be concerned about the unique abilities of Dillard. I also give you my assurance about Robert Follmer and Philip LaHann. Those two know every back alley in the Middle East. They've been in Jordan half a dozen times over the years and always on 'sneak-in' assignments. The Jordanian D-4 don't even know they exist—Dillard either, for that matter."

The three are here with me in Jordan. Let's see how good they are.

Kelly Dillard said, "Hussein Park is only four blocks from here." His low voice became mocking. "Of course you realize what will happen if the police stop us for some reason? The

2

operation will go down the sands and we'll be kicked out of the country as being personae non gratae.''

"It seems to me," mused the Death Merchant, "that there are a lot of public conveniences named Hussein. His Majesty seems to have a good thing going for him."

"Hussein has. Don't kid yourself about Jordan being a moderate Arab state. Hussein and his family own the entire country. His rule is actually a quiet, unofficial dictatorship. People who get in the way and are considered dangerous by Department 4 simply disappear. Not even their relatives ask questions—at least not openly.''

The Death Merchant wasn't concerned about the weapons that he and Dillard carried. Underneath their suits and topcoats the Hawes/Sig-Sauer D.A. auto-pistols were not noticeable; the Walther P-38Ks in Safariland ankle holsters might as well have been invisible—*Unless we're stopped and searched. I'm not about to let us be searched. If the regular police found all this armament on us—and the transmitter—they'd turn us over to the Department-4 sadists, and Dillard and I too would simply vanish.*

Grateful that the temperature was only forty-six degrees Fahrenheit,[2] or their light topcoats would have been out of place, the two "consulting engineers of Ryan, Colt & Webber Construction Company, Inc." turned the corner and started down Hisrudi Street.

The Death Merchant, who was not about to enter Hussein Park as an optimist, carried an ultraminiaturized cycle-signal transmitter, a 300 milliwatt unit that operated into a 60-ohm load, the power furnished by two 9.6 volt batteries.

At this very moment, Phil LaHann and Marie Dine were picking up the pulses with the interferometer receiver and were keeping track of Camellion and Dillard with the Relative Direction Meter. It wasn't that the two Company people didn't know that the destination of Camellion and Dillard was the water fountain fifty feet north of the "Circle," the center of the park in which there was a tall statue of the king, Hussein ibn-Talal. LaHann and Dine were backups. If necessary, it was their Volkswagen Quantum station wagon that would carry Camellion and Dillard to safety—if fireworks started—if Camellion and Dillard were lucky.

"Phil and Marie should be in position on the Street of the

[2]The idea that most Arab nations are all sand and heat is erroneous. For example, in November the average low temperature in Amman is fifty degrees.

3

Palms by now, wouldn't you think?'' remarked Dillard. In step, the two men crossed the street when the light turned green.

"They had better be," Camellion said gruffly. "This could well be another Jonestown disaster. This meeting in a park is carrying security beyond the point of ridiculousness. We happen to be on a very special mission. We should not be engaged in anything that might even faintly draw attention to ourselves."

"Don't bring your troubles to me." Dillard shrugged. "I agree with you. Since the contact came into Jordan by way of Aqaba,[3] no doubt he's in the country illegally. I can understand why he doesn't want to take the chance of being seen going into our embassy. He still has to make contact with the Station. He could have relayed the message to us through Anderson. Department 4 wouldn't give us a second glance. The secret police would expect us to go to the American Embassy. We're here in the open."

"It's the Fox,"[4] said Camellion. "He's more cautious than a married man going into a whorehouse. I've seen this kind of thing happen before. It's part of the tradecraft, something we have to take in stride."

Nine more minutes, a short distance, and they were entering Hussein Park—a half a block square, a fairly well-lighted area of white poplar and pistachio trees. On the ground were privet and other shrubs and oak ferns.

The Death Merchant's eyes were everywhere, probing the dark shadows, analyzing the darkness. He noticed that Dillard was relaxed and walked easily, and he could see that the man's eyes were constantly on the move, especially when anyone passed them going in the opposite direction. A lot of survival always depends on pure chance and the fine-tuning of one's mental warning signal. You can spin around and look at a man or woman who has just passed you on the sidewalk, but you can't see behind every tree and bush and shrub.

Only a couple, a man and a woman, and a lone man passed them by the time they were halfway up the southwest walk that terminated at the Circle.

"How do you want to do it?" Kelly Dillard was impatient. Yet as he spoke, his eyes did not deviate from probing the flanks and the forward section of the park. "Both of us go to the water

---

[3]Jordan does have twelve-miles of coastland on the Gulf of al-'Aqabah. This is where Aqaba—in English—the nation's only port, is located.

[4]Grojean.

fountain, or what? You're the honcho in charge. I have the cigar that's supposed to be lighted three times as a signal. I'll go, if you want.''

"Don't be so anxious," warned Camellion. "Keep your eyes on the trees to the right of the fountain; I'll watch the trees to the left. Any trap would have to be a circular one.''

He glanced up at the moon again. The damn thing was still there—big, bright, bold. —

They were only fifty feet or so from the Circle when Camellion spotted a man's head pull back behind a tree that was south of the northeast sidewalk that ended at the corner of al-Sahadi Street and Street of the Palms. The four sidewalks in the park formed an *X,* with the Circle in the center of the *X.*

Almost simultaneously, the sharp-eyed Dillard caught a brief movement to his right—a man's pulling his leg behind a tree, the white poplar south of the southeast sidewalk that ended (or started, depending whether one was entering or leaving the park) at the corner of al-Sahadi and ibn-Abdullah streets.

"I just saw the contact," Dillard said in a pleased tone. "He's behind a tree south of the Circle and of the southeast sidewalk. I would say about twenty feet due south of the water fountain.''

"In that case, the contact is either twins or else he's brought a friend," Camellion suggested facetiously. "I saw a man pull his head back behind a tree at 2:30 from the east side of the Circle. Don't break step. We're only out for a stroll. You're sure you saw someone?''

"I'm positive. It was his leg." Dillard's voice was steady, not showing any nervousness, his lack of fear pleasing the Death Merchant. "I saw him clearly by the light from the circle, at about 5:00. We can't turn around and go back to Hasrudi. We'd tip them off.''

They were almost to the southwest side of the Circle as Camellion whispered, "We'll stroll around the Circle to the left. Once we're on the north side we'll move fast—run to the north and take cover behind the first trees we come to. If the men are enemies—there must be more than two—they'll react, one way or another.

"Surround and capture," Dillard said. "What else?''

"And kill us if they can't!''

They came to the Circle, a stone wall fifty feet in diameter and three feet high. The inside of the wall was packed with hard earth, the sides inclining upward to the large black marble block in the center, on which rested the twenty-foot-tall red marble statue of King Hussein.

5

Calmly, calculatingly, the Death Merchant and Kelly Dillard walked around the west side of the Circle, gradually, with each step, moving to the north side.

"Now!" Camellion said. "RUN!"

They raced north from the circle for almost thirty feet, Camellion zigging and zagging with such speed that he almost collided with a poplar as he got down behind it. Dillard braked, almost slipped on the grass, and jumped behind a large cypress that looked so ancient it must have been planted when God was a child! In an instant both men had pulled their Hawes/Sig-Sauer pistols and were thumbling off the safety catches.

Four loud gunshots cracked the stillness of the night, several slugs thudding into the tree protecting Camellion, one of the shots sounding very close, less than twenty-five feet to the east. Even more projectiles stung the tree harboring Dillard, only six feet from the Death Merchant, who whispered, "We'll give them a few shots to draw their fire. I'm going to try an old trick."

"We must do this fast," Dillard cautioned. "The police will investigate in one damn big hurry!"

Camellion and Dillard shoved their Hawes/Sig-Sauers around the sides of the trees and triggered off two quick rounds, firing toward the east, the roar of their own autoloaders creating more police-bringing noise. At once the enemy—whoever they were—answered. This time six or seven pistols cracked!

"OHHH-OH-OHohhhhhhhh!" Camellion yelled loudly, letting his wail trail off in pretended agony, as if he had been struck by a bullet.

He and Dillard heard a voice call out, "You, to the south! Have your men close in on the other man. Kill him. We must leave and get to the cars!"

The language used by the man was *Russian!*

Pig farmers! DAMN! Camellion dropped flat to his stomach, moved his head and gun arm to the right of the tree, glanced over at Dillard, and saw that he had done the same. *Good! He's experienced in this kind of business.*

It wasn't exactly a surprise when Camellion and Dillard saw two men slink from behind trees seventy feet to the southeast, at the 4:00 position, two more from trees at 3:00, another man from a cypress at 6:00, and a sixth gunman from behind a tree only twenty feet directly east of the Death Merchant's position.

Camellion and Dillard fired, Camellion first taking out the man twenty feet to the east of him. The 9mm jacketed hollow point projectile struck Wafi Teloria just below the chest bone,

6

knocked him back on his feet,[5] and slammed him down as though he had been hit in the head with a twenty-pound sledgehammer.

Dillard's first bullet chopped down Rudolf Lyalin, a KGB *Mokryye Dela* ("blood-wet affair") agent, who was one of the men moving from the 4:00 position, while the Death Merchant's second projectile bored into Ali Zadok, the Jordanian gunman who thought he was closing in from the 6:00 position, but not before Zadok, firing by instinct, had gotten off a slug from his M-92 Beretta. No luck! The 9mm Parabellum bullet missed Camellion's head, but by only half an inch, the hunk of metal coming so close it almost left a burn line on the side of the Death Merchant's houndstooth check wool hat.

"Good bye! Farewell! Be damned!" Smiling, the Death Merchant fired, the gilded metal bullet slicing into the groin of Sirry Kubeisy, the second slob from the 4:00 position. The fat Kubeisy yelled in pain and fear, dropped the Heckler & Koch P9S pistol, and sank unconscious to the ground.

Seeing their men whacked out by the most accurate pistol fire they had ever seen, Andrew Kholivshek and Sergei Chogli, the other two blood-wet-affair assassination agents, began firing wildly at Camellion and Dillard, Chogli using a Vitmorkin machine pistol, Kholivshek firing a DM Makarov.

Chogli's first two 9mm slugs came at the Death Merchant— one stinging the dead grass and splattering the left side of his face with dirt, the second going through the crown of his hat and knocking it off. At the same time, the Death Merchant fired at Boudi Sirkis, one of the men moving from the 3:00 position. The bullet zipped into the Jordanian, punched him high in the chest, and pulled from him a high-pitched scream before he spun and went down.

Dillard fired at Abdul Burarrak, the second man who had come from behind a pistachio tree at the 3:00 position. He missed. The bullet hit only bark. The instant the firing had begun, Burarrak turned and raced back to one of the trees, reaching safety a second before Dillard triggered his Sig auto.

The Death Merchant snuggled back behind the tree and quickly

[5]An individual struck by a bullet is not actually knocked to the ground by the impact of the bullet, although the victim does appear to be slammed down. What really happens is a muscular reaction to *nerve trauma* caused by shock and damage from the bullet. The victim is not knocked down by the sheer energy of the bullet's delivery.

shoved a full magazine into his Hawes/Sig-Sauer D.A. Dillard also jerked back behind his tree and reloaded as Sergei Chogli switched the Vitmorkin MP to full automatic fire and raked Camellion and Dillard's former position with a full sixteen rounds, the machine pistol sounding like a mini submachine gun. All the sounds found were trees and grass.

Dumb, damned pig farmers! They're all six feet lower than the bellybutton of a cockroach—if a cockroach had a bellybutton!

Holding the Sig Fed style, his left hand grasping the edge of his right hand, the Death Merchant fired the entire clip of eight rounds, spacing out the slugs—a cloudburst blast.

Chogli and Kholivshek now knew that, while they had thought they were going to capture or kill a wildcat, they were tangling with a tiger—two tigers, because Kelly Dillard was also firing off a full magazine in the direction of the KGB agents.

Lying prone and well concealed, the two blood-wet-affair agents knew it was time to retreat and get to the cars on al-Sahadi Street. Nine-millimeter slugs sliced the air and stung the ground all around them. There wasn't any way they could get to the two *Amerikanski* agents, and soon the Jordanian police would be arriving in force.

Abdul Burarrak, taking advantage of the firing directed at the two Russians, had already left his place of concealment and was moving backward, keeping the tree in front of him. He would only have to move thirty feet or so before he could turn and run. There was a large open space around the water fountain. Beyond, the trees and bushes were thicker and there wasn't any light. In the distance—police sirens.

Chogli and Kholivshek used the same tactic as Burarrak while they, too, moved east. So did the Death Merchant and Kelly Dillard, after reloading their Sigs, except that they moved west, quickly getting behind trees to their rear. They would move forty or fifty feet, then change course and race northeast in the darkness to the Street of the Palms—and to safety.

Camellion and Dillard were racing northeast when they heard loud firing from the southeast of their position, toward the southeast end of the park. One of the weapons was a submachine gun, another an automatic rifle, the rest pistols.

"It would appear that the fuzz has arrived and trapped our 'friends,'" Dillard said, the words staggering as he tried to catch his breath.

"We'll be next if we don't get the anvils off our feet," warned the Death Merchant. "Even with the station wagon, we could be in for serious trouble."

8

They were, which would become very obvious in another four minutes!

They reached a section of trees only twenty feet from the wide sidewalk, thirty feet from the narrow parkway and the road. There waited the Volkswagen station wagon, fifty feet west of the corner of al-Sahadi Street and the Street of the Palms. As Camellion and Dillard watched, two jeeps pulled up thirty feet behind the station wagon and twelve members of the Jordanian Administrative Police,[6] wearing "Faisal" caps and verdigris uniforms, began piling out. Each man carried either a Beretta M12 SMG or an FN-5041 automatic rifle.

Dillard made an ugly sound under his breath. "Those cops are the frosting on the cake—and it's all crap." His low voice was deadly calm. "They'll be coming in our direction. We can't duck 'em, and we're going to have to be damned good to get all twelve before one of them gets off a spray. Good God! Look!"

The police stood on the sidewalk checking their weapons, all but two, who started toward the Volkswagen. It was the last short walk of their lives. Marie Dine, the Amman Station's girl Friday,[7] opened the left front door and stepped out, her back to the policeman, one arm in front of her. Philip LaHann eased out on the driver's side.

Suddenly—the two cops were only eight feet from Marie Dine—the young woman spun around and triggered the Czech Vz61 Skorpion in her hands, the vicious little weapon, its metal-frame stock folded over the top of the weapon, the curved end of the stock fitted over the short barrel, spitting out a stream of 7.65mm (.32 cal.—ACP) projectiles in three-round bursts. Half a blink, and the top cops were as dead as two citizens of planet

---

[6] The Jordanian police force is divided into the Administrative Police—the regular police—the Judicial Police—drugs, aliens, serious crimes like murder, etc.—and the Auxiliary Police—accounts, budgets, equipment, public relations, etc. All three are under the control of the Jordanian Public Security Department, controlled by the Ministry of the Interior. The Chief of Police is the Director-General of Public Security—P.O. Box 935, Amman, Jordan. Department 4 is the "CIA" of Jordan. It is a special section of the Ministry of the Interior and has its own director. As of 1982, Mr. Rahamin Hudassi.

[7] Keeps records, doles out money, often acts as a radio operator; clerical duties at the Station. She always has top clearance. She's fired if caught testing a mattress with any of the male Company personnel connected with the station.

Earth could be. They sagged, their eyes wide open in shock, staring, the front of their uniforms ripped, torn, and dripping blood.

Caught completely unaware, the other ten didn't have one chance in a hundred trillion, mainly because Philip LaHann (who resembled Richard Nixon) was also firing, his Vz61-S on full automatic. In addition, each machine pistol was fitted with an extra-long magazine that held sixty rounds.

It was massacre to the nth degree! Shot to pieces, tiny bits of their uniforms flying off into space from the impact of the 7.65mm slugs stabbing into their bodies, the policemen went down in death faster than an Appalachian moonshiner running from an Alcohol, Tobacco and Firearms agent.

"Come on," Camellion urged. "Let's get to the car while we have the opportunity."

"Yeah, Phil and the broad will leave in minutes," Dillard said excitedly.

They raced across the dead grass toward the station wagon, the Death Merchant yelling, "DON'T FIRE! IT'S US!" at LaHann and Dine. LaHann had gotten back into the station wagon and started the motor. Dine was reloading the two Skorpions, LaHann and she oblivious—up to a point—of passing cars, whose drivers speeded up when they saw the mount of corpses on the sidewalk.

Camellion and Dillard raced from the trees, ran across the sidewalk and the parkway, and piled into the rear of the Volkswagen Quantum.

"You heard the firing from the east center of the park," Camellion said LaHann and Dine. "The police came in from al-Sahadi. They might be headed this way. Get the hell out of here!"

"I certainly didn't intend to stay to play chess!" LaHann said nervously. "From now on it's all luck."

"All I can say is that this is a poor way to spend an evening," Dillard said bitterly. "Christ! We walked right into it back there." He gave a little laugh. "Ironic! That's what this mission is all about—Jesus Christ and good old Judas!"

Without a word, Marie Dine handed the Death Merchant, sitting on the left, one of the Skorpions.

The station wagon shot from the curb. Right into a maelstrom, a razzle-dazzle of utter confusion. The intersection of the Street of the Palms and al-Sahadi Street was a four-way stop. On the Street of the Palms the light was red, and cars were moving normally north and south on al-Sahadi—including two police

10

jeeps heading north. One jeep had turned off Hasrudi Street and had joined one of the police vehicles that had stopped on al-Sahadi. Both jeeps had their sirens on and were moving fast.

LaHann didn't stop. He didn't slow down either. He gunned the engine and swerved like a madman between two cars, one coming from the south, the other from the north. The driver coming from the north jammed on his brakes, the rear end of his Audi skidding around to his left, but the car missed the speeding station wagon. The driver coming from the south just managed to miss the rear right side of the Volkswagen. Two other drivers, coming from the south, put on their brakes, their tires screaming in protest on the concrete.

The two drivers going north were lucky. The hail of 7.65mm slugs fired off by Camellion and Marie Dine from the Skorpion SMGs missed the two cars and flooded all over the two police jeeps. BANG! The front right tire on the first jeep exploded. Both windshields dissolved from the rain of slugs. Policemen screamed and yelled in pain and confusion. Within seconds the drivers of both jeeps were dead and the vehicles were out of control, one cutting to the left in front of a Honda Accord. The driver of the Honda didn't have time to even begin to put on the brakes. He slammed right into the left side of the first jeep with its five corpses and a sixth cop, who, in the rear seat, had not even been wounded, yet was helpless. He was catapulted from the rear seat and slammed to the pavement when the Honda overturned the jeep.

The second jeep veered to the right, its dead driver like a floppy doll behind the wheel, which was turning first to the right then to the left, as if being moved by invisible hands. The other five cops were also as limp as old rags, falling in all directions, back and forth, as though held in place by wires that would only reach so far.

The jeep missed the other vehicles as it turned at an angle to the left, struck the curb, and turned over, dumping out its cargo of corpses.

LaHann took the Volkswagen east on the Street of the Palms, dodging cars like the expert he was (he had once qualified to drive in the Datona 500).

"I'll go several blocks, turn off to the right, go south, hit the first alley, and slow down," he said in a loud voice, at the same time trying to steady the station wagon that was rocking from left to right. "Any objections?"

"We'll make it, if you don't wreck us—maybe!" muttered Kelly Dillard, doing his best not to fall against Camellion, who

11

had leaned over the front seat and was asking Marie Dine for another Skorpion magazine. It came to Dillard that Camellion was remarkably calm.

The Death Merchant was—for good reason. He knew that they would be able to drive to safety—

None of them have a deep purple or black aura. . . .

CHAPTER TWO

The hardest thing to keep to oneself is one's opinion. Roy Anderson did not even have to make an effort. As Chief of Station of the U.S. Embassy CIA Station in Amman, Jordan, Anderson could say anything he pleased—and he didn't give a lopsided damn if Richard Camellion was in charge of Operation Green Glow. At the moment, Anderson was saying plenty, voicing his opinion in a loud, angry voice. He might as well have roared like a lion. No one outside the eight rooms of the station could hear him. Not only were the rooms soundproof, but "white sound" generators were going full blast in each room, although they were unnecessary. Twice a day and three times at night, a technician used a ULD30-A transmitter locator to check each room for a hidden bug—even if it would have taken God Almighty Himself to get inside any of the rooms to plant a "button-mike transmitter."

"I guess the four of you know what you triggered off last night?" raved Anderson, who was pacing back and forth in front of his desk. He suddenly stopped and glared down at Marie Dine, who, sitting in front of the desk, next to Cyrus Dillon, the assistant Chief of Station, was filing her nails—as unconcerned as a rock! "The Jordanian D-4 boys will be watching every foreign embassy with double effort, especially ours and the Soviet Union's."

"Oh hell, Roy," snorted Robert Follmer, "they've always watched the embassies."

"You didn't tell us what your dangle[1] in Department 4 reported," drawled Camellion, who was sitting in a stately red-leather easy chair, to one side of Anderson's desk. Kelly Dillard sat to the left of the Death Merchant. Phil LaHann and Robert Follmer, two CIA career employees, were on the red-cushioned chrome couch.

With the red-leather chairs and couch, pink wallpaper, and red

---

[1]Company slang for a double agent. *Double-O* is another term.

shades on three lamps, Camellion felt that he was in a modern bordello, or in a six-bit restaurant in California, a fancy gyp joint that used period atmosphere as a substitute for good booze, good food and good service—*All we need is a lineup of floozies!*

Anderson, stolid in build and (usually) in temperament, turned and faced Camellion, staring at him as if he would have liked to cut his throat with a dull hacksaw.

"The dangle reported that Colonel Hamshari is yanking in suspects all over Amman," Anderson said heavily. "I can't say that I blame him, what with twenty-two regular policemen terminated." He swung to his right and tossed visual daggers at Marie Dine and Phil LaHann. "Damn it! Did you two have to blow them all up?"

"I killed a lot myself while we were pulling out onto the Street of the Palms," interrupted the Death Merchant. "I didn't see any reason to let Miss Dine have all the fun."

"No, by God! We didn't have to!" LaHann answered Anderson angrily, leaning forward and putting his hands on his knees. "We could have let those twelve Jordanians capture Camellion and Dillard—or more likely, kill them. I'm sure D.C. would have danced a jig over our sitting by and doing nothing."

Marie Dine, looking up, said, "I had no choice with the first two. They were coming to the car to question us. I'm not being paid to spend the rest of my life getting raped by Jordanian prison guards."

Twenty-nine years old, she was a tall woman with blue green eyes in an oval, small-featured face. The Death Merchant wondered why she wore her silver blond hair piled up in a bird's-nest coiffure.

The Death Merchant didn't give Anderson time to find fault with Dine and LaHann's explanation. He said, "We didn't have any choice with the Jordanians on al-Sahadi Street either. It was stop them before they could follow and stop us. We stopped them forever. Miss Dine and Mr. LaHann saved my life and Mr. Dillard's. I intend to report to Mr. G. that they did outstanding work." He paused, a thin smile curling over his mouth. "You can report otherwise if you want."

For a moment, Anderson looked like a man who had a choice between blowing out his brains or fighting a tiger barehanded. The Death Merchant easily gave him a chance to escape from his embarrassing dilemma by asking, "What did the dangle report about the Russians in the park? Naturally they carried phony identification."

"They had West German passports," sighed Anderson. "There

were three of them. The rest of the men were Jordanians.'' He leaned back and half sat on the front center of his desk. "We're lucky that one of the Ruskies fired at the Jordanian police. The police fired back and killed two Russians and a Jordanian trying to reach al-Sahadi Street. The Russians might not have broken, but the Jordanian would have told everything.''

"The Jordanian couldn't have told the secret police anything of importance,'' LaHann said, putting a hand to the back of his head. "They were only hired guns. The KGB didn't tell such trash about the Judas Scrolls.''

"The Russians had three cars waiting on al-Sahadi,'' Anderson went on. "The dangle said all three were sanitized. All three rented. No prints and false license plates.''

"Just like the station wagon,'' said Kelly Dillard with a grin. "We're in the clear. If Department-4 suspected us, they would have closed in on us at the Caravan this morning, or this afternoon. It was almost three in the afternoon before Phil, Dick and I left the hotel to come to the embassy.''

"Not necessarily,'' Phil LaHann said slowly. "We're American engineers. Colonel Hamshari's boys wouldn't play gang busters with us the way they would with their own people or other Arabs. If they suspect us—and I doubt if they do—they'll watch and wait and watch some more.''

"The hell with Hamshari and his sand crabs,'' muttered Dillard. "We automatically assumed our rooms at the Caravan might be bugged. All we've been talking about is stress analysis, foundations, and wind factors, getting it all out of a book.''

"Yeah,'' LaHann said. "I thought I'd go nuts this morning, putting that page about stress into conversation. All that crap about the rigidity of the riveted or welded joints of a truss that was deflected—what was it again? Oh yeah—'deflected due to axial deformation of its members.' ''

Robert Follmer, a solid dark-haired man with a meaty, dark face, loudly cleared his throat for attention. He looked younger than his thirty-six years. Whereas the Death Merchant, Dillard, and LaHann had flown together from New York City to Amman, by way of Beirut, Follmer had arrived that same day, landing at Amman International Airport at 1330 that same afternoon.

"Gentlemen, this is all very interesting,'' Follmer said businesslike. "However, I would appreciate someone giving me the details of Operation Green Glow. All I've been told is that I'm a consulting engineer for Ryan, Colt & Webber Construction Company, the outfit that's building the experimental solar power station in southern Jordan.''

15

The Death Merchant recrossed his legs, locked his hands in back of his head, and looked up steadily at Roy Dean Anderson, who was cutting off the end of a cigar with a foot-high guillotine cutter. The blade dropped. The end of the Santa Ynez Emperadores fell off.

"You haven't given him the details?" Camellion said, deadpan.

Anderson rolled the other end of the long cigar around in his mouth, pulled it out, and blinked rapidly. "I assumed you had more facts," he said, giving Camellion a hating look. "You were briefed at the Home Office. All we did here in Amman was report what Mahmoud Khalil told us. The Center back home already knew about the scrolls—only they had the wrong mountain range."

Nodding, Camellion removed his hands from the rear of his head, put his elbows on the arms of the red-leather chair, and let his gaze drift to an interested Bob Follmer.

"The whole nine yards started—"

"Uh—'the whole nine yards?' " questioned Follmer.

"I gather you have never been in any branch of the military?" A slight frown creased the Death Merchant's head. He suddenly wished he were back home in the Big Thicket.

Follmer seemed puzzled. "Should I have been? I mean, does it make a difference that I wasn't?"

"Never mind (*I have a feeling he's going to be deadweight!*). The real beginning started several months ago in September," Camellion explained. "It started with Professor Gordon Alsworth Aimes, a British archaeologist who was working in some old ruins near Mount Hebron in the West Bank.[2] He discovered some scrolls—twenty-seven of them, to be exact hidden underneath the floor of what had been a temple. The scrolls were papyri and the writing was in Aramaic, the same language spoken by Jesus Christ. Professor Aimes—he's connected with the British Museum in London—was not a linguist as such, although he did speak nine languages, including classical Greek. However, Professor Ramon deCastés, a Spanish archaeologist with the expedition, was an authority on ancient Semitic languages and partially deciphered the strange writing on portions of six of the scrolls. To their astonishment, Professors deCastés and Aimes discovered *that the man who had written the scrolls was none other*

---

[2]As a result of the Arab-Israeli War of June, 1967, Israel occupies the territory on the west bank of the Jordan River. About 2,270 square miles, this occupied area represents about 6 percent of Jordan's territory and one-half of the nation's agricultural land.

than Judas Iscariot, the archtraitor who had betrayed Christ and whose name was synonymous with treachery of the blackest kind.''

The twenty-seven scrolls were undoubtedly the greatest discovery in the history of archaeology. There was a major problem: getting the prize out of Israel. Originally, the Aimes expedition had requested permission of the Israeli government to explore ancient Jewish graves around Rishon Le Ziyyon, in Israel proper, the main interest of the scientists being ancient Jewish burial customs. The Israelis refused. Explorations within Israel were reserved for Israeli scientists. The Ministry of the Interior did give the Aimes expedition permission to explore two sites in the West Bank, the first a few miles south of Ariha, or Jericho, the second a mile to the northeast of Mount Hebron. It was in the ruins of the second site that the scrolls were discovered.

Professors Aimes and deCastés, realizing that the Israelis would never permit them to take such a treasure out of the country, knew they would have to smuggle out the scrolls. Before the two men and others in the expedition could put together a plan, the immensely important historical find was stolen in the middle of the night by members of the PRL, the Palestinian Resistance League, a small group of fanatic terrorists, extremely dangerous in that they advocated total violence against Israel.

The PRL learned of the Judas Scrolls through Abdul Haj Zaid, an Iraqi "digger" working for the Aimes expedition. A secret member of the PRL, Zaid had spied on Professors Aimes and deCastés and had heard them discussing the valuable find in their tent. Zaid relayed word to the PRL. Five days later the scrolls were stolen.

Robert Follmer put down his glass of vodka on the rocks, from which he had just taken a drink, and looked quizzically at the Death Merchant.

"I can readily understand the immense importance of the scrolls," he said. "Anything written by Judas, provided it could be authenticated, would have tremendous religious and historical value. Why should the KGB get in on the act? The Ruskies would hardly stick out their necks for such a find. They'd just pooh-pooh the discovery as being another fraud of religion, like manufactured relics, as a lot of people call the Shroud of Turin. How did the Company obtain all these facts—or is Zaid one of our Middle East informers?"

It was Cyrus Dillon, a pudgy, pink-cheeked butterball of a man, who answered. "Not hardly, Follmer. Zaid was and is a die-hard fanatic. He's out there somewhere. He stayed with the

Aimes expedition until Aimes and the rest of them returned forlornly to England.''

"There were two Jordanians in the PRL," Camellion said. "One was named Ghassan Nazzal, the other, Mahmoud Khalil. Both were on the informer payroll of the KGB. Furthermore, each man knew the other was working for the pig farmers; in fact, they were working as a team. What Nazzal didn't know was that Khalil was a double agent and that Khalil was an informer for the Company. The CIA was paying him four times as much as the Russians.''

"It figures," commented Follmer. "The KGB always pays informers in low places a piddling sum.''

Continued Camellion in an easy tone, "There was something that neither Nazzal nor Khalil realized: a highly trained KGB operative was in the inner circle, or Council, of the PRL. A Russian national who spoke and read Arabic perfectly, who knew the customs and religion. He went under the name of Kamal Essawy and for all intents and purposes was an Arab, supposedly a Palestinian.''

Bob Follmer's eyes narrowed and he nodded. "No doubt he was a graduate of one of the KGB's *barich dyuzh i dor'iteli*[3] schools.''

Roy Anderson, who had sat down at his desk, let out a cloud of cigar smoke. "We think Essawy was Major Vladimir Josef Rokanovitch. We can't be sure. We did know that Rokanovitch was operating somewhere in the Middle East. It doesn't make any difference. Essawy is dead.''

The Death Merchant resumed the briefing of Robert Follmer. "The PRL desperately needed money for its war chest. To obtain this money, the Council—including Kamal Essawy—set up a bold plan. They . . .''

. . . Sent two emissaries to Rome, Italy, one to the Foreign Office of the Vatican, the other to the Soviet Embassy. The plan was practical. The PRL offered to sell the Judas Scrolls to either the Vatican or the KGB, to the highest bidder, the starting price: $30 million.

The reasoning of the PRL was diabolically logical. The Russians would be more than happy to have anything that would help them undermine Christianity and/or prove that the Christian

---

[3]There isn't any literal translation into English. The closest would be "fake" or "false training." The KGB has special training centers—entire towns—in which an agent learns to live, speak, and think like the citizens of the nation he is to infiltrate.

religion was based on fraud and superstition. In contrast, the Vatican would be equally anxious to keep such proof hidden, to maintain its power and spiritual authority over more than half a billion Roman Catholics.

As proof that the scrolls were genuine, each emissary took an eight-inch square of a scroll with him.

The Vatican didn't know what to do.

The KGB did. *The Russians stole the scrolls!*

"Essawy and the two Jordanians working for the Russians—correct?" said Follmer. "The Agency got all this from Mahmoud Khalil."

Camellion said, "Even before the PRL contacted the Soviets in Rome, the KGB knew about the scrolls—through Kamal Essawy. Moscow Center sent word back to Essawy or Rokanovitch—take your pick. He was to steal the scrolls; and that's what he did, with the help of Khalil and Nazzal and a dozen for-hire-to-the-highest-bidder Jordanians. They grabed the scrolls from the main PRL stronghold outside of Ma'an in southwest Jordan."

The theft was not successful. Kamal Essawy and the fourteen Jordanians were only half a mile from the PRL fortress when the theft was discovered. The PRL fanatics got into trucks and other vehicles and pursued Kamal Essawy to the Jabal Hārun (or Hārun Mountains), forty miles to the northwest of Ma'an. Here in the Hārun Mountains, a fairly low range, a fierce gun battle took place. When the shooting was finished, most of the PRL terrorists were dead. Only five were left in good shape. Not knowing how many of the enemy were dead, or rather, how many were still alive and able to pull a trigger, the five terrorists wisely retreated. It was a serious mistake on their part because Kamal Essawy—or Rokanovitch—and twelve of the Jordanians were dead.

But Ghassan Nazzal and Mahmoud Khalil were very much alive.

The two men knew they couldn't hide the precious scrolls in the Hārun Mountains. Sooner or later the PRL would find the scrolls. The two men took a jeep and the case of scrolls and drove thirty-three miles straight south to the Jabal Arqā. They hid the scrolls in a long cave and carefully covered the cave with rocks.

No sooner were the scrolls hidden than Ghassan Nazzal shot Mahmoud Khalil twice in the back with a Walther P-38 pistol. As Nazzal saw the situation, the scrolls were now his and his alone. He realized he alone could not sell them to the KGB; the

Russians would kill him on sight for being a traitor if he attempted blackmail. The Vatican was also impractical. The KGB would be watching Vatican City. There was, however, another agency that would love to get its hands on the scrolls—the CIA.

"Did Nazzal make contact with the Agency?" asked Follmer.

The Death Merchant acted as if he hadn't heard the question.

There was a serious flaw in Ghassan Nazzal's scheme. Mahmoud Khalil was not dead. He was not even seriously injured, except for his back, which was bruised in several places. The clever Khalil had been wearing a full bulletproof vest—chest and back—under his robes. He had no choice but to pretend to be dead. After shooting him in the back, Nazzal had pulled his pistol from its holster, dragged what he thought was a corpse to one side of the cave, and covered the body with loose rocks.

As soon as Nazzal left the cave, Khalil pushed aside the rocks and began the long journey to Amman, 200 miles to the north. He knew he would either have to obtain supplies on the Hujāz highway or he would never reach the capital. Another risk was that he might encounter members of the PRL, or even Ghassan Nazzal. He had no way of knowing that Nazzal had taken the jeep and was headed toward the West Bank. He would abandon the jeep at the proper time and smuggle himself into the West Bank, a fairly easy task, since the Shin Bet[4] couldn't be everywhere. He had forged papers to prove he was an Israeli Arab once he was in the West Bank. His business? Why, he had visited his dying grandfather in al-Ajqib, a small village close to the Judean mountains. His destination was Yerushalayim (Jerusalem), his purpose twofold. In Jerusalem he would "cover" himself with the KGB by reporting to his contact in that city that the Judas Scrolls were hidden in the Jabal Hārun and that Khalil and Essawy were dead. Nazzal would then move on to Tel Aviv and attempt to make contact with the CIA at the U.S. Embassy. He didn't dare return to Jordan. Too many PRLs were still on the loose.

Ghassan Nazzal managed to get into the West Bank. Twice his forged papers got him past Shin Bet security patrols. His luck failed the third time. One of the guards searched and found Nazzal's P-38 taped to his left ankle and Khalil's Beretta strapped to his right ankle.

The Shin Bet, convinced that they had bagged a dangerous terrorist—and they had—turned Nazzal over to agents of Mivtzan

---

[4]Israeli Department of Internal Security.

Elohim,[5] a special section of the Mossad that deals only with terrorists. By the time the Wrath of God agents were finished with Ghassan Nazzal, a day later, he was ready to confess to the plotting of the assassination of Abraham! They had drilled his teeth, pulled out his fingernails and toenails, and had boiled his hands in scalding water. More dead than alive and in agony, Nazzal was still an Arab and a realist. He knew that once the Wrath of God sadists had extracted all the information from him they could get, they would put a bullet in the back of his head. He didn't mind death; all people die. But he hated and despised the Israelis and was determined to have the last laugh.

He confessed the entire story about the Judas Scrolls, from beginning to end, telling only one lie: that he and Mahmoud Khalil had hidden the scrolls in the Hārun Mountains. And he stuck to the story, even though the Israelis tortured him with an "electric bed"[6] for another six hours. At length, they had him give a detailed description of the area where the cave was located.

The Israelis didn't have to execute Nazzal. His heart gave out from the strain of the torture.

Robert Follmer inspected the Death Merchant with puzzled eyes.

"How could Khalil have revealed those details?" he asked. "He and Nazzal separated in the cave in the Arqā Mountains!"

Roy Anderson laughed scornfully and leaned back in his plush executive Recaro chair ($1,000).

"Kahlil wasn't aware of what had happened to Nazzal any more than we were," he said happily, "until our own highly placed A. in Israel sent us a full report."

"The Agency has penetrated the Mossad?" Follmer looked more than a little surprised.

"Better than that," corrected Anderson. "The Sheruth Modiin.[7] We've had an agent inside for two years."

"Anderson, tell him the next development," the Death Merchant said.

Anderson looked across his desk at Follmer. "You're wondering what happened to Mahmoud Khalil. As you know, he made it to Amman and made contact with us through an S-M . . ."[8]

[5]Means the "Wrath of God." Mrs. G. Meir had Major General Aharon Yariv form the organization in 1964. Yariv had been a brilliant commander of military intelligence and was totally ruthless.

[6]Electricity is forced through springs. The Israelis refer to the device as the "jumping springs."

[7]Military Intelligence. The Mossad is the "CIA" of Israel.)

[8]"Street man."

. . . Khalil told the full story to the CIA contact. The Company man was flabbergasted, then angry—but didn't show it—when Khalil demanded the equivalent of $100,000 JDs (Jordanian dinars) to reveal the location of the Judas Scrolls.

Jerry Buckley played it smooth, telling Khalil that, while he thought the Agency would pay the sum, he would have to consult with his superiors.

"We kidnaped the son of a bitch and brought him here to the embassy," Anderson said grimly, "and got the truth out of him, every single bit of it. We immediately sent the information to the Home Office. In the meanwhile, the agent in the Sheruth Modiin had related the same information to the Home Office, but with a difference. The agent in the Sheruth Modiin reported that the Judas Scrolls were hidden in the Jabal Hārun. The Center radioed back to us for confirmation. We explained that the true location was the Arqā Mountains and that we had Khalil to prove it. We still have him. He's locked up in the basement, with a man watching him day and night."

Lighting a cigarette and glancing after Marie Dine, who was leaving the room, Follmer leaned back on the red-cushioned chrome couch.

"Now the pieces are starting to fall into place," he said. "That's why we're going to the solar station at Ra's an Naqb. That god-awful place is only twenty-five miles southeast of the Arqā Mountains."

"Correction, old buddy. The solar station is only nineteen miles from the Jabal Arqā. The station is six miles from the settlement," said Kelly Dillard, opening a roll of Rolaids.

"Us and two Catholic priests," the Death Merchant said. "Father Bernard Norton, an American, and Father Victorio Gatdula. They're both Jesuits, experts in the Aramaic language."

Cyrus Dillon (who would have looked like an overgrown cherub except for his small, mean eyes) explained. "The Agency made contact with the Vatican. Those holy joes were only too anxious to help us find the Judas Scrolls. They want the scrolls as much as we do."

"What I don't understand is how—"

"How the KGB found out about us," the Death Merchant cut Follmer off. "We know that the Russians did because of the attack in the park. We can only surmise that someone at the experimental solar station is working for the KGB and tipped them off that four new engineers were on the way."

Cut in Phil LaHann, "The KGB thinks the scrolls are in the Jabal Hārun. They figure the four 'engineers'—us—are agents going to the solar station because the Hārun Mountains are fifty-five miles from Ra's an Naqb. We show up in Amman. KGB agents watched the hotel and kept track of us. Of course, that doesn't explain how the Russians knew about the man we were to meet in the park.''

"Yeah, and the order for the meet came from the Fox himself," Dillard said crankily. "There's only a few answers that make any sense. Either whoever we were supposed to meet sold us out to the KGB, or else the Russians grabbed him and made him talk.''

"Either way, we pull out tomorrow for the solar station, including the two Jesuits." Camellion stretched out his long legs and crossed them at the ankles. "Welcome aboard, Follmer. I hope you can get used to A-rabs. You're going to see plenty of sand crabs before this deal is over and done with.''

Follmer, who had walked over to the liquor and was pouring another vodka, said, "Almost anything would be better than the mess back in the States. I don't have to tell you about the race policy of the current crop of idiots in D.C. You know how we're being invaded by aliens. For example, 80 percent of the babies born in Los Angeles County hospitals in 1981 were to illegal aliens, to illegal immigrant mothers, almost all of them from Mexico—and all their medical expenses were paid by taxpayers.''

Kelly Dillard laughed sinisterly. "Why you shouldn't talk like that!'' he chided. "After all, the nonwhite trash mean more votes for the politicians, more money for businessmen, more souls for the two-faced clergy, and more opportunities for the goddamn race mixers to destroy America's white heritage.''

"Ordinarily, I'm a fair-minded person," Phil LaHann said thoughtfully. "I must agree with you. We can see what the nonwhite morons have already done to the American educational system. The lowering of scholastic and disciplinary standards in order to accommodate the huge influx of black and Chicano students into previously all-white schools has resulted in one big mess. Whites are learning less, while the coons and spics are learning nothing, which is normal enough. But no one should be surprised that white students do not learn in a school system that sees more than 5,000 of its teachers assaulted each month. What a joke! One might as well try to 'educate' apes!''

The Death Merchant, who seldom involved himself in useless discussions, felt like saying *Folks! You ain't seen nothin' yet!* Knowing world history as he did, Camellion was only too aware of the road the United States was taking—*For the federal government, for America's teeming nonwhite minorities, and even* for a very substantial portion of the white majority, the choice is clear: they will continue straight ahead—

And into oblivion!

They will continue to clamor for more racial mixing in the schools, in residential neighborhoods, and on the job. They will continue to allow millions of nonwhite aliens to pour across U.S. borders from Mexico, the Caribbean, and the Orient; and the U.S. economy and the standard of living will grow steadily worse. They will continue to push for more handouts for those who will not work, more indulgences for the least productive elements of society, more of the same permissiveness and lack of discipline that have helped bring on present problems.

The massive influx of aliens is rapidly transforming the character of America's population and the appearance of its cities. The principal beachheads of the foreign swarms—New York City and its environs, Florida, southern Texas, and California—are in the process of acquiring nonwhite majorities. The intruders—with the morals of camels—are taking over entire neighborhoods that once were home to native Americans of European stock.

It will end in a race war. The nonwhites will lose. They have neither the intelligence nor the firepower to win.

"There's something else I don't understand, and so far none of you have explained it," said Robert Follmer. "Why are the Russians so anxious to get their hands on the Judas Scrolls." He looked steadily at the Death Merchant. "It seems to me that the KGB is going to a lot of trouble to acquire the scrolls."

The Death Merchant's voice was as expressionless as his face, flat and almost toneless. "Company agents had a long talk with Professor Aimes and Professor deCastés. According to them, the scrolls give a true account of what actually happened to Jesus Christ. *Judas got the short end of the stick and didn't hang himself. Nor did Jesus Christ die on the cross. He survived and died in Jordan at the age of sixty-four!*"

Follmer's low whistle could be heard throughout the room. . . .

CHAPTER THREE

"An armored caravan." That's what Captain Gamal Nashibi laughingly called the thirteen vehicles. No matter what the Jordanian army officer called the string of machines, they actually composed an armored column. The first vehicle on the Hujaz Highway was a six-man British Hubbler scout car on which was mounted a .30 caliber Browning machine gun. In back of the scout car were two Saladin armored cars, two armored troop carriers (twenty men and two drivers to each T-C), then the command van, in which rode Captain Nashibi, Lieutenant Nitzan Hatumin, the radio operator, and the two drivers. After the command van was the $125,000 motor home, as large as a Greyhound bus, that belonged to Ryan, Colt & Webber Construction Company, Inc.—a company that transported key personnel in the best comfort available. Behind the Century-Flash motor home was a Centurion MK III heavy tank, followed by two six-wheeled light cross-country supply trucks, a Centurion tank chassis and turret, on which was mounted twin Oerlikon 35mm AA guns, together with radar and fire control instruments, then two more Saladin armored cars.

The reason for all the armor and firepower was that—in spite of what the Jordanian Tourist Bureau said—90 percent of Jordan was as primitive as in the days of Jesus Christ. All too true of the Ard As Sawwan, the great desert that composed four-fifths of the territory east of the Jordan River. As inhospitable as the anteroom of Hell, this desert—that moved south right up to the border of Saudi Arabia—was sand, outcroppings of sandstone and granite, basalt, flint, and volcanic lava, all of it as ageless as time, all of it eroded by wind.

The harsh and dreary landscape was impersonal. Sand and rock could not pull a trigger. Rocks could not cut a throat. The Bedouin, or Bedu, could, roving bands of them armed with modern weapons. Sometimes the Jordanian camel patrols caught some of these vicious marauders and executed them on the spot. More often than not, the Bedu escaped. The Ard As Sawwan was too vast and patrols, both in Jordan and in Saudi Arabia, too few.

Before the column had started out that morning, Captain Nashibi had explained to Camellion and the five other "engineers," including Fathers Norton and Gatdula, that "the bandits wouldn't be so much of a problem if we could use all our helicopters to patrol the entire area of the desert. We must use most of our helicopters to patrol the border between our nation and that section of our country that Westerners refer to as the 'West Bank.' Imagine! Having to patrol a 'border' of a section of territory that was stolen from us by those Israeli thieves!"

The murderous Bedu[1] made it necessary that the experimental solar station be protected constantly. The Jordanian army always had men and vehicles at the station—"Or the Bedu would slaughter those Americans in a single day," said Gamal Nashibi.

Moving on the wide concrete highway, the line of vehicles moved through the southern outskirts of Amman, passing new housing projects, blocks of sterile-looking multistoried apartment buildings—a vast wasteland of undifferentiated slabs, totally rationalized dwelling units that offered no public space. At the very edge of the city were ten-story apartment houses that resembled two O's melded with a support bracing in the form of an X in the center; but toward the open country, farther out, there were small homes with charming central patios and colorful red-tiled roofs.

All pure luxury, the Century-Flash motor home was all chrome, stainless steel, and plush cushioning inside. Sleeping seven, the "penthouse" on ten wheels had two color television sets, $4,000 worth of AM/FM stereo equipment, and a Yaesu FRG-7 short-wave radio. In the well-equipped kitchen section, there was even a large deep freeze next to the extra-wide and extra-deep refrigerator, all of it powered by a row of Celtine batteries that were constantly being recharged from the motion of the vehicle. A portable generator, powered by batteries, would keep the Celtine batteries recharged when the vehicle was at rest for any length of time.

The Death Merchant and Robert Follmer had carried a portable ice chest into the motor bus. The ice chest did not contain ice. It did contain and protect a very special shortwave radio transmitter, along with a "black box" and double G-13v scram-

---

[1]Not all the Bedouin are robbers. Most are a simple people who exist by raising sheep, goats, and camels. They have a nomadic existence, living in goat-skin tents.

bler, either for code or voice transmission. Various weapons, including two silenced SIG *Maschinenpistole* 310s, were included in other luggage.

Seated in a chair with a button-tufted back and lavish padding, the Death Merchant harbored the suspicion that his first task would be to achieve peace in his "little family." *It's like having diehard liberals and conservatives in the same room—damn it!*

An atheist, Kelly Dillard did little to hide his dislike of the two Jesuits. Robert Follmer was a racist who blamed the Catholic Church for constantly urging the United States government to admit more Mexicans into the United States.

"Any person with the sense God gave a rock knows why the Church wants millions of chili peppers running around all over the country!" Follmer had lashed out the previous night, as he and Dillard, Camellion and LeHann were returning to the Caravan Hotel. "Because the Mexicans don't use birth control. Because they turn out kids as fast as rats. Because more brats mean more 'souls' and more money for the Church."

Kelly Dillard had readily agreed, saying, "Organized religion has killed more innocent people than Hitler, Stalin, and Attila the Hun all rolled into one. If religion had its way—I'm speaking of religion all over the world—the human race would still be in the Dark Ages. I tell you, civilization has progressed not because of religion but in spite of it!"

"Maybe so, but where has the race progressed to?" mocked Philip LaHann. "Worldwide, we're poisoning the air, the water, and the soil, and are only a step away from destroying civilization in a nuclear war. I don't think of that as progress."

Dillard didn't give a single millimeter. "Indirectly, we can blame organized religion for hurting our national defense effort. Do you realize the billions of dollars that could be generated if the churches paid their fair share of taxes?"

The Death Merchant knew that Father Norton and Father Gatdula themselves would be a problem. Father Gatdula, S.J., had flown from Rome to New York City. He and Father Norton had made it clear to Camellion and the CIA briefing officer that, while they would help in any way in regard to the Judas Scrolls, they would not—as Father Norton had put it—". . . participate in any act of violence against our fellow man."

Which means we're going to have to play shepherd to those two sheep!

Camellion did feel rather guilty about the two Jesuits, who were under the impression that, if the scrolls were found, they would be turned over to the Vatican.

Sorry, boys! The CIA has plans for those scrolls—I wonder whom they are going to blackmail with them?

Paradox! Camellion was too much of a psychologist to let himself become the victim of conflicting emotions. The two Jesuits would be a pain in the department of practicality. Nonetheless, the Death Merchant admired them, and the rest of the Jesuits, for the same reason he admired the Jewish people—*They have intelligence; they stress education. I wonder what Kelly and Bob would say if they knew I had spent six years at Saint Louis University—a Jesuit university?*

The Jesuits did have their enemies. They always had, as predicted by Saint Ignatius Loyola, who had founded the Society of Jesus in 1534. Over the centuries the Jesuits were accused not only of seeking to undermine various rulers, but of plotting to assassinate no fewer than four European kings. By the eighteenth century they had become so powerful that enemies referred to the superior general of the Jesuits as the "Black Pope." The word *Jesuit* eventually became synonymous in the popular—though mainly Protestant—imagination with duplicity, intrigue, and equivocation. But even their enemies had to grudgingly admire them, for their demanding training, rigorous discipline, and pioneering work in education also earned its members a reputation as the "schoolmasters of Europe."[2]

Originally, the Society of Jesus was formed as a kind of spiritual marine corps to check the advance of Protestantism during the Counter-Reformation—*And now the Jesuits are in trouble with the Pope, because their theologians are advocating sweeping changes in the Church. They'll survive. They always have. They are still the largest single Catholic order.*[3]

The motorized column was in open country, with Amman miles to the north. Camellion glanced at Bernard Norton, S.J., who taught at Loyola University in Boston, and at Victorio Gatdula, who was a professor of languages at the University of Milan. Both men, sitting across from Camellion on the other side of the bus, were dressed in cargo side-pocket pants and tan desert-cloth shirts. No one would have suspected the two men were Jesuits.

[2]The Jesuits trained, among others, Molière, Voltaire, Descartes and James Joyce. In missionary work, the Jesuits have been "superhuman" on five continents.

[3]But its ranks have thinned, due to the turmoil in the Church since Vatican II—have dwindled from an all-time high of 36,038 in 1965 to 27,015 in 1980.

28

They wouldn't take up arms; yet Camellion knew they weren't cowards. Cowards do not become Jesuits who spend at least fifteen years in the Society before taking final vows, which include a special pledge of fealty to the Pope. Just the same, throughout the history of the order, Popes have accused them of arrogance and disobedience. In 1773 Pope Clement XIV even suppressed the order because European governments and jealous clerics complained that the Jesuits had too much power. The order was not revived until 1814.

Furthermore, not all the Jesuits are like Norton and Gatdula, thought the Death Merchant, turning and looking out a window at the bright sunshine pouring out over the countryside. In contrast to Norton and Gatdula, many Jesuits were extremely active in politics. One activist Jesuit had already been murdered in El Salvador and two had been snuffed in Guatemala for advocating greater social reform. Another reason why the Jesuits were in trouble with the "Head Office" in Rome—they couldn't keep their holy noses out of politics. In 1979, Pope John Paul made it clear to Latin American bishops in Puebla, Mexico, that he did not approve of priests defending the rights of the oppressed by a political activism that had more in common with communism than with Catholicism. For the first time in its long history, the Jesuits were divided among themselves, some believing in political intrigue, others in obeying the pope.

"Tell me, Norton, now that Superior General Arrupe[4] has retired, who do you think the pope will appoint as head of the Jesuits?" the Death Merchant asked of Father Norton, a medium-sized man in his early fifties. With a bony face, he had colorless cheeks and he lacked the verve of a man who was no stranger to the outdoors. His hair was gray and wispy; yet his eyes, although narrow and deep-set, were alert, bright, and shining with intelligence.

Both Jesuits seemed slightly startled by the Death Merchant's question. It wasn't because he hadn't addressed Norton as Father Norton. It had been agreed that at no time would the two Jesuits be addressed as priests. Or the Jordanians (and/or the Americans at the solar station) might wonder why two priests were also engineers! The two priests were surprised that Camellion was capable of asking such a question. To Fathers Norton and Gatdula, he was only a ruthless manipulator, a modern corsair making a net profit from the international power game.

---

[4]Father Pedro Arrupe, who retired after having a stroke in August of 1981.

Father Norton quickly regained his composure. "I really have no idea, Mr. Camellion," he said seriously. "I presume it will be someone who will follow Pope Paul's conservative doctrines. That is how it should be. The Pontiff is the representative of Christ on earth."

The Death Merchant was not about to discuss who represented whom. For those who believed, no explanation was required; for those who didn't, an explanation was not even possible.

Camellion rubbed the end of his nose with a forefinger, his thoughtful eyes steady on Norton and Gatdula, the latter of whom was short, in his forties, and had a round, heavy face, a thick mop of curly black hair, and a precise and controlled manner. His table manners were excellent, and it was a pleasure to watch him eat.

The Death Merchant said, "I should think that the present crisis in the Society of Jesus—that is, the sharp differences between the liberals and the conservatives—will greatly influence the Pope in his decision. I have read that the younger members of the Jesuit order are extremely impatient for change."

"To the conservatives, the real problem is not political activism," said Father Gatdula, speaking with only a slight accent, "but the loss of discipline and intellectual rigor that set in during the experimental sixties. The stagnation is still there."

"Yes, that's all too true," said Father Norton. "During the sixties, many younger Jesuits were influenced as much by the radical politics of antiwar activist Father Daniel Berrigan as they were by the society's venerable manual, *Spiritual Exercises*. I believe it was Catholic historian James Hitchcock of Saint Louis University who described it as a 'self-probing, inward-looking, almost narcissistic mentality' that has crept into the order."

"Self-renewal can often be a good thing overall," Camellion said. "We all should know who we really are, at least in this present time continuum."

He glanced around the interior of the motor home. Every two hours the men would spell one another in the driver's compartment, including the two Jesuits. At present Robert Follmer was driving. Kelly Dillard was in the kitchenette, putting a crown of pork roast into the oven. An amateur chef, Dillard had offered to do all the cooking. At present he was muttering because the well-stocked larder lacked ingredients for an oyster dressing.

Philip LaHann, sitting to the right of Father Gatdula in a slumber-seat lounger, said with a kind of vague graciousness, "Once we have the scrolls penned by Judas, I just wonder how their contents will shape the future of the Christian faith."

"Assuming we are able to get the scrolls," Father Norton said. He looked at the Death Merchant. "Have you any kind of plan yet, Mr. Camellion?"

"No, I haven't," lied Camellion. "I want to look over the lay of the land around the solar station before deciding on a course of action."

"The scrolls have to be forgeries," Father Gatdula said tentatively. "I cannot believe that our Lord Jesus Christ did not die on the cross and did not rise from the grave on the third day." His gloomy eyes moved to the Death Merchant. "Do you not agree, Camellion?"

The Death Merchant refused to be pinned down. "My opinion is totally irrelevant. Getting the scrolls is the only thing that matters. The task will not be easy, considering that the Russians and the Israelis are after the same prize."

"The Jordanian secret police might also be a problem," Philip LaHann said in a low voice. "They don't know about the scrolls. They do know that something very unusual is going on."

"You are referring to last night's tragedy in Hussein Park?" asked Father Norton, almost in a whisper.

LaHann smiled slightly. "That, plus the battle between the Palestinian Resistance League and the Russians and their Jordanian helpers in the Hārun Mountains. A Jordanian camel patrol found all the corpses. We can be sure that Department 4—that's the secret police—is doing its best to unravel what happened."

Added the Death Merchant, "It's also possible that the secret police might make a connection between the shoot-out in the park and the gun battle in the mountains. There isn't any point in worrying about it. It's out of our hands."

Father Gatdula shifted on the couch and looked at LaHann. "The scrolls, forgeries that they are, will not cast fresh light on the authenticity of the Bible. As you may know, a wave of archaeological discoveries have already altered old ideas about the roots of Christianity and Judaism and affirmed the the Bible is more historically accurate than previously thought by many scholars."

"The Shroud of Turin?" Doubt was clearly in LaHann's voice.

"There has been a lot of digging going on in the Middle East for the past twenty years," Camellion said. "Among confirmed or suspected discoveries—correct me if I'm wrong—are King Solomon's Mines, ruins of the cities of Sodom and Gomorrah, and evidence of a catastrophe that might explain the Red Sea miracles in the Book of Exodus."

31

"Proof of God's miracles!" Father Gatdula said smugly.

Logician that he was, Camellion couldn't stand stupidity. "Evidence that an event happened is far from proof that the Creator of this Universe made it happen. For example, the story of the Deluge was obviously borrowed from the Babylonian tale of Gilgamesh; and fragments of wood, often said to be fragments of Noah's Ark, are always popping up. Not too many years ago there was a documentary film that offered 'proof' that such a fragment was from Noah's boat. Carbon dating proved that the wood came from about A.D. 700, a long long LONG time after the Deluge."

"Well, they did find the Ark of the Covenant!" Kelly Dillard called out loudly from the kitchenette. "They even made a movie about it!" he laughed, "*Raiders of the Lost Ark!*"

Fathers Norton and Gatdula ignored Dillard's sly dig and insult.

"The oldest ark ever found was in Palestine," Father Norton said mildly. "Three American scientists found it in August of 1981. It was a ceremonial imitation dating back to about A.D. 300."

Father Gatdula said quickly, "It was Italian Professor Giovanni Pettinato who found seventeen thousand cuneiform tablets in Syria, in 1967. The tablets . . ."

. . . Were found in ruins of the 4,500-year-old city of Ebla and were initially hailed by at least one expert as the "most important find ever made" in relation to the Bible.

According to Pettinato's translation, the tablets recorded commercial transactions involving at least two biblical places whose existence was previously unproved—Sodom and Gomorrah.

"Another newly translated tablet may shed light on the Bible's miraculous account of the Hebrews' Exodus from Egypt. This valuable historical document reportedly gives the Egyptian side of the story, describing how the Pharaoh allowed 'rebellious Asiatic immigrants' to depart the land and how their 'footsteps' were 'swallowed' by a flood."

Father Norton glanced at Father Gatdula. "You forgot to mention the significant variation in the date ascribed to the event—1477 B.C., about two-hundred years earlier than the previous dating of the exodus."

"You know, it's an odd coincidence, but scientists also know that the Santorin volcano exploded during the same period," the Death Merchant said softly. "The blowup wrecked the Mediterranean island now known as Santorin, which is sixty miles north of Crete in the Aegean Sea. Evidence indicates that it was the largest volcanic explosion known to man, a blast that was twenty times as powerful as the Krakatoa explosion in 1883. The magnitude of the explosion supports the theory—it was proposed in 1939 by the Greek archaeologist Spyridon Marinatos—that the Santorin explosion caused a shift of power from Minoan Crete to mainland Greece. The explosion can also explain many of the 'miracles' regarding the Exodus.''

Inserted LaHann, ''Santorini is also one explanation for the origin of the Atlantis story, although Plato in his dialogues of Timaeus and Critias dates the destruction of Atlantis at about 9600 B.C.''

Father Norton's face remained calm and unruffled. Father Gatdula's expression changed to instant resentment (Camellion would have bet Damon and Pythias, his pet pigs, that if Pope Paul had said the moon was made of papier-mâché Father Gatdula would have been the first to shout, ''That's right!'')

''The Santorini explosion!'' Father Gatdula sounded almost angry. ''How could such an explosion indicate anything about God's miracles?''

''Quite a bit,'' explained Camellion. ''The magnitude of the explosion could have unleashed monstrous tsunamis that produced the flood that inundated the Pharaoh's troops. The actual explosion could have been the biblical 'pillar of fire.' ''

Father Gatdula motioned with a hand. ''Nonsense! It's nothing but pure speculation.''

''The same can be said for theology, father,'' the Death Merchant said breezily, ''and theology has changed quite a bit over the centuries. It's always in a state of flux, this slowness not surprising me, considering it's part of a religious system that only now is even considering vindicating Galileo. Or does the Church still maintain that the earth is the 'center of the universe' and doesn't revolve around the sun?''

Father Gatdula betrayed his discomfort by squirming on the couch. ''I must admit that Rome has made some serious mistakes in the past. The Galileo affair is most regrettable.''

''It's more than that,'' said Kelly Dillard. He had come out of the kitchenette and was taking off an apron. ''It's a lot of humbug and superstitious nonsense. Why relics used to be such a big business that, at one time, during the Middle Ages, no fewer than twelves churches possessed the prepuce of Jesus Christ.''[5] His loud laugh was one big sneer. ''They even gave 'Hell' a

[5]This is a fact. We refer the reader to G. Rattray Taylor, *Sex in History* (New York: Ballantine, 1954), p. 44.

33

topography, flora, fauna, and climate.[6] According to the Jesuit Cornelius a Lapide, hell was only two hundred Italian miles across, but he figured this was big enough since a cubic mile could contain 100 billion souls—provided they were packed tightly! I ask you, Who believes such nonsense?''

The Death Merchant interrupted, changing the subject and addressing Father Bernard Norton. ''As I understand it, there are other discoveries that are very unsettling to some people, especially the fundamentalists, who don't even want a comma changed in the Bible.''

''Yes, that is true,'' Father Norton said openly and honestly. ''For example, Christ was not wholly original in all of His teachings. A translation of the Dead Sea Scrolls indicates that Christ wasn't a radical original as previously believed. One of the scrolls more or less proves that a tiny sect of Jews preached an end to Old Testament practices of polygamy and divorce several generations before Christ did.''

''The Essenes,'' said Camellion in a positive tone.

''Exactly. One of the scroll's translators, Professor Jacob Milgrom of the University of California, thinks that John the Baptist, Jesus' cousin, could have picked up these and other beliefs when he lived near Qumran. Moreover, the Gospels tell us that Christ spent three years in the wilderness. Where else but among like-minded people, such as the Essenes?''

''That, too, is only supposition!'' declared Father Gatdula harshly. ''Far too many biblical scholars are turning theory into fact. It's the great immorality of our age.''

''Possibly, but we must be honest and open-minded in these matters,'' responded Father Norton. ''We can't pass over lightly a series of inscriptions and drawings found in a very ancient shrine in the Sinai. These drawings show God, possibly, with a female goddess. Professor Ze'ev Meshel, an Israeli expert who deciphered some of the ancient Hebrew writing, reported in *Biblical Archaeology Review* that two of the pictures may even be Yahweh—Jehovah, if you prefer—and his consort.''[7]

''That's heresy, pure heterodoxy!'' Shocked, Father Gatdula turned and stared in disbelief at Father Norton. ''I'm surprised that you should even mention such a fatuous hypothesis.''

''It isn't heresy but fact that the drawings were found in the Sinai desert. They are there.'' For the first time, Father Norton seemed annoyed. ''It's our duty to investigate such discoveries

[6]A. Graf, *The Story of the Devil* (New York: Macmillan, 1931).
[7]*U.S.* News & World Report, August 24, 1981.

that may provide new evidence on whether distortions have crept into the Bible through centuries of copying and translation."

Father Norton turned from an angry-faced Father Gatdula and looked at Richard Camellion, who knew that Father Norton was an intellectual first and a priest second.

"Several major discoveries have been made by accident," Father Norton said. "That's what happened in 1981 when Greek Orthodox monks tore down a wall of their ancient monastery, Saint Catherine's, at the foot of Mount Sinai. Inside the wall, they found thousands of parchment and papyrus fragments, some containing Bible passages from A.D. 300. The most dramatic discovery was eight pages previously missing from the *Codex Sinaiticus*. This is a priceless fourth-century Greek version of the Old Testament uncovered at the same monastery 132 years ago."

"It's more than likely that the Judas Scrolls will be called the greatest religious discovery of all time," Camellion said, "or rather, I should say, would be regarded as such." He furthered the belief of the two Jesuits, and of the Vatican, that the precious manuscripts, if found, would be turned over to Rome. "If the writings are by Judas, I don't see how their contents could be made known to the world."

Interjected Phil LaHann in a sly tone, "But here's the rub. Even if the scrolls are proved to have originated during the era of Christ, how can it be proved that Judas is the author? If we can prove that he is, how can we be sure he told the truth. We have a dozen tigers by the tail, with each tiger holding a five-pound block of RDX in its mouth."

"The scrolls have to be forgeries," Father Gatdula said with a suavity that the Death Merchant found infuriating. Like all unsure people, Gatdula was too sure of himself. "We know that Judas hanged himself," Gatdula went on. "The Bible says so. We know that Christ died on the cross and rose from the dead on the third day."

"The Bible tells us so!" mocked Kelly Dillard, who was leaning against one side of the doorway between the kitchenette and the lounge.

"Why, the death and the resurrection of Christ is the very cornerstone of our faith. I believe that the Vatican will expose the scrolls for the forgeries they are. By exposing the lies, our faith will be strengthened."

Grinning from ear to ear, Kelly Dillard shook his head and went back into the kitchenette.

The motor home suddenly gave a slight jolt, throwing the men off balance as its front wheels ran through a large rut that Follmer, the driver, could not avoid, the unexpected jar prompting Father Norton to say, "It seems this highway is in need of repair. I suppose we won't reach the solar base until sometime tomorrow."

"Tomorrow afernoon," offered the Death Merchant. "We're not trying to break any speed records. The Centurion tank and the Centurion vehicle carrying the two AA guns can only go 35 mph. Nor can they keep up such a sustained speed without their engines overheating. Every few hours, we'll have to take a fifteen-minute break."

Philip LaHann said speculatively, "All this discussion about the scrolls is academic. We're still a long long way from getting our hands on the Judas Scrolls."

The Death Merchant thought: *Men make gods in their own image, and if the Creator was an image of their better selves, the Devil was an image of their worst selves.* But he said, "All of it could be totally irrelevant in view of the changes in the planet that are taking place. The 1980s and the years that follow will bring drastic weather changes unlike anything modern man has ever experienced."

LaHann and Norton gave the Death Merchant a long, thoughtful look.

Father Victorio Gatdula was immediately skeptical. "I suppose that is only your opinion, Camellion?"

"It's also the opinion of Dr. Douglas Pine, associate professor of atmospheric science at Cornell University, as well as the beliefs of various climatologists throughout the world," Camellion said promptly. "They are all in agreement that a new glacial age has begun."

Camellion proceeded to explain that the experts' alarming forecast was based on a number of incredible factors:

—The sun is shrinking at a rapid rate—much faster than scientists have predicted over the years. *Already, over the past 400 years, the sun has lost a total area equivalent to that of 80,000 Earths!*

—The temperature of the Earth is falling. A drop of only 4.9 degrees would result in the same freezing temperatures as those of the last Great Ice Age.

—The growing season in the food-producing temperate zones has shortened by three weeks in the past forty years.

—*Sizzling summers and vicious winters have killed more than 1,000 people during 1981 in the United States alone,* and there

36

are not any signs that the freakish weather will subside over the next decade.

—Shifts in the position of the sun, Earth and the other planets will change terrestrial climate dramatically. The result will be a new Ice Age. Colossal cold will creep throughout the Northern and the Southern Hemispheres, killing off agriculture altogether in many areas and severely reducing food production in others. Result: a worldwide famine.

Habitable zones on Earth's surface will be greatly restricted, leading to incredible densities of population in warmer zones and extreme hardships in the arctic areas. Millions of people will die from hunger, fuel shortages, and inadequate housing.

"The Four Horsemen of the Apocalypse will be in all their glory," the Death Merchant said. "Death, War, Plague, Famine will be in all their glory."

"I'm thinking of a similar prediction," said Father Norton, "made by Johann Friede, a thirteenth-century Austrian monk. "He said that toward the end of the world, mankind will face its last, hard trial. That the end would be foreshadowed by striking changes in nature, that the alternation between heat and cold will become more intense. He said storms will have more catastrophic effects. Earthquakes will destroy many lands and the seas will overflow into many lowlands."

LaHann said easily, "I'd be safe in saying that we can find clues to these troublesome times to come in a study of the zodiac. History—"

"Astrology is superstitious claptrap!" Father Gatdula said flatly.

"History and legend show an analogy between the archetypal temperaments of man and the twelve signs of the zodiac. A lot of historians feel it is these analogous relationships which underlie the twelve tribes of Israel, the twelve apostles of Christ, the twelve nights of King Arthur's Round Table, and the twelve labors of Hercules."

"That's some more humanist nonsense," Father Gatdula said gruffly.

"No, it isn't." LaHann easily brushed aside the Jesuit's objection. "Ancient man recognized the relationship betweens the heavenly bodies and his early condition thousands of years before the humanists were around. That's why he devised architectural buildings to observe the stars and the planets. We can see this in the ziggurats of Sumeria, the legendary Tower of Babel, the temples of Central and South America, and the Great Pyramid at Gizeh in Egypt."

37

"There's also the prophesies of the Church's own saints that foretell great disaster," Camellion said, his gaze fixed on Father Gatdula. "The amazing seer Saint Malachy[8] has had a number of his prophecies fulfilled. He not only foresaw that two Popes would follow Pope John Paul II, but he also predicted the end of the reign of Popes and foresaw extreme persecution of the Catholic Church. He said the last Pope would be *'Peter the Roman,'* who would lead his flock amid many tribulations. The *'City of the Seven Hills'*—Rome—would be destroyed and the 'Great Judge' would come. I would presume he was referring to the end of the world—or, symbolically, the end of an age."

"There is a tradition of belief in the Church that the last Pope will be named Peter," Father Norton said nervously.

"There is also the prophecy of nineteenth-century Saint Don Bosco," the Death Merchant said, "and the vision of Pope Pius X. Both foresaw the Vatican in flames and the Pope fleeing the Vatican through Saint Peter's Square, over the dead bodies of cardinals, bishops, any number of religious, both men and women, and thousands of laymen."

"That ties in with the predictions of Nostradamus," remarked LaHann. "By the mid-1980s, Italy will see its death pangs and a third world war will begin by then. But this war—it will last almost four years and end in 1986 or 1987—will not be the biblical Armageddon. The inhabitants of Rome will flee for their lives, and for whatever reason, the French army will be in on the act and will be defeated in Italy. The Pope will flee to France but will be killed near the city of Lyon in December of—? Who knows?"

Camellion was debating whether to spring on the two Jesuits certain facts that the Fox had revealed to him when LaHann made it easy for him by mentioning Sister Lucia, one of the children who had seen the Blessed Virgin at Fátima.

"You know," mused LaHann contemplatively, "I wonder if any of what we have been discussing was one of the Fátima prophecies that Lucia revealed to Pope Paul VI in 1967. Could it have been the end of the Roman Catholic Church? Could that have been what she told the Pope?"

"No one knows what she told His Holiness," Father Norton said. "Pope Paul VI never did reveal the secret, and naturally no one dared to ask."

[8]1095–1148. Irish churchman; successively the abbot of Bangor, bishop of Connor, archbishop of Armagh, and bishop of Down.

The Death Merchant began tapping the tips of his fingers together.

"Or Sister Lucia might have told Pope Paul VI *that Satan would penetrate up to the very head of the Church*," Camellion said, slyly watching Father Gatdula. "That was the prediction made by La Salette, the French mystic, in 1846."

Father Norton's eyes widened. Father Gatdula looked as if he were about to have a stroke. "T-That's monstrous!" gasped Gatdula.

Camellion continued, "Some see in La Salette's prophecy a change in the form of Church leadership. Or it could mean a literal takeover of the Vatican by conspiratorial, heretic forces. Both known and unknown seers, as well as A. C. Emmerich, Don Bosco, Pope Leo XIII, and Pope Pius X have foreseen the dire tribulations that will befall the Catholic Church; these are frequently suppressed or denounced as inaccuracies by the hierarchy of the Vatican."

"They're all false, all lies," said Father Gatdula. He straightened up, his eyes blazing. "More likely than not, it's the communists who start these rumors."

Nuts to that joker. If I didn't know better, I'd think he was an ex-member of the New York City—or Mesa, Arizona—Police Department!

The Death Merchant dropped the verbal bombshell. "Gentlemen, I've news for you. Voice . . ."

. . . Recordings offer virtual proof that an imposter Pope was making public appearances while posing as the real Pope Paul VI. Pope Paul VI was heard to have said, *"The smoke of Satan has entered the Church."* Soon after that, he was replaced by a double and held prisoner in the Vatican. His private quarters were bugged. No one, except the conspiring usurpers, were allowed within Pope Paul's private rooms, not even the Swiss Guards. There is a good deal of evidence that a continuous cover-up has been undertaken by the Church, including suppression of incriminating, documented evidence of imposters within the Vatican.

"The 800-year-old *De Labore Solis* of Saint Malachy had been interpreted to mean 'Rising Sun,' which denotes the East," Camellion said. "This could apply to the present Pope John Paul II, who came from Eastern Europe, from Poland. If so, then Pope John Paul II may be the Pope referred to in Saint Malachy's prophecy. Other Popes used only one name—Paul, John, Leo, etc. Cardinals Luciani and Wojtyla used two names. Thus the

Malachy symbol of the 'half-moon' and 'nothing whole' could fit Wojtyla's name perfectly.''

"None of this can possibly be true—none of it!" Father Gatdula was furious and almost shaking with rage. "Mr. Camellion, it's men like you who do the work of Satan, who spread rumors and add to lies and gross distortions.''

"Pish 'n' tosh!" Camellion said gaily, waving a hand. "I'm talking to two Jesuits, not circulating handbills. There's been a power struggle within in the Vatican for years—the traditionalists versus the modernists. It's common knowledge among people in the know. And you can't deny it!''

Father Gatdula regained control of himself, loudly clearing his throat. His jaw tightened, but he relaxed and stopped glaring at the Death Merchant. "I suppose you'll be telling us next that some psychic or saint predicted that those scrolls, supposedly written by Judas, would be found?''

"Not that I know of,'' Camellion replied. "I'm neither saint nor psychic, but I can predict that if the scrolls are where they are supposed to be, we'll find them, and we'll get them out of Jordan.''

"I see you're not modest about your abilities!" Father Gatdula cleared his throat again, this time with less respect and more admonition.

"Modest? I?'' Camellion smiled maliciously. "Why, you've no idea what a poor opinion I have of myself—and how little I deserve it.''

In spite of his cheerful manner, Camellion was deeply concerned about Father Bernard Norton. Unlike Father Gatdula, who had been shocked at Camellion's statements, considering all of them sacrilegious and debased to the extreme, Father Norton had not appeared even mildly concerned. Not even when Camellion had mentioned an imposter pope had Norton registered surprise or mild amazement.

It's as if he already knew!

Kelly Dillard appeared in the entrance between the lounge and the kitchenette, his expression sullen.

"We're not going to have Waldorf salad,'' he announced bitterly. "No apples. We'll have to settle for green salad.''

If I'm right about Father Norton, what else does he know?

CHAPTER FOUR

A fanatical believer in the old truism that God helps those who help themselves, the Death Merchant and Courtland Grojean had planned with the utmost caution down to the last detail. The Company had done its part; and because it had, the New York City home office of Ryan, Colt & Webber Construction Company, Inc., had instructed Colin Burtch, the manager of Jordanian Experimental Solar Station One, to give the six "engineers" a free hand. Oh, by the way, one of the engineers was an Italian from Milan, Italy. He was a representative of Galabino Industries, a large manufacturing corporation that was speculating about getting into the solar energy field.

None of these details bothered the Death Merchant, who was driving the motor home, as the armored column approached the solar station—an hour ahead of schedule—at 1500 hours.

As dreary looking as a junkyard, the general landscape was not the type that would ever appear on any travel folder printed by the Jordanian Travel Bureau. The only things that even vaguely resembled civilization was the highway (that ran two kilometers east of the solar station) and the solar station, half a kilometer to the southeast. Otherwise, this part of the Ard As Sawwan appeared as it had been for centuries, bleak, barren, unfriendly. Uneven, the entire area was filled with golden-colored sand dunes whose surfaces were marked with diminutive ripples. Around the dunes and between them were black basalt rocks of various sizes and solidified lava, or rock froth, of the type called scoria, all this wilderness of stone intermingling with slabs of broken sandstone. Here and there was exfoliation of small slopes. The only vegetation was scanty sagebrush and twisted and tortured looking *put'qad'* shrubs.

"God, it looks as useless as stilts on a stork!" said Kelly Dillard, who was riding in the driver's compartment with Camellion.

In a few more minutes, the Death Merchant turned the motor

41

home northwest. The ride became bumpy, for now the "road" was only hard, uneven rock covered with sand. The only consolation was that the solar station continued to grow larger.

Captain Gamal Nashibi, who had instructed Camellion to follow the command van, called on the intercom system that had been established in the column and, as the "caravan" was moving to the north side of the station, told the Death Merchant to park between "the silver domes and the goat-hair tents of the Bedu workers."

The solar station wouldn't have won any beauty prizes either, although it wasn't as desolate as the desert. Ringed by Jordanian armor, the station was large, a couple of thousand feet from north to south and the same distance from east to west.

In the northwest section of the circle were the seven large silver-colored domes—or steel igloos that had actually been the roofs of silos—where the forty American construction workers lived. Each dome, joined to its neighbor by an arch assembly, contained half an inch of spray-on cellulose coating as an acoustical barrier and round windows of double-paned glass sealed in a car-type gasket. Louvers over the windows could be opened and closed by a cord from inside each dome.

East of the domes were the black goat-hair tents of the Bedouin workers. Toward the center of the circle was the kitchen attached to the common mess—barracklike buildings of the prefab type, of the kind that could be hauled on large flat-bed trucks.

South of the kitchen/mess was the General Office, another prefab job painted a sickly pale yellow. To the southeast of the GO was the generator shack and its seventy-two-foot tall "windmill" that wasn't a windmill. The "windmill" looked like a giant clothesline draped with very straight beach towels; yet it was actually a very efficient wind turbine, with the beachtowels being thirty-foot-tall airfoils that generated 340 Kw.s[1] of power. The turbine's six aluminum symmetrical airfoils rode along cable loops suspended between the two sets of large lightweight pulleys. As the wind pushed the foils along the cables, the pulleys rotated. The electric generator was coupled to the pulleys.

To the west were rows of army tents in which the Jordanian soldiers lived. Farther to the south was the work shed, another prefab building that was shaped like half of a swastika.

[1]Kilowatt. The turbine is manufactured by the Free-wing Turbine Corporation, of Murray, Utah.

42

South of the work shed was the Solar Breeder building—432 feet long, 72.3 feet wide, and shaped like a triangle, the wide base of the triangle being the foundation. The slanted sides of the Solar Breeder building contained 36,410 square feet of solar cells. The interior of the building contained the solar-heat storage systems.

The Death Merchant parked the motor home while Captain Nashibi's armor moved into position alongside the vehicles that were already there. The Jordanian soldiers who had been at the station for weeks would begin the return journey the next morning.

Colin Burtch, the chief engineer and the manager of the station, was a tall, sandy-haired, raw-boned man with a deeply lined face marked by wind, rain, and years of sunshine. Friendly, he laughed readily and seemed to be an amiable man.

Assistant Manager Elmore Fradenbach, ten years older than Burtch, was a balding man in his early fifties, tallish and on the thin side. He had an oval-shaped face, eyes that could have been gray marbles, and didn't seem to know what to do with his large hands after Burtch introduced him to Camellion and the other "engineers."

"I know you're all tired from your long journey," Burtch said congenially to the Death Merchant and the others. "I suggest all of you settle in today and we'll show you the station tomorrow." He smiled broadly, showing crooked but white teeth. "All of you are guests of honor tonight. The cooks are preparing *hu'jinq*.[2] And when Captain Gamal Nashibi and Major Suleiman Franji, the latter of whom was the commander of the soldiers that Nashibi and his men would replace, were out of earshot, Fradenbach whispered nervously, "If any of you are Jewish, please don't mention it. The soldiers and the Arab workers have an unreasonable hatred of the Jewish people."

"None of us are Jewish," Camellion replied levelly. He wasn't worried about the three CIA men; they had been through many many deceptions. As for the two Jesuits—with more belief in "miracles" and "God's will" than common sense—Camellion had told them to say as little as possible and to think five times before they answered any questions. "There won't be any trouble in that direction," Camellion told Fradenbach and Burtch.

---

[2]Lamb, chicken, and mixed vegetables cooked in a rich, spicy sauce.

There wasn't a problem at supper that night either, nor later, during the early morning hours, when Camellion and Kelly Dillard opened the portable ice chest, carefully removed the special DL-14j shortwave radio with a built-in "black box" and a double G13v scrambler. The radio had sixty-four channels, each 10,000 hertz (cycles) wide on the ultrahigh frequency, and transmission and reception could be effected either by voice or code key. In either case, the transmission would first go through the scrambler, then through all sixty-four channels simultaneously; the final stage would be the "bumblebee," or "black box," which would complete the "demuxing" and shoot out the message over the air at the rate of 610 words per second. Only an identical radio/scramble/bumblebee could receive and decipher the transmission. To Israeli and Soviet monitors, the transmission would be very rapid static, similar to the type that comes from an X-ray star.

An identical DL-14j radio was exactly 89.2 miles southeast of the solar station, the final 13 miles inside Saudi Arabia, at the small settlement of At-Turayf. There, outside the village, the CIA, with the help of the Saudi General Security Directorate[3] had set up a special station to send and receive communications from Onion-Feathers-Four.

Onion-Feathers-Four pulled the coiled red cord from the open ice chest. At the end of the cord was a heavy-duty claw-type jumper which he clipped to one of the rings over one of the burners on the bottled-gas stove, thereby turning the entire motor home into a giant antenna.

In case someone had planted a high-gain "bug" outside the motor home, Dillard had turned on a small white-sound generator close to the radio, all the while muttering vindictives against President Reagan and his administration. "I tell you, Camellion, if I didn't know better, I'd think Reagan and his people were all working for the damned liberals. After the next election we're likely to have Teddy Kennedy, that 'gun-control' idiot, for President. Hopefully, some good soul will kill him before he can get nominated."

"With a brick or say a two by four," finished the Death Merchant. "That way the liberal trash can scream for a ban on bricks and lumber. Heh, heh, heh . . . Bricks 'kill.' So do two by fours."

<hr>

[3]We refer the reader to Death Merchant #49, *The Night of the Peacock*.

"At least we got rid of the ATF," chuckled Dillard.[4] "Those storm trooper bastards won't cripple any more innocent people. And if the Secret Service starts any bullshit about weapons, they'll also get plenty of pressure from 50 million gun owners who are sick to death of idiot judges slapping rapists, muggers, and other pieces of trash on the wrist and turning them loose. It's time the American people start protecting themselves, because the courts sure as hell won't. Or don't you agree?"

"Add to that that we should execute 90 percent of the judges in the United States and you'll have something." Camellion flipped a toggle switch, turned the fine-tuning dial, and went to work, his finger on the NYE Viking code key.

The next morning, under a deep blue sky with only a few powder puffs of clouds to the south, Colin Burtch and Elmore Fradenbach took the Death Merchant and the five other men on an inspection tour of the base. Camellion, Dillard, and the others were quick to notice that Major Franji and his armor were gone and that Captain Nashibi's vehicles were in place—an armored car to the north of the encampment, three others to the south, east, and west. The Centurion MK III heavy tank and the tank chassis and AA gun turret were positioned in the center of the circle, northeast of the tool shop. Jordanian soldiers were at all times either close to or in the vehicles. In addition, two men were always in the seventy-five-foot-high watch tower in the center of the camp. At night the men would scan the terrain through night-vision devices.

Colin Burtch, a man who talked as much with his hands as he did with his mouth, explained in a very serious low tone, "You see, it's not only dangerous bands of Bedouins we must protect ourselves against, there is always the possibility that the Israelis might make a strike against us. They're not anxious to see this solar station completed, much less see it operate successfully. Then there's those fanatical Palestinian Resistance League killers. They hate Americans as much as they hate the Jews."

"Why Americans?" inquired Victorio Gatdula. "I suppose it's because the United States is supplying Israel with arms."

"That's right," said Burtch. "Personally, I worry about the

[4]The Bureau of Alcohol, Tobacco and Firearms. It was disbanded. Firearms now belong to the Secret Service; tobacco and alcohol to Customs. The ATF was disbanded because the agency constantly went after honest citizens, over some obscure law, while ignoring genuine criminals.

Israelis. The Israeli border is only thirty-eight miles to the west."

"Twice, during the past year," started Elmore Fradenbach as the group walked toward the Solar Breeder building, "the PRL tried to infiltrate the camp—men with bombs, that sort of thing. Each time, the Jordanians caught them. They executed all ten by a torture called *hu'timq*. Have you heard of it?"

"I can't say that I have," Camellion said innocently—and he hadn't.

Fradenbach pulled the brim of his green felt bush hat lower over his yellow-tinted sunglasses. "Well, sir, the Jordanians staked the captives out in the sand." He lowered his voice. "They're a sadistic bunch of bastards. They staked the poor devils out in the sand, with their eyes staring into the sun. Then the soldiers cut off their eyelids. It was terrible. The terrorists took hours to die. They died screaming—insane."

"Disgraceful," muttered Philip LaHann. "This is indeed a savage country. But we're here and must make the best of it I suppose."

(The Death Merchant again thought of how he and Kelly had been set up in the park back in Amman. It hadn't been that much of a surprise. He had suspected an ambush. All right. So it was over and done with—up to a point. There was still the matter of the contact—*And I don't like loose ends!*

The report from the Company Green Gables team at At-Turayf, via the DL-14j shortwave, had not been good. The contact had not reported in to the CIA station in Amman. Conclusion: he—or it might be a she!—was playing it ultracautious or else he (she) had been taken. By whom? The KGB? The Israelis? Or could Department 4 have blacked-bagged him (her)? The contact's message—passed on by Green Gables to Camellion—had been vital: the Saudis had finally agreed to let the CIA fly attack and troop-carrying helicopters from Arabia into southern Jordan; furthermore, the Saudis would provide Saudi army commandos. *I wonder what Big Uncle had to give the Saudis in return? They never do anything for nothing!*

Another unanswered question that was a thorn in the Death Merchant's mental file compartment: *If there is a spy at this solar station, how is he getting out reports?* Answer: *He has to be using a transmitter with a black box. OK! He's either a pro or a talented on-contract man.*

Where was the radio hidden? Obviously not in the domes or the office. Not in any of the buildings where more than two persons gathered. *It has to be concealed in a very private place. That leaves me with three answers—the three motor homes.*

Fradenbach, the assistant manager of the solar station, had a Caper mini motor home mounted on a Chevy S-10 pickup truck. Burtch, the manager, had a twenty-five-foot Southwind. The red and white Winnebago van belonged to Clint McPictrick, the chief solar-cell technician. Now the problem became how to get into the vans and find the radio.

Once inside the Solar Breeder building, Colin Burtch waved a hand toward the hundreds of five-foot-tall cells all in a row and started explaining how they worked. "As you know, it's a chemical called sodium thiosulfate pentahydrate. We call it hypo for short. It's really the basic chemical in our heat-storage system derived from the solar cells on the sides of the building."

Each heat-storage cell, or unit, had five nozzle pipes in a salt tank. When the tank was fully discharged, salt crystals would block the nozzles. The actual charging would begin when hot water (above forty-eight degrees centigrade) from the solar collector circulated through heat-exchange coils, warming thermal oil; an electric pump would then start, pumping oil via a bypass pipe up to a simple automatic distribution valve, the pressure lifting a piston to its highest position and opening a top outlet to circulate the oil.

"What happens then is that heat from the bypass pipe melts the salt, blocking the bottom nozzles," Burtch said. "This opens oil passages from the lowest valve outlet. The resultant pressure drop causes the piston to fall to that level. Oil flowing through the cleared nozzles causes further local melting."

Interrupted the Death Merchant, "But there are snags in the system." (*I hope!*)

"I know you've seen the reports at the Home Office," Burtch said nervously, wiping his high forehead.

"Naturally, we all have," replied the Death Merchant. And they had, for the construction company in New York had provided the CIA with any number of reports and reading material in order that the Death Merchant and the rest of the CIA men could familiarize themselves with the solar station. Even the two Jesuits had spent hours reading up on the heat-transfer system.

Father Gatdula now proved he remembered what he had read. "All the reports indicate that hypo has ideal characteristics for solar-heat storage," he said matter of factly. "New York is very pleased."

And so was Burtch, who, nodding, smiled. "I'm glad to hear

that. Hypo is ideal," he said. "It's thermal-storage capacity is exceptional, and it melts at a higher temperature than Glauber's salt—48 degrees centigrade, 118 degrees Fahrenheit. That's high enough to provide hot water and space heating, yet not too high for the normal collector panels to tolerate."

Robert Follmer said, "Yet there is a problem with the formation of the salt crystals? We understand you're solving that problem with mineral oil, a special kind of mineral oil?"

Burtch nodded. Fradenbach's ovoid-shaped face deepened with lines of concern for a moment before he spoke. "The system combines a heat-exchanger coil in the solar panel and domestic-plumbing circuit with a tank of phase-change salts. That's the heart of the system. The snag is that the salts gradually solidify when latent heat is released and cling to the surface of the coil, building up an insulating crust. I don't have to explain what happens then. This stops further extraction of heat."

"But we think we've solved that problem with the special mineral oil," Burtch said quickly. "It's a nonmechanical answer, yet it seems to work."

"You mean the use of the mineral oil as a two-way heat-transfer medium between coil and salts?" said Kelly Dillard, who then lighted a cigarette.

"Yes. The mineral oil—it's an immiscible fluid—is pumped through the molten salt." Burtch's hands moved like two flags waving in a hard breeze. "Since the oil's specific gravity is lower than the salt's, the oil rises to the top of the tank, where the exchanger coil is immersed, and transfers the absorbed heat to it."

"What Elmore is saying is that a crafty multilevel arrangement for dispersing the oil through the salt solution whips the crusting snag," said Burtch. "I'll show you the drawing and blueprints we have in the office after we finish with the rest of the installation, although there isn't really all that much more to see."

Fradenbach hooked his hands on the lapels of his tan cruiser jacket. "We can tell you for sure that the oil-feed arrangement, plus direct salt-to-oil contact, speeds the heat-transfer action," he said confidently. "That means that fleeting bursts of solar warmth are captured, and even small reserves of heat can be extracted—and quickly too. We have the efficiency and phase graphs to prove it. You can check them when you look over the blueprints."

"There's plenty of time," Camellion said nonchalantly. "We'll be here for a month and will return to Amman with Captain Nashibi.''

"Surely, there's more than enough time." Burtch's hands moved from his thighs to his rib cage. "The truth is that we were somewhat surprised—all of us here at the station—that New York should send five of you to study the problem of salt solidification."

"Gentlemen, I am only an observer," Victorio Gatdula said stiffly, "as a representative for my company, Galabino Industries of Milan."

"Oh, yes yes, I forgot for a moment," apologized Burtch condescendingly.

"Speaking of things to see"—Camellion looked at Colin Burtch—"I'm interested in the silo top domes. I've never seen anything like them. I'd like to see them from the inside."

During the day and the following night, and the next day and the next night, the Death Merchant and the Company men accomplished almost next to nothing. Most of the time, the two Jesuits remained in the motor home, twice a day saying their Office. Twice Camellion warned them in stern tones not to let any of the solar station personnel see the thick manuals, *Spiritual Exercises*, from which they read.

Kelly Dillard, who seldom, if ever, spoke to the two priests, was convinced that "They're nothing but trouble, Camellion—excess baggage who'll get our butts blown off."

The second night Camellion did manage to slip out of the motor home, at 0330, and attach thimble-size DW14 transmitters to the undersides of the Caper mini motor home, the Southwind, and the Winnebago—a task that required a lot of time and considerable crawling since the three vehicles were a hundred feet southwest of the silo domes, three hundred feet west of the Century-Flash bus.

For the remainder of the morning—that is, until 0745—Camellion monitored the three bugs with a panoramic surveillance receiver—and heard nothing but "silent" static (known as "black noise" in the trade).

"For Christ's sake, when are you going to sleep?" demanded Robert Follmer. "It will look damned odd to Burtch and Fradenbach if you sleep all day!"

"Don't worry about it," Camellion said. "The amount of sleep gotten by the average person is about an hour more than he needs. With me it's six hours less. Another thing, there has to be one of us at the surveillance receiver at all times. Of course, if he's using a silent code key, we'll never hear it.''

"Suppose none of the three is the spy?'' said LaHann. "The target might be one of the other Americans, or one of the Jordanians. What then?''

"I don't know.'' Camellion sighed. "We'll have to play it by ear.''

During the second day, the Death Merchant had his hands full giving excuses why he and the other engineers should not go to the office and check blueprints, "coefficient computations,'' and other data which only professional engineers could discuss with any semblance of intelligence. Within ten minutes it would have become obvious to Colin Burtch and Elmore Fradenbach that Camellion and the others were as phony as a prostitute's smile.

The panoramic surveillance receiver continued to pick up only black noise . . .

On the third day, to keep from going to the office and checking data, the Death Merchant pretended to have a sick stomach and remained in the motor home most of the day. He spent the time going over various plans; yet all his logic and experience informed him that there was only one sure way to know for certain if the Judas Scrolls were in the Jabal Arqā. A lightning strike straight into the Arqā Mountains from Saudi Arabia! *By air, from the south. Somehow, we can link up with the force. At the same time, a diversionary attack from northern Saudi territory, at the junction where the Jordanian, Iraqi, and Saudi borders converge!*

Again there were several difficulties. Coordination of the two attacks. The second was the exact location of the cave in the Jabal Arqā. For the force to be guided by only a vague map drawn by Mahmoud Khalil would be as ridiculous as expecting one of Father Gatdula's "miracles.'' It would be much more practical to take Mahmoud Khalil with the force. Once the Jordanian saw familiar landmarks, he could guide them directly to the cave. This meant that Khalil would have to be smuggled from the U.S. Embassy in Amman to Saudi Arabia. A difficult task, but it could be, and would be, done very soon.

On the third night, at 0300 hours, the Death Merchant discussed the entire plan with Green Gables at At-Turayf. He had signed off when the siren on the watchtower began to scream its shrieking warning, its piercing blare blasting the stillness of the night.

The siren meant only one thing! The guards on the watchtower

50

had spotted an enemy. Very soon the solar station would be under attack.

Triple dirty damn! An attack—by whom, I wonder?—is all we need!

Camellion was locking the lid of the ice chest and thanking all the gods in the realm of mythology that the DL-14j shortwave was protected by concealed armor plate within the top, the sides, and the bottom of the chest as the accordion-type door to the lounge opened and Kelly Dillard, followed by the other men, rushed into the kitchenette. Fully dressed, for he had been monitoring the three bugs, Kelly Dillard carried a mini-Uzi with a forty-round magazine. He had a bag of spare clips over one shoulder and a Dan Wesson .357 magnum jammed in his waistband. Wearing only pants and in their bare feet, Robert Follmer and Philip LaHann were armed with M-12 Beretta submachine guns that hung from their shoulders by straps. They were buckling on basic A.L.I.C.E. belts whose holsters held Astra A-80 auto-pistols.[5] Unarmed and wide-eyed, the two Jesuits were in pajamas.

"We're damned lucky that the Jordanian government gave us permission to bring in weapons," Dillard said roughly. "If—"

He stopped and, with the other men, jerked his head up and to the right at the sound of the voice coming through a bullhorn from the watchtower, the frantic words first in Arabic, then in English—"ENEMY VEHICLES APPROACHING FROM THE WEST! ENEMY VEHICLES APPROACHING FROM THE WEST! ENEMY VEHICLES APPRO—"

There was another sound, a familiar sound, the run-together *thump-thump-thump-thump* of a helicopter rotor—coming from the southwest and getting louder all the time! *The damned Israelis! Terrorists don't use choppers!*

"You guys get the hell out of here and see what's going on," Camellion said calmly. "I'll arm myself and join you."

"W-What d-do we do?" cried Father Norton.

"Outside and under the motor home—and pray!" Camellion said. "Move it!"

While the three Company men and the two Jesuits rushed outside, the Death Merchant raced into the lounge, opened one of the side lockers, pulled out a Swedish M-37 *Automat Gevär* (a modification of the U.S. Browning "BAR"), a cotton duck

---

[5]A new weapon, the Astra A-80 is a double-action semiautomatic pistol that comes in 9mm, .38 Super, and .45 ACP. Models in 9mm and .38 Super have a fifteen-round magazine.

ammo bag filled with eight spare magazines for the weapon, and a Safariland garrison belt on which were two leather holsters, each one filled with an M-200 International Auto Mag pistol. Additional magazine pouches for the two Auto Mags were attached to the back of the garrison belt.

The Death Merchant was leaving the motor home the same time that the Israeli helicopter, a Westland-Aérospatiale Lynx, roared in from the southwest, at an altitude of only several hundred feet. During those few moments, Camellion saw by the camp lights that the three Company men and the two Jesuits—*Damn!*—were crouched by the east side of one of the silo domes with Colin Burtch, Elmore Fradenbach, and a dozen other American engineers, all of whom were armed with 310 SIG *Maschinenpistoles*. Moreover, Captain Nashibi and his men were far from idle. The four Saladin armored cars were rolling toward the west. So was the heavy Centurion MK III heavy tank, groups of Jordanian soldiers behind the tank and the armored cars. The Bedu workers had left their goat-skin tents and were running full speed into the desert, many carrying their few possessions with them. This fight was not their fight and they wanted no part of it.

The Jordanian gunner began firing the twin Oerlikon antiaircraft guns at the Israeli chopper when it was only 1,500 feet from the southeast perimeter of the encampment, on a course that would take it at a very sharp angle to the northeast. Thirty-five millimeter shells began streaming toward the chopper as the Israeli copilot/gunner shot off two S16 Temple missiles from the pods. The high-explosive laser-guided missiles streaked toward the Solar Breeder building that was three-quarters completed. The missiles struck the slanted south side of the building and exploded with crashing roars and huge flashes of yellow fire. In an instant, $8 million dollars worth of sun-gathering cells and heat-storage units were destroyed, the wreckage flying up and out, over a wide area.

"Get to the north of the domes—quickly!" yelled the Death Merchant. "They'll be opening fire with either cannon or machine guns."

In only a few seconds, Camellion was proved correct. Gunners in the Westland Lynx opened fire with FN-MAG machine guns, from both port and starboard, the rain of solid metal-jacketed slugs first chopping through the roof of the work shed, then exploding the two soldiers on top of the watchtower into big bloody chunks of flesh. More 7.62-mm slugs whipped into the windmill, the generator shed, the mess/kitchen, the command van, and the Hubbler scout car, a flood of metal that demolished precious equipment and, where the slugs hit the hard ground, made geysers of dirt jump upward a foot, often hundreds of spouts at a time.

There were three Jordanians in the turret on which the twin Oerlikons were mounted. FN-MAG slugs found the gunner and blew him apart. With the dead man's blood splattered all over them (including bits and pieces of his uniform), the other two Jordanians, cursing in Arabic, pulled the corpse from the gunner's seat and refilled the bins of the two AA guns with 35mm shells. The Jordanians didn't have the training of the Israeli crew in the chopper; however, they did have a slight edge. They weren't afraid to die. In fact, if they died fighting the Jews—the worst infidels of all!—they would go straight to heaven with all possible speed. They knew this to be truth. It was one of the articles of faith in the Islam *īmān,* or "doctrine."

By the time the AA guns were reloaded, the Israeli gunship was ripping to shreds the black goat-skin tents, hundreds of 7.62mm slugs sending a dark cloud of material into the air. The pilot then began to pull-in-pitch and take the Westland Lynx upward. Behind the chopper, the encampment was a wreck. The Solar Breeder building had all but disappeared, and every light had blinked off, now that the generator was good for only junk. The petrol in the Hubbler scout car and in the command van had exploded and wrecked both vehicles. The two piles of junk were burning, thick, oily black smoke pouring upward into the no longer clean early-morning sky with its half-moon. There was the disagreeable odor of hot metal, burning rubber, cloth, and other material, while the crackling flames caused giant shadows to slide and glide silently over the camp.

"Oh, my God! Oh, my God! What are we going to do?" moaned Clint McPictrick, the chief solar-cell technician. Skinny, pale faced, and nervous, he made the Death Merchant think of a woodpecker without a pole to peck on.

"A year of work wrecked!" Colin Burtch, down on one knee against the east side of one of the housing domes, complained bitterly. "Goddamn those Israeli bastards."

Elmore Fradenbach said fiercely, "Let's try to take out that helicopter with our machine guns. If we all fire together—"

"Stay down," Camellion warned him. "We're not a match for a chopper with thirty calibers. They'd cut us to pieces."

"Now see here," began Fradenbach angrily. "You're not in charge of how we—"

"Shut up and do what I tell you if you want to live. Watch it! The gun bird is returning."

The Israeli chopper had made a sharp turn; the pilot had revved down the rotor and was preparing for another run, this time coming in straight from the east. Once more the four FN MAG machine guns roared. Then abruptly they stopped.

Fate! Luck! Or intense hatred of the Jordanians! Whatever it was, the Jordanian gunner at the Oerlikons got lucky. A 35mm HE shell exploded in the cockpit of the enemy helicopter and killed the pilot and copilot, leaving nothing but shattered instruments and a bloody mess. Completely out of control, the dying Westland Lynx jerked like a mortally wounded bird, which it was. At a very steep angle, wobbling back and forth, the chopper headed toward the ground, crashing a short distance from the burning scout car. A *WOORRRRUUUMPH*, a rolling ball of flame, and it was all over with, the only remains burning scrap and four roasting corpses.

"La ilah illa Allah!"[6] yelled the two Jordanians in victory.

The Death Merchant put a hand on Colin Burtch's right shoulder. "Where are the rest of your men, the American workers?"

"They're in the domes," answered Burtch like a little boy. "They don't have machine guns or rifles, only maybe a couple of dozen pistols and revolvers. I figured that if we were ever attacked, they would be safest inside the living quarters."

"Get them out of there and out here," Camellion said fiercely. "The Israelis have armor and they'll start shelling this base as soon as they get within range. Have your people—"

"The Israelis aren't dumb," interjected Kelly Dillard, thrusting his big face closer to Camellion and Burtch. "Think about it, Camellion. Nine times out of ten, they use a forward stab and a pincer from the flanks. There could be Jew commandos coming at us from the north, or south or east."

The Death Merchant almost said *affirmative*, but checked himself before the first syllable could be formed by his vocal cords.

"You're right," he agreed. "I was thinking along the same lines. For that reason we'll (he almost said *deploy*, but again caught himself) space out men along the north, east, and south perimeters—a hundred feet apart and hope for the best."

"I'll go get the other men," offered Clint McPictrick as he turned to go to the main entrance of the domes. He stopped and looked at Camellion in confusion when the Death Merchant reached out and grabbed him by the left arm. "Listen, send the men with handguns to us," Camellion said. "Tell the others to

---

[6] "(There is) no God but Allah."

54

get their butts to the goat-skin tents. The Moses' boys aren't going to waste shells on goat-skin rubbish—and you can bet they know where everything in this camp is located. Get going.''

Camellion turned to a silent but fearful Father Norton and Father Gatdula. "The two of you go with the workers and dig in under the tents.''

"Damn it to hell! If we only had some heavy machine guns or grenade launchers,'' growled Robert Follmer to no one in particular.

"Where is Captain Nashibi and Lieutenant Hatumin? No one's mentioned them,'' said Phil LaHann. "It's chilly!''

Inquired Father Norton in a quiet voice, "What will happen if the Israelis, or whoever is attacking, get through?''

Another man, one of the construction engineers, said, "We'll be taken prisoner, won't we?''

Camellion gave the Jesuit and the engineer a look of disdain. "If our armor doesn't stop their armor, we'll all meet God or the Devil before sunrise. Yeah, does anyone here know where Hatumin and Nashibi are?''

"I can't be sure, but I believe they are in the tank,'' said Colin Burtch, taking a large, shuddering intake of breath. "Captain Nashibi once remarked that in the event of an attack, he and Hatumin would use the tank as a command post. Both were trained to be tank men, so I understand—Nashibi as a tank commander.''

"I hope he's good,'' Camellion said.

Soon men were pouring out of the main entrance of the domes—some of them running in the low light cast by the burning-down fires of the command van and the scout car—toward the goat-skin tents, which lay on the ground in confusion and shot full of holes. Other men stopped by the side of the dome, all of them more angry than afraid. Altogether, twenty-nine men were armed with either pistols or revolvers, although one man did have two Walther P-38s.

Speaking rapidly and in a voice steady with authority, the Death Merchant told them what to do and how to do it.

"You seem to know what you're talking about, fella,'' one man said in admiration. "You must have been in a lot of wars!''

"A few!'' Camellion commented.

In a very short time, the Death Merchant and the men were moving from the side of the dome and dispersing, some of them heading north, others moving to the east and the south—darting silently and quickly, except those in bare feet. They moved more slowly, almost as if walking on egg shells and trying not to break them. There were small pebbles on the hard ground.

Camellion, Robert Follmer, and seven other men, two with 310 SIG machine pistols, hurried toward the southeast perimeter, the Death Merchant willing to bet his *Memento Mori* ranch that he was right about the Israeli attack force. The border to the West Bank was only thirty-eight miles to the west. The strike would have to be fast. In very quickly. Do the job, then out again—*Before the Jordanians could send choppers or whatever. Tanks are too slow, and the Israeli High Command wouldn't want to risk a tank on a sneak-in black operation. What would I do? I'd use armored cars, light trucks for troop carriers, and jeeps with recoilless rifles. I'd count on surprise. And the Jew boys have already lost that advantage.*

BBBLAAMMMMMMMM! The first enemy shell—it had been fired at random—hit the center of the encampment, the explosion tearing the three girder "legs" of the watchtower from their foundations. Slowly at first, then faster and faster, the tower began to topple toward the west. With a loud crash it hit the ground, the two riddled corpses of the soldiers bouncing six feet.

The Death Merchant's estimation was correct. The Israeli force, under the command of Major Lev "Tank" Mosshin, was composed of five Israeli-manufactured armored cars that had been modeled after the British Daimler. The Israeli designed vehicle was more efficient than the Daimler, however. While it carried the standard two-pound gun, it weighed six and a half tons, had 17mm armor, and could go 62 mph top speed on a flat surface. The Daimler had 16mm armor and a maximum speed of 50 mph.

The Israeli force also had seven jeeps, similar to American jeeps of World War II, except that the Israeli-built jeeps were 100 pounds heavier than the American-made vehicle of 2,424 pounds. The Israeli jeeps did have better-performing engines. The jeeps were there for one reason only: to the rear of each jeep was mounted a 75mm recoilless gun.

Way down in the basement of his heart, Major Mosshin knew the attack had failed even before the battle between the armor began; he knew because the helicopter was supposed to knock out the Jordanian Centurion MK III heavy tank. The last report by radio he had received from the Westland Lynx was that Amram Avrahamin, the pilot, and Jacob Meir, the copilot and gunner, had missed the tank. They would do better on the second run (they said). They would fire the remaining four S-16 Temple

56

missiles. Avrahamin and Meir didn't have the chance. Their luck had run out. The Jordanian AA gunner had destroyed the chopper.

Captain Joseph Bar-Hebin suggested the entire force retreat as quickly as possible, pointing out to Major Mosshin that if the tank even got close enough—"Sir, we don't have anything to stand against it. We were counting on speed and surprise. Major, we've already lost those advantages. Sir—I see no other course but to retreat."

It was Major Mosshin's fierce pride that forced him to make a decision he knew was wrong, but he rationalized that his luck would never desert him. During the Syrian assault, in the battle for the Golan Heights (October, 1973), his tanks had annihilated the Syrian armor. And now he should turn tail and run before a *single* Jordanian tank? *Never!*

"We fight," Major Mosshin said grimly. "We'll concentrate all the recoilless guns[7] on the tank. We might get lucky; and we still have the advantage: the hundred commandos who have slipped around to the south. They will make the difference between victory and defeat. They will kill every Jordanian and every American at the solar station."

"It's madness!" said Bar-Hebin emotionally. "Why, it's just a little out-of-the-way station. In the name of Jehovah, why are we even attacking this place?"

"Joseph, I have told you," Mosshin said acidly. "For some reason the Mossad wants the base destroyed and everyone there killed, especially the Americans. And I think the Mivtzan Elohim boys are in on it. You know as well as I: you never ask them why about anything."

The Israeli advance had been made with the four armored cars ahead of the seven jeeps. Behind the jeeps were ten trucks, twenty soldiers to a truck. Five of the trucks were empty; they had carried the commandos they were slipping in on the camp from the south. The advance now came to a halt, and Major

[7]The Davis Countershot gun, just prior to the First World War, was the first recoilless weapon. The next use of recoilless guns was by the German airborne troops who invaded Crete. They were equipped with the 75mm Light Gun—the LG2. The recoilless weapon works on the principle that, if it is possible to fire equal weights at equal velocities in opposite directions and achieve recoillessness, then it is also possible that one can fire half the weight at twice the velocity, and so on, until one arrives at the point where it is possible to fire a stream of high-velocity gas to the rear and still have the gun without recoil. This is exactly what happens in a recoilless weapon.

Mosshin gave the order that the armored cars move to the left flank, that the jeeps move up, load their recoilless cannon, and that one fire a range round. The men quickly cranked down the weapons to horizontal level and waited, most of them wondering why the force was not retreating. They found out when Mosshin gave the next order: all the 75mm guns would concentrate on the enemy tank.

The Israelis waited. Not for long. The Centurion MK III appeared, two armored cars on either side of the clanking monster. Jordanian soldiers behind the tank and the armored cars quickly spread out and raced to rocks and got down, four of them setting up B.S.A. general purpose machine guns.

In the gunner's seat of the Centurion, a determined Captain Gamal Nashibi got off the first 120mm shell when the Centurion was only 500 feet from the Israeli line. A roar, a flash of smoke, and the HE shell shot through the muzzle brake of the long barrel, screamed the short distance, hit the ground, and exploded only twenty feet in front of a jeep, the concussion knocking over four Israelis and turning over the jeep with its 75mm gun. Quickly, Nashibi, his entire body soaking in sweat, began to adjust the range, compensating in the range finder for the forward movement of the tank. He fired another shell at the same time that five of the Israeli 75mm recoilless guns fired. Four of the 75mm shells missed the Centurion and two of the Saladin armored cars that had speeded up and had crossed in front of the tank to engage, with the two other armored cars, the four Israeli armored cars.

The fifth Israeli 75mm shell hit the sloping glacis plate of the Centurion and exploded with a thunderous roar. The Centurion was not hurt. No one was surprised that it wasn't. The armor plate of a Centurion tank is 187mm thick. Trying to stop a Centurion with a 75mm gun was like trying to bring down a rhinoceros with a BB gun.

It was the Israelis who got off the first shots from the armored cars. Both Israeli gunners fired at the same Jordanian Saladin, their two-pound guns belching flame. Both 40mm shells hit the Saladin and exploded, killing the driver and the gunner. The Saladin erupted with flame, then blew itself apart as the third man, the machine gunner and radio operator, was trying to pull himself through the wrecked turret.

BLAAAMMMMM! One of the Saladins, far to the right of the Centurion, got off a 76mm shell and blew one of the Israeli armored cars apart, the HE armor-piercing shell catching the

Israeli armored car in the left side—one of the Israeli armored cars that had destroyed the first Saladin.

BLAAAMMMM! Another Israeli armored car got off a 40mm round, the shell burning its way into the turret of the second Saladin that had raced ahead and in front of the Centurion. Another big bang and a sheet of flame. The turret disintegrated and so did the gunner, his head soaring upward—like a basketball—thirty feet.

During those 3.6 minutes, there were other thunderclaps, small ones followed by explosions that sounded monstrous. Five Israeli 75mm shells had struck both sides of the tank and its mantlet (in front of the turret). No damage, except for Captain Gamal Nashibi and his tank crew, all of whom felt like firecrackers had exploded inside their heads. It didn't matter. The pressure did not interfere with Nashibi, who, with the rest of the crew, was on a hell-bound train of revenge. In rapid succession he destroyed three of the parked jeeps and the Israelis trying desperately to stop the Centurion with their 75mm recoilless guns.

It was then that Major Lev Mosshin and the men of his command jeep and the crew of another jeep got lucky. Their 75mm shells struck the bazooka plate, on the right front of the Centurion, the long plate that covered the top rollers and the upper part of the road wheels. The explosions sent a length of the plate rocketing outward and twisted a suspension-unit arm, which pulled five top track links free, two of which shot off into space. The rest of the track links were now free of the track idling wheel. There was a loud grinding sound as the links dislodged from the back sprocket. The Centurion turned sharply to the right and stopped. As far as movement was concerned, the Centurion was wrecked. But there wasn't anything wrong with the turret and the 120mm gun.

Captain Nashibi worked the controls and turret and gun began to move . . .

Another Israeli armored car exploded when a Saladin's 76mm shell hit below the front of its turret. Then the third Saladin dissolved from its being found by a 75mm shell ripping into it and tearing apart its insides, including its crew.

The last Jordanian Saladin rushed straight at another Israeli armored car and fired at almost point-blank range. And so did the Israeli armored car. The explosions and sheets of fire rolled together, the twisted metal rubbish of both cars falling in the same general area.

The Centurion, which could not move, was now alone, with

the exception of the Jordanian soldiers behind small rocks, 700 feet to the east.

The three remaining Israeli recoilless guns sent 75mm rounds at the Centurion—a useless gesture, the explosions doing nothing to the tank, but shocking further the nervous systems of Captain Nashibi and the rest of the tank crew, all save Suleiman Franji, the driver. Franji was already dead from concussion. Although blood was dripping from Nashibi's ears and nose, the concussions had not doused the fire of his determination to win, a pathological determination generated by his insane hatred of the Israelis, of the Jews. Abu Iyad—totally deaf from concussion—forced himself to shove another shell into the breech and shove down on the lock arm. Nashibi sighted in and pulled the trigger on the firing handle, the long barrel of the 120mm cannon spitting flame from the firing that sent the shell on its way. Four hundred feet to the southwest there was a tremendous crash, a ball of blossoming flame, and the jeep and its recoilless gun were dismantled, the bloody and dismembered corpses of Major Lev Mosshin, Captain Joe Bar-Hebin, and three other men tossed twenty feet into the air.

The ten trucks had already turned and were in full retreat. The crew of the last two jeeps now tried to save their lives. They piled into their jeeps and the drivers started the engines. It didn't do them any good. Nashibi fired again. One jeep that had started to move vanished in smoke and fire.

Shouting curses in Arabic at the Israelis, Nashibi began getting the range on the last jeep . . .

The Death Merchant, the three Company agents, and the construction workers waited behind small rocks, their bodies prone on the sandy, pebbly ground, Camellion nursing the fear that one of the construction men would become overanxious (and/or overfrightened), and fire at only a shadow and thereby tip off the Israeli commandos—*If they're out there. We can't be sure that they are.*

The defenders did have formidable firepower. In addition to Camellion and the Company men's automatic weapons, there were the SIG *Maschinepistoles* of Burtch, Fradenbach, and the twelve other Americans. Eighteen automatic weapons against— *how many Israeli commandos? A minimum of a hundred. And the Israelis are among the best in the world. All we're looking at is twelve miles of pure dirt road. We're playing David to Israel's Goliath!*

The other men didn't know what was going on to the west.

The roaring of the guns on the armor only told them that a helluva battle was going on. The Death Merchant, however, knew that the Israelis were losing in the western sector, the proof being the deep roaring of the Centurion's gun. One by one, the other guns grew silent. Not the 120mm cannon of the Centurion MK III. *Ironic! Nashibi and his boys will smear the Israelis there, and the Israeli commandos will smoke us here. Tit for tat. Score: zero!*

The Death Merchant detected movement in the darkness at about the same time that Robert Follmer, lying three feet to his left, whispered, "Did you see it? About twenty meters ahead, at about 11:30. I don't think it was a shadow."

"It wasn't a drifting tumbleweed either," Camellion whispered back. "They'll be here shortly and try to crawl all over us four ways to Friday. Another few minutes and we'll have them."

Half a minute crawled by. By now, Camellion, Follmer, and several dozen other men saw a figure darting here, a figure zigzagging there. Either singly or in twos or threes, the Israelis would race to rocks, fall flat, hunch down, wait, then run forward again—sometimes straight ahead, at other times to one side, depending on the terrain, on the size of the rocks ahead, the largest of which was the size of the largest old-fashioned wooden washtub.

The Death Merchant couldn't help but admire the enemy commandos. They had to have moved six to seven miles ahead of the armor and have crept in very slowly in order not to be detected by the two Jordanians using night-vision devices in the watchtower. It must have taken them five to six hours, maybe more. It wasn't luck either on the part of the Israelis. It was training.

There was light from the moon in the sky, not a lot but enough. For that reason, Camellion had ordered the men to be extremely cautious and to stay down. "Fire when they're twenty to thirty feet away, that is when you have a clear shot. Make every bullet count and don't waste ammunition. You won't have time to reload. When this is over, only the quick will have survived; the slow will be dead."

A burst of gunfire from a SIG machine pistol exploded several hundred feet to the left of Camellion, to the east. The Israelis were still fifty to sixty feet away, spread out in two lines three hundred feet long.

It didn't matter. The commandos were too close to the perimeter to retreat without risking being shot in the back. They might get greased in front, but at least they would have a fifty-fifty

61

chance for victory. Without wasting any time, the Israeli commandos charged, firing short bursts with Uzis SMGs and Galil assault rifles. Instantly, Camellion and the other men returned the fire.

The Death Merchant and Robert Follmer, lying flat with large rocks on either side and in front of them, fired from between weirdly shaped scoria rocks, Camellion's *Automat Gevär*, on semiautomatic, snarling out 6.5mm (patron m/96) 100-grain semipointed projectiles, Follmer's M12 Beretta chatterbox spitting 9mm Parabellum slugs. They didn't necessarily hit an Israeli commando each time they pulled the triggers. It was the same with the other defenders. The enemy commandos were darting and ducking and weaving as they raced in and fired three-round bursts. A dozen construction men, not at all familiar with firefight tactics, had already been killed by their overeagerness. They had made the fatal mistake of rearing up to fire. Galil 5.56mm or Uzi 9mm slugs smeared them instantly.

Nine millimeter boat-tailed bullets screamed and cut into the rocks and ground in front and on each side of Camellion and Follmer. Other slugs whizzed over their bodies, many of the lead-alloy-core slugs coming dangerously close. One Galil bullet cut through the loose high crown of Camellion's heavy-knit Laker cap and pulled it back from his forehead. Another slug— this one a 9mm projectile—skimmed by his left cheek.

All around Camellion and Follmer, and most of the other men in the southwest sector, were the bodies of dead commandos. Nonetheless, the Death Merchant, Follmer, and most of the other defenders did not have time to reload; the enemy was now too close, practically on top of them. Those who had sidearms— other than the twenty-nine men with either pistols or revolvers— now resorted to firing them. Those who did not have sidearms stayed down and pretended to be dead and hoped that soon they *wouldn't* be.

The Death Merchant pulled his twin stainless-steel M-200 International Auto Mags. Follmer resorted to his Astra A-80 autoloader. They fired with deadly precision, each round finding a target—an Israeli commando. Be that as it may, Camellion had time to fire only four rounds, and Follmer only two, before they were forced to jump to their feet and defend themselves against commandos coming at them from all sides except their rear. Some of the commandos were pulling daggers or sidearms—9mm Berettas—while others were beginning to swing their empty Galil assault rifles.

Easily, Camellion ducked an assault rifle a commando swung

at his head and shot another Israeli coming at him with a double-edged fighting dagger, the blade painted black for night use. *This is almost as bad as going into a bar in Phoenix on a Saturday night!* Twice more the Auto Mags roared, the .357 137-grain projectiles almost lifting two commandos off their feet and killing them instantly, the big, brutal bullets stabbing into the midsections of the two men who had been trying to come in at Follmer to the CIA man's right.

Follmer's Astra barked and another commando, pulling a 9mm Browning from a shoulder holster, went down, his mouth slack, blood spreading from a burn hole in his chest, although the wine red on the camo desert fatigues could not be readily seen.

"Shalom, sap!" murmured the Death Merchant, jumping back and to the left to avoid a knife swipe and pulling the trigger of the left Auto Mag, the weapon jerking in his hand. The Israeli was so close that Camellion could see his young face, a face smudged with dark camo paint, a face that dissolved in a miniexplosion of flesh and muscle, bone and blood from the force of the .357 magnum projectile that broke apart his skull and brain.

All up and down the line of the south perimeter, the defenders of the experimental solar station were fighting for their lives, were in hand-to-hand combat with the Israeli commandos who had survived the streams of slugs. The Americans were losing, even though the construction men who had been positioned to the north and the east had rushed to their aid.

First of all, the Americans were at least ten years older than the Israelis, who were in their mid-twenties, were in prime physical condition, and possessed first-rate training in one-on-one combat. One commando was easily worth two American construction workers. As for the Americans who had seen combat in either World War II or the Korean fracas, they were rusty and their age was against them. They did not have the wind, the stamina, the staying power.

Once you're past forty, you either get in the first crippling blow—or run like hell. This does not apply to firearms. In this area, a physically weak pro with a handgun—he might be seventy! —can blow away a novice of twenty, especially if the old guy has a killer instinct.[8]

---

[8]Does not mean "love of killing" as many believe. It does mean *proficiency* in specific killing techniques and, especially, *when* and *how* to use them. Or, "He who hesitates—is dead!"

It was different with Camellion and the three CIA men, none of whom would ever see thirty again. They were, however, in top physical condition. The Death Merchant himself was one of the deadliest bare-handed killers in the world, possessing black belts in four different karate systems, all fused into the Camellion School of Quick & Silent Death. Philip LaHann was a black belt, 5th Dan, in *Kenpo* karate. Kelly Dillard was a master in *Bwang,* the spear and hand (and feet) combat technique of Micronesia, and in *Chin-Na,* the grappling art of defense that originated in southern China. Robert Follmer was an expert in *Shotokan* karate and *Tai Chi,* Chinese "grand ultimate boxing," the most common and the least understood system of *Kung Fu.*[9] All four were using what they knew in these various techniques to keep themselves alive and healthy and to kill astonished Israelis who proudly thought that they, and they alone, were the world's best.

Kelly Dillard, too busy and too angry to be afraid, was more than holding his own. He didn't have a spear or a pole, but he did have his left hand wrapped around the middle of a Galil assault rifle, his right hand filled with an Astra autopistol. Very quick for a man who was thickset and of medium height, he jabbed a commando viciously in the stomach with the barrel of the Galil, a savage poke that ruptured the lining and brought the man down in agony. All in the same motion, Dillard twisted to his right, kicked backward with his left leg, and, using the Galil, jabbed backward and outward to his left. His left foot landed solidly on the abdomen of one commando, the heel digging six inches into the Israeli's gut while the end of the Galil's metal-frame stock half buried itself in the other commando's stomach. From Dillard's right, another commando rushed in and, with his left hand, grabbed Dillard's right wrist, and, with a dagger in his right hand, tried to bury the blade in Dillard's stomach. Dillard first blocked the blow by knocking aside the commando's right arm, then slamming the end of the barrel underneath the man's chin, the rounded metal muzzle making mush of the commando's voice box and the upper portion of his trachea. Choking to death, gasping loudly, the commando started to sink into the timelessness of Death, a horrible look on his face.

LaHann ducked a long-bladed knife thrown by a commando ten feet in front of him and charged the disappointed man before he could pull another knife from a combat boot. In those two hair slices of a second, LaHann caught sight of Elmore Fradenbach

[9]*Chen Tai Chi* is the oldest, most combat-oriented style.

and did a triple take. The assistant manager of the solar station may have been in his early fifties, but he was as agile as a twenty-year-old! Furthermore, he was a one-man army winning his war against two Israelis. He had executed a perfect wheel kick to one man's face and was putting away another commando with a lightning series of *Shuto* chops and *Nukite* spear stabs.

Eli Lodtz, the commando in front of LaHann, attempted a very fast high spin kick. He not only made a fatal error, he made a fool of himself. LaHann grabbed the Israeli's left boot with both hands and twisted. With a loud yell of pain and surprise, Lodtz found himself being completely turned around, getting only a flash of Mother Earth before he fell heavily to the ground, the fall stunning him. He didn't have time to roll or squirm away, not even to say his prayers. LaHann jumped high and came down on the small of the commando's back, his heels digging into the spine. A low, sickening snap. The commando lay still. He was stone dead in the Jordanian marketplace.

The Israeli who tried to brain Robert Follmer by swinging a Galil rifle at his head met his god a microsecond later. Follmer ducked, grabbed the man's arm, and kicked him in the left armpit. He jerked the dazed man to him and, employing a from-behind neck break, snapped the top four of the man's vertebrae. Follmer than flung the corpse into another commando who was rushing Camellion with a partner, who was also armed with a knife. It wouldn't have made any difference to the Death Merchant.

"All I want for Christmas is—your life!" Camellion had muttered. He had reached to the back of his neck, had pulled out "Baby" from her special holster between his shoulder blades, and had thrown her. The ice pick with its lead-filled handle had buried itself in the chest of one man a split second before the corpse, shoved by Follmer, crashed into the commando and both dead men tumbled to the ground.

The other commando with the knife hesitated, having second thoughts about his charge. It didn't do him any good. The Death Merchant charged him and, before the commando could pull back, let him have a high forward kick full in the face, a grand slam that broke the Israeli's chin, nose, and seven front teeth. A few moments later, Follmer grabbed the man from behind in a rear break-neck hold. Snap! Crackle! Pop!

There were wild, furious yells from the southeast and the southwest and a series of shots. Automatically, Follmer and Camellion fell to the ground; only then did they look to see what was happening. They liked what they saw. Several dozen

Jordanian soldiers had arrived on the scene and were killing the remainder of the commandos with sidearms. Within minutes it was all over and done with, and there were only bodies: the dead, the dying, the wounded.

Of the forty-one Ryan, Colt & Webber construction men who had taken part in the fight, twenty-six had been killed and six wounded, four seriously. Colin Burtch, the manager of the solar station, was among the dead. Of the Jordanians, the twelve men in the four Saladins, the two men who had been on the watch-tower, and Suleiman Franji, the driver of the Centurion MK III, were dead. Captain Gamal Nashibi, Lieutenant Nitzan Hatumin, and Abu Iyad were in a bad way from concussion, from the barrage of Israeli shells that had exploded against the Centurion tank. All three would have to be hospitalized.

Five of the Israeli commandos were still alive, two probably dying.

There was another casualty, the Century-Flash motor home. Half a dozen FN-MAG 7.62mm had zipped through the hood and wrecked the engine. The only way the motor home would move was when it was towed back to Amman for repairs.

"At least the rest of the weapons and the grenades and the DL-14j are safe," Kelly Dillard remarked as he and Camellion and the two Jesuits inspected the interior of the motor home.

"We can hook up the portable generator to give us light," the Death Merchant said briefly. All the while thoughts tumbled about in his mind. He still didn't know the identity of the spy at the station—*I don't even know if there is an informer!* He didn't have to think twice about what the result of the Israeli raid would be. *All of us will have to return to Amman and leave the country. This station is wrecked. Damn! We'll be right back to zero!*

Robert Follmer hurried into the motor home, which was lighted by only a butane lamp and had become the residence of numerous drifting shadows.

"What did you learn?" Camellion asked, watching Follmer drop onto one of the deep-cushioned couches.

"Nashibi's too rattled for command," reported Follmer. "He's put Sergeant-Corporal Rif Jaffersi in command. Jaffersi has radioed Amman. Four transport choppers are coming with reinforcements. Two of the birds will fly Nashibi and the rest of the wounded, including the Israelis, back to Amman. And an armored column is on its way. It will get here late tomorrow night. The choppers should be here by dawn." Follmer stared at the Death Merchant. "Here's the 'good news.' Some of the Department 4 secret police are coming with the choppers. Camellion, that could mean serious trouble for us."

Kelly Dillard cut in roughly, almost angrily. "Why? We're American engineers! We helped save the bacon for the Jordies."

"And the Jordanians saved our butts toward the last," cracked Phil LaHann, who had just come out of the toilet. "We're lucky that Nashibi had the presence of mind to send the soldiers back to the station."

"He didn't," corrected Follmer. "Sergeant-Corporal Jaffersi did. He was in command of the soldiers behind the rocks. He got to thinking that the Israelis wouldn't be dumb enough to put all their eggs in one armored basket. He ordered thirty to come back here. He and his men also got the last Israeli armored car. The used a hand-fired missile to do the job."

"Let's get back to the secret police." The persistent Dillard spoke in a low, tense voice.

"It's not difficult to figure out," the Death Merchant pointed out. "The construction men have already bragged to the Jordanians how I took charge—'just like a military man' Fradenbach said. The Department 4 boys are going to start wondering about me and the rest of you. It's already probably struck them as odd that the Israelis should go to all the trouble to send a couple of hundred men and armor to destroy an out-of-the-way nonmilitary installation."

LaHann gave the Death Merchant a faintly sardonic smile. "I've been wondering about that myself. Let's see if your theory meshes with mine."

Unexpectedly, Father Victorio Gatdula spoke, sounding remarkably calm, so much so that the Death Merchant wondered if the priest might be suffering from D.S.R.[10] "Deductive reasoning should tell us that the Israelis suspect that this solar station is to be used in some way, perhaps as a focal point, to acquire the scrolls."

"Good thinking, Boy Wonder!" Dillard was sneeringly polite, his granite visage as hard as the lava rock on which he had recently lain. "You're right, father (of what?). We didn't get all the Israelis. They did succeed in what they came here to do. They wrecked the station. As Hitler said of Nazi martyrs, *'Und ihr habt doch gesiegt!'*—'in defeat they have won a victory.' "

Camellion shook his head. "No, they haven't. It was all a waste on the part of the Israelis. We were only going to use this base as a pickup point. We still can—and will. We have to."

[10]Delayed stress response.

No one said anything for a long moment.

"When?" Dillard asked straight out.

"Right now I'm going to do some monitoring on the surveillance receiver," Camellion said, getting to his feet.

"It's a waste of time," growled Kelly Dillard. He felt disappointed that the Death Merchant hadn't answered his question, but consoled himself with the knowledge that he had not really expected a direct answer from the strange man about whom he knew nothing, except that Richard Camellion was man who—in the words of Juvenal—could cut a throat with a thin whisper. "A sheer waste. Burtch is dead, a cold cut. McPictrick is more cold than warm from the slug in his shoulder and the one in his leg. He'll croak before the Jordanians can get him to a hospital in Amman."

"That still leaves Fradenbach." His mouth tight, Camellion went over to a wall locker above a couch, opened the locker, and removed the surveillance receiver. He placed the receiver on the floor, turned it on, set the controls, and put on the headphones.

There was only black noise from the Southwind and the Winnebago. Camellion almost said *I'll be double-damned!* when he tuned in on Fradenbach's Caper mini motor home on the Chevy pickup truck and heard the distinct waveform influence, that is, the change in meter indication caused solely by a change in waveform from a specified waveform, of the applied current and/or voltage.

The Death Merchant knew exactly what he was hearing, a code key that had been made silent by an RC phase-shift oscillator that was only half working. The result was that the key was only half silent; yet still not loud enough for Camellion to hear the actual dots and dashes.

By the pleased look on Camellion's face, the others knew he had zeroed in on something.

"Fradenbach?" Robert Follmer's eyes widened in surprise.

The Death Merchant removed the headphones and handed them to Follmer. "A key," he said. "Only half quiet. Concussion or whatever must have jarred loose one of the connectors."

Once he had the headphones on and was listening, Follmer agreed.

"It's a key. No doubt about it, and it's from the Caper. It's Fradenbach—that son of a bitch."

"I'm going to the shortwave," Camellion said and headed for the folding door between the lounge and kitchenette.

Camellion was determined, now more than ever, to leave the solar station before the armored column arrived from Amman.

The only course open to him was to radio Green Gables at At-Turayf and request that the Saudis send a helicopter to lift him and the five other men out. In the meanwhile, Camellion and the three Company men would have to do the impossible: immobilize the Jordanians at the base, including the reinforcements due to arrive in the Jordanian choppers.

The Death Merchant switched on the DL-14j.

We'll blame it on the Israelis, on the Mossad. . . .

CHAPTER FIVE

Nobody can give you wiser advise than yourself! In effect, that is what Green Gables informed the Death Merchant when they radioed back that the Saudi General Security Directorate had discussed the situation and had decided not to send helicopters into southern Jordan to pick up Camellion and the other five men. Sorry. Camellion and the five were on their own—out in the cold. If caught, the CIA would deny even knowing them.

"Their refusing doesn't surprise me," Phil LaHann said drily. "The Saudis have always run scared. They have 95,000 men in their armed forces. Their men are the best paid[1] in the world, and they couldn't wage war with Luxembourg and win!"

"Neither could we win, considering all the blacks we have in our armed forces!" Robert Follmer's expression was as bleak as his voice. "Or don't any of you know the latest test results from the University of Chicago?"[2]

"Oh God! Here we go again!" LaHann shook his head and sank down on one of the couches. "Another lecture on the superiority of the the white race! You would have made a fine Nazi, Bob!"

"What's that supposed to mean—another lecture?" lashed out Follmer. He swung angrily to LaHann, shadows playing on his savage face by the light of the butane lantern. "The Pentagon is putting out the lie that the all-volunteer army is attracting recruits

[1]An air force captain gets $60,000 a year, three times what his U.S. counterpart earns. A Saudi army private earns $12,000 a year. But money cannot replace skills.

[2]In 1982, the University of Chicago's National Opinion Research Center conducted verbal and mathematical tests among 11,878 civilians age eighteen through twenty-three. Scores averaged 56 out of a possible 80 for whites, 31 for Hispanics, and 24 for blacks. Among military recruits scores have run 58 for whites, 41 for Hispanics and 33 for blacks—*U.S. News & World Report*, March 8, 1982.

a 'cut above the average.' It's a lot of hot air. All the military is getting is near morons!'' His eyes swept around the lounge. ''Why don't all of you open your eyes to reality and admit who's helping wreck America—and don't give me that myth about 'equality' between blacks and whites! Put two Krauts together and they'll plan a war. Two Greeks will start a political party. And two coons will plan a crime,[3] as sure as God made onions!''

More than a little disgusted over Follmer's racism, Camellion sank to a chair and said in a cold voice, ''You might have a different opinion if your skin were black. Consider for a moment what's happened recently. The rich got big tax breaks, but poor people—black and white—lost jobs, food assistance, training opportunities, and a lot more. As for the blacks—they exist in a cocoon of poverty and defeatism that's been handed down, from generation to generation, like some deadly inherited disease. The entire pathetic mess has congealed into a *Lumpenproletariat* of female-headed families, jobless men, and bitter young people. In short, my friend, don't profess to know all about another people until you've walked for a while in their moccasins.''

''More excuses!'' spit out Follmer, glaring at the Death Merchant. ''You're saying that poor people have a right to mug, murder, and steal. That's as ridiculous as the nonsense that mixing the races in the schools will give minorities a better education. It hasn't[4] in all these years and it never will.''

''It seems to me I recall some other 'racial specialists,' '' said Father Victorio Gatdula, peering up at Follmer. ''Hitler, Darre, Himmler, Goebbels, and hundreds like them. In spite of their preoccupation with *Rassenreinheit,* the *Lebensborn* homes, and all the rest of the hellish nonsense of Nazism, Germans still

---

[3]The FBI's Uniform Crime Report reveals that blacks commit violent crimes 8.5 times as often as whites, relative to their numbers in the overall U.S. population. Blacks are 7.2 times as likely to commit rape, 11.2 times as likely to commit murder, and 14.1 times as likely to commit robbery. *Violent black crime is typically spontaneous rather than planned and reflects a general lack of inhibition and foresight.*

[4]In a newly published study, ''Black-White Contacts in Schools: Its Social and Academic Effect,'' Purdue University sociologist Martin Patchen concludes: ''Available evidence indicates that interracial contacts in schools does not have consistent positive effects on students' racial attitudes and behavior *or on the academic performance of minority students.*'' Italics mine—JRR.

continue to be born blond and blue-eyed like Hitler, tall like Dr. Goebbels, and—'' he laughed—''slim like Göring!''

Father Bernard Norton sounded funereal as he said, ''Mr. Follmer, you should realize that racism is not only an emotional illness, but a spiritual sickness as well.''

''Shut up, you damned hypocrite!'' Follmer said in disgust. ''You Jesuits are in enough trouble over your stupid 'Theology of Liberation' that combines Marxism with Catholicism. Your order has helped the left-wing Sandinista commie trash in Nicaragua and you've helped the rebels in Guatemala and El Salvador. In your stupid sentimentality and half-witted concern for 'human rights,' you're helping the Soviet Union. If you were realists, you'd know that 'human rights' is another myth. There isn't any 'social justice,' only greed and power politics.''

Father Norton opened his mouth, then closed it again and looked away from Follmer, who continued to shoot triumphant visual daggers at him.

The Death Merchant broke the short silence, saying caustically, ''Now that the seminar on human rights is over, I suggest we get down to the business of getting out of here—should anyone be interested.''

''We can't walk to Arabia,'' cracked Kelly Dillard. He fondled his Dan Wesson .357 revolver tenderly, the way a lover would fondle the breast of his loved one.

Philip LaHann was more practical. ''We have all the Jordanians out there, and shortly there'll be forty or fifty more when the helicopters arrive,'' he said slowly. ''The construction men don't know what the real deal is. They'll fire at us if they think we're an enemy.'' Suddenly startled, he drew up and looked at the Death Merchant. ''I assume you can fly a chopper?''

''I can lift off and get us to Arabia, but that's all,'' Camellion said.

''I can do slightly better,'' said Dillard.

''Then you're elected pilot.'' Camellion tugged at the chest strap of his shoulder holsters. He had put them on since entering the motor home. Each holster was filled with a .45 Safari Arms Enforcer.

''Just one thing,'' began Phil LaHann. ''How do we swipe a chopper and not get snuffed doing it?''

''What about the construction men?'' Follmer was deeply concerned. ''We're supposed to be 'engineers.' What's going to happen to the construction men after we're gone and the Jordanians know it was all an act with us? We can't have Department 4 taking it out on them. One lousy Jordie is worth ten Americans. Besides, the home office of Ryan, Colt & Webber would scream all the way to D.C. and might go to the press. Camellion, what do you have in mind to get the construction workers off the Jordie hook?''

''I'd like to know what we're going to do about Fradenbach,'' Dillard said harshly. ''We should kill the son of a bitch. But we can learn more by taking him with us. He's KGB. He has to be.''

''Do any of you speak Hebrew?'' The Death Merchant smiled thinly, a light mockery in his sky blue eyes.

''Ahha! That's it!'' LaHann sounded happy. ''Now we're Israelis! Yes, I speak enough to fool the Jordanians.''

''Mossad, I presume?'' Dillard said, a hint of excitement in his voice.

''Not just Mossad,'' Camellion said. ''We're Mivtzan Elohim. Elmore Fradenbach is going to be proof to the Jordanians that we're Wrath of God agents.''

''God help us all,'' whispered Father Gatdula.

''God helps those who help themselves!'' Camellion said cheerfully.

The four Jordanian transports—they were French-built Super Frelons—landed as the first rays of the sun crawled across the horizon. Two of the helicopters were filled with supplies—food, medicine, extra tents, a powerful shortwave transmitter, extra ammunition, a dozen light machine guns, two heavy machine guns, several 2cm AA/AT guns, five 10cm mortars, and thirty-one antitank hand-held missiles. The other two choppers carried twenty-three soldiers each—and four members of Department 4, the secret police of Jordan.

''That's forty-six more we have to worry about,'' muttered Kelly Dillard. ''And one finger on the trigger of one sub gun could smear all of us.''

With Camellion and the others, Dillard watched the soldiers of the Fourth Jordan Commando erect cook and mess tents and a large headquarters tent. Other soldiers set up a canopy for the supplies. The Jordanian dead and the American corpses had been gathered and neatly laid out in rows and covered with pieces of the black goat-skin tents. The Bedu workers at the station had not returned. They had kept right on running.

For the time being, the dead were ignored; they were beyond help. They would be returned to Amman on the second run, after the wounded were flown to Amman. The rotor of one Super Frelon didn't even stop revolving, but kept idling as the wounded were taken on board, strapped to stretchers, these including the three wounded Israelis. The other two Israelis had died during the night. Their bodies had been thrown into the desert—to find the wind and wild animals.

The Death Merchant was not at all worried about anything the three captured Israeli commandos might reveal to Department 4—the poor bastards didn't even know why they were attacking the solar station. They might have known it was a Mossad deal, if that much!

Camellion, the two Jesuits, and the three CIA men watched the helicopter with the wounded lift off and head north. All around them was activity, especially at the perimeters, where soldiers had dug in and set up heavy machine guns, light machine guns, and mortars. They saw Sergeant-Corporal Rif Jaffersi conferring with Major Yosef Aboussan, the new commander, who had arrived in one of the choppers.

"They'll be getting around to us shortly," Robert Follmer said.

The Jordanians did, half an hour later, Ami Sidki sending a soldier who politely requested that the Death Merchant and the others follow him to the headquarters tent.

In addition to Sidki and the three other D-4 agents, Major Yosef Aboussan, Captain Basi Hunada, and Frank Tiflorton, who was now the senior American engineer, were present in the tent.

A narrow-chested man with gray hair and shiny ebony eyes, Ami Sidki stood up from the folding table and smiled as the Death Merchant and the other men entered the tent. Sidki's blue suit needed pressing, but he was clean shaven.

"*Salam alaikum*, Sahib Camellion," Sidki said in a friendly manner. However, he did not raise his right hand in the Arab custom, but extended it Western fashion.

"*Alaikum as salam*," Camellion answered, shaking hands with Sidki. He noticed that the Jordanian had a very strong grip—deliberate or natural?

Camellion introduced the five other "engineers." In turn, Sidki introduced the three other secret-police agents, Major Yosef Aboussan, and Captain Basi Hunada. He then motioned for Camellion and the rest of his group to sit down in camp chairs of the folding variety.

Ami Sidki got right to the point. "I want to congratulate you

74

Sahib[5] Camellion and the rest of you for the way you helped repel those stinking Israeli commandos." His voice rose half an octave. "I understand you took charge of the defense, Sahib Camellion. Tell me, have you had military experience?"

"It was Captain Gamal Nashibi who deserves the credit. It was he who destroyed the Israeli armor," Camellion said magnanimously. "If the Israeli armor had reached this station, we would have been defeated."

"The station would have been destroyed if the Jews had managed to gain access to the base," pointed out Sidki slyly. "That did not happen because of your quick action, Sahib Camellion."

"Yes, I suppose you could say that" (*You son of a bitch!*), the Death Merchant said, quick to sense that the secret-police officer was determined to give him half the credit for repelling the Israeli commandos. The Death Merchant knew why: Sidki wanted to keep the conversation on him. *He wants to discuss my military career. He suspects, but isn't sure that I'm not what I claim to be. Mercy, mercy, Mother Percy. Since he suspects me, he suspects the other five. But he can't afford to make a false move, a wrong decision.*

Still overly friendly, Ami Sidki smiled and began tapping the eraser end of a pencil on the table. "Would you not also say, Sahib Camellion, that you and these other engineers showed extraordinary courage?"

"As well as a professional knowledge of tactics," added Zaid Quamiylin. Another Department 4 agent, Quamiylin was olive skinned and had black eyebrows slanting upward toward a high, narrow forehead above a narrow face.

"It's like I said, I saw plenty of action in Korea," Camellion said, trying to downplay his part in the firefight. "The others only followed my orders. There's another factor: when it's either kill or be killed, you find extra reserves of strength. And don't forget, quite a few men did die."

Major Yosef Aboussan, a large man with very hairy hands and black curly hair, leaned forward and peered at Frank Tiflorton. "Sahib Tiflorton, I recall your saying that Sahib Camellion and three of the other engineers exhibited an amazing knowledge of karate. Is that not so?"

Tiflorton nodded, grinning like a cat who had just cornered a mouse.

[5]Actually means "Friend." The Arab equivalent of "Mister," but only when one is addressing a Westerner.

"That's right," he said proudly, thinking he was paying not only Camellion and the other men a compliment, but Americans in general. "I didn't see all the action. I was too busy fighting for my own life. What I did see—well, sir, Camellion, Dillard, Follmer, and LaHann—I tell you, it was like watching a karate match on television. I've never seen anything like it."

Philip LaHann said lazily, "The martial arts are a hobby with me, ever since I was in college."

"I took up karate as a body-building exercise," Robert Follmer offered.

"A most remarkable coincidence," said Ami Sidki, smiling. "All four of you being such experts."

Sakar Jalkuto and Amersi Karamesh, the other D-4 agents, exchanged *I-told-you-so* glances. Like Sidki, Jalkuto and Karamesh were as phony in their "friendliness" as a Soviet diplomat. To the Death Merchant, they were the type of men who specialized in that kind of *Gemütlichkeit*[6] that is never genuine.

"The two other engineers who came from Amman," Sakar Jalkuto said. He looked at Fathers Norton and Gatdula. "Are you not also adept in some killing art?"

"We understand you didn't even take part in the battle," Captain Basi Hunada said matter-of-factly.

Father Norton spoke up, surprising the Death Merchant with his calmness and false sincerity. "Vic and I have heart conditions. I have aortic stenosis and he suffers from mitral stenosis. We were under the goat-skin tents. We didn't see how we could help anyone by having heart attacks and dropping dead."

"A logical action," Ami Sidki said, his voice having the faintest inflection of reproof. A twisted little smile formed on the secret-police agent's thick lips. "I don't know what decision my government will make regarding this station. The work here may or may not continue."

"As far as I'm concerned, we might as well return to Amman," Camellion said, wanting to throw Sidki and the other Jordanians off guard. "There isn't anything here we can do."

Sidki looked for a long moment at Camellion. "Yes, I am sending all five of you back to Amman as soon as the helicopters return."

"Fine." Camellion smiled with fake enthusiasm. "I'd sure hate to see those damned Israelis again."

Frank Tiflorton said, "The Solar Breeder—" He stopped and

[6]"Geniality," "Friendliness" (standard German).

glanced at Elmore Fradenbach, who was entering the tent. "I was about to tell them, El, that the Solar Breeder is totally wrecked. To rebuild it—well, we'd have to start from scratch."

Pulling up a folding chair, Fradenbach sat down, wiped his face, took off his hat, and wiped his bald head. "That's right. I just finished inspecting the entire installation. I doubt if we can salvage two dozen solar reflectors," he said wearily. "I swear to God, those damned Israelis must hate you Jordanians with a passion. I still find it impossible that they should go to all the trouble to destroy our work. Why, damn it, there wasn't anything military about this station. It was so senseless!"

"They do hate us," Major Yosef Aboussan said vehemently. "The Israelis think they're the 'Supermen' of the Middle East. They hate all Arabs and are actually practicing a quiet genocide against the Arab peoples. That is difficult for you Americans to understand. You're so used to being nice to your so-called minorities that it's become your national pastime; and you're nice to foreign nations. Your government has sent them vast amounts of aid and all you have received in return is insults."

"You Americans have been particularly nice to Israel," Ami Sidki said in a coldly vicious manner. "It was Moshe Dayan who gave the orders for the brutal attack on the U.S.S. *Liberty*. The attack killed thirty-four of your countrymen. Yet when he went to Washington, your President shook his blood-stained hand. When that murderer Menachem Begin goes to Washington, he wags his finger in the face of your President, snarls out his demands, and your government meekly hands him what he wants, as if the American people owed it to him. Oh, you're nice folks, you American goyim!"

"One moment, Sahib Sidki," Camellion said, pretending to be angry. "You act as though we personally were responsible! We're only average American citizens. We're not the government. It's not our fault that the United States is led by the sorriest set of figureheads who ever graced the prow of a sinking ship."

"I resent that, Mr. Camellion," snapped Fradenbach. "We are Americans. It is our government in Washington!"

The Death Merchant pretended to be contrite. "Yes, you're right. It was poor taste on my part"—*You son of a bitch! Are you going to get yours!*

The Jordanians speaking of "nice Americans" was more

77

than enough to trigger Follmer, who began playing his favorite record.

"They're right about our being 'nice' to everyone," he said in an unpleasant voice, his eyes raking Camellion. "Look how 'nice' we've been to the blacks. Since World War II, we've made fools of ourselves by restructuring our entire society in a stupid attempt to uphold the myth that we're all 'equal.' We've handed billions to those brillo heads to finance their idle ghetto loungings—and look at the result. Our streets and parks have been turned over to black punks, and then they plea-bargain and are turned loose on early parole so they can prey on us again. We've handcuffed our policemen, lest they make the slightest infringement of blacks' 'rights.' We've forced our kids to go to school with those moron asses, and we've rubbed our kids' nose in lies about white guilt. And when none of it has worked, when the blacks remain as far as ever from 'equality' but are ten thousand times more surly, we bow our heads, go into a white Step'n' Fetchit act, and humbly beg their forgiveness—and give them still more. Yeah, we're 'nice' people. We're unrealistic idiots!"

"Oh, we're suckers in other ways too," Dillard said. "It's not just the jungle jigs we're 'nice' to. We've let millions of aliens swarm into the States and deprive our people of jobs. Spics, those gooks from Vietnam—you name it! We let 'em come in. The only Orientals who have any intelligence and culture are the Japanese—and they have too much sense to want to live in the United States."

While the Death Merchant totally disagreed with Follmer and Dillard, he was not putting on an act when he got in his six-and-a-half cents' worth.

"You're forgetting the traitors in our midst," he ground out. "All the scum who ran off to Canada; and when mobs of demonstrators—during the Vietnam years—paraded in the streets behind the banners of the Vietcong and spattered our nation's flag with filth and dragged it in the gutter, the police had to stand by and be careful not to violate the 'civil rights' of the scum. Later, the Washington, D.C., idiots welcomed home with open arms and forgiveness the thousands of traitors and deserters."

"They should have been shot," growled LaHann.

"Wrong!" snapped Camellion. "They should have strangled slowly with piano wire. There's nothing lower on this earth and in any society than a yellow belly who deserts his country.

Except a Russian who defects. But the Russians don't have a nation. They exist in a pig sty. And it's not just their government either. Show me a Russian and you'll show me an 'it' that should be living in a cesspool. They're the kind of scum who are blowing up hundreds of innocent children in Afghanistan with toys rigged to explode in their faces."

"I read in a newspaper that the Russians are using more than dolls and other toys rigged with explosives," Phil LaHann said. "They're using pens, matchboxes, anything that a child might pick up—dropping them all from helicopters. The sons of sluts and whores are playing a waiting game and the bodies of children have become their tools of war."[7]

Ami Sidki stood up, the smile gone from his face. "Gentlemen, you must excuse us. We have private matters to discuss." His eyes swept the Death Merchant and the other Americans. "I suggest that you pack a small bag of the possessions you wish to take to Amman." He looked straight at Camellion. "You, Sahib Camellion, and the other five with you will be flown back on the first available helicopter."

Camellion pretended to be pleased. He rubbed his hands together.

"Fine. The sooner the better."

Once the Death Merchant and the other men had left the headquarters tent and Frank Tiflorton and Elmore Fradenbach had gone their separate ways, Kelly Dillard said murderously, "I'd like to meet Sidki in an alley, and all by himself. You know why he's like a prostitute and a computer, don't you?"

"I have a feeling you're about to tell me," drawled Camellion as the group walked back to the motor home.

"Because he's a fuckin' know-it-all!"

"Uh huh, and if you screw an Arab gal you'll get sand crabs!" Robert Follmer's voice was controlled and even, but it had a dogged iron conviction to it and a slight trace of concern. "The D-4 boys suspect we have a whole bag of skeletons in our closet. We're going to have to act fast." He glanced speculatively at the Death Merchant. "You're sure we can blame all this on Fradenbach?"

[7]Fact. The Soviets think that by maiming and/or killing little tots, they will demoralize the Afghan people and prevent them from helping the rebels.

"Positive!" Camellion said. "We'll make our move as soon as the choppers arrive."

"Your plan had better be foolproof," Robert Follmer said.

"You can say that again," sighed LaHann. "I'd hate to go the L-pill[8] route."

---

[8] An abbreviation for a suicide pill—or "self-destruct device" in Company lingo. Ironically, the L stands for "lifelessness." The agent is anhydrous hydrocyanic acid for stabilization, 2 percent oxalic acid is added. Dosage: an even cubic centimeter. Diameter: 9mm. Length after annealing: about 32mm. Death is instantaneous.

There is a smaller L-pill that can be attached to, or inside of, a tooth. Death from this pill will take about four minutes.

CHAPTER SIX

It has been said that coincidence is a small miracle where God prefers to remain anonymous. There would no co-working inter-twinings of fate to help Camellion and his group of five escape from the experimental solar station. Nor was God about to work even a tiny miracle.

To have been able to get the drop on all the Jordanians—more than 150 of them—would have been ideal. Impossible! The Jordanians were scattered all over the area, helping the Americans clear away the rubble. Others were walking guard duty around the perimeter and around the supply depot. Worse, there were the four heavy machine guns at the four points of the compass. The soldiers at the guns could easily swing the weapons in on the camp. If they had to!

Sitting in the motor home, Camellion and his men discussed the situation. "Well, we might take out one group of machine gunners with a silenced Ruger," said LaHann. "But all four groups? No way. We'd be noticed. We'd be gunned down."

Robert Follmer leaned back on a couch, folded his arms, and studied Camellion. "Let's face it, Camellion. There's too many of them—and how are we going to get from the motor home to the chopper carrying sub guns? Sure, they don't mind our wearing sidearms. But SMGs? Hell, we're not being attacked. And Sidki, even if he suspects us, knows we can't do anything with pistols, not against men armed with automatic weapons."

"No matter what we do, the risk will be terrific," Kelly Dillard said. "Well—no one said it would be easy."

The Death Merchant sighed audibly, a tacit admission that he was in agreement. "Even a blind horse knows when the trough is empty," he said. "We're going to have to grab the bull by both horns and hope he isn't willing to die."

Kelly Dillard was visibly unimpressed. That was his way. He would have acted bored if the end of the world had begun. Like Camellion, he was confident that, somehow, they would escape.

If they didn't—so what? Everyone dies. It's only a question of when and how.

The two Jesuits looked like two men staring into the muzzles of double-barreled shotguns held by madmen. Follmer and LaHann did their best to look unconcerned.

"How do we do it?" Dillard demanded bluntly. His voice took on a note of deep solemnity "These choppers are due to return any moment." Unexpectedly, he chuckled. "At least none of this will be in Freedom of Information files. Those liberal bastards, wrecking the CIA, will never know what took place here.[1]"

The Death Merchant stood up and scratched the back of his head.

"The first thing we do is plant a two-pound block of PETN on the DL-14j," he said. "We can detonate the stuff by remote control from the chopper."

"You mean if we get inside a chopper!" Follmer said in an undertone.

Camellion looked at LaHann, who was checking a Ruger .22 pistol with a noise suppressor built around the barrel. "Phil, take four offensive grenades and remove the primers and the fuses. I'll go put the PETN in the ice chest. And pack a small bag with a few clothes. It will all look normal. Sidki did suggest we take a few belongings with us."

"Yeah, we can put thermite canisters in the bags," Dillard said; he then inquired distantly, "What do you want the rest of us to do, Camellion?"

"Make sure all your sidearms are in shape and that your backups are ready to fire. The two of you"—Camellion smiled at the two Jesuits—"do what you do best—*pray*."

Fifteen minutes later, they left the motor home, the remote control detonator in an inner pocket of Camellion's jacket, and looked around the large area. To the southwest, Elmore Fradenbach was talking to Frank Tiflorton, who was making notes on an aluminum clipboard. Two other construction workers were tak-

[1]The CIA has been forced to operate in a fishbowl. The entities responsible are the American Civil Liberties Union, Church Committee, Philip Agee, Freedom of Information Act, Organizing Committee for a Fifth Estate, Covert Action Information Bulletin, National Lawyers Guild, American Friends Service Committee, and the National Emergency Civil Liberties Committee. It's these spineless fools who would rather be RED than DEAD. . . .

ing photographs of the wrecked Solar Breeder building, which was a total mess. Hundreds of solar cells were smashed. Girders were marred, the Temple missiles having twisted them like rubber bands. The heat-storage cells were wrecked beyond repair, parts of them scattered for hundreds of feet. Even where Camellion and the other men stood, there were parts and pieces of pistons, bypass pipes, and smashed copper coils.

Only a short distance from Fradenbach and Tiflorton stood four soldiers of the Fourth Jordanian Commando, British B.S.A. 9mm submachine guns cradled in their arms. Dressed in modern battle fatigues, the only piece of clothing that distinguised the soldiers as Arabs and as members of the elite commando group was their checkered red and white *kaffiyehs*, the traditional Arab headdress bound with black ropelike material around the forehead, the sides, and the back of the head.

The early morning was bright sunshine, zippers of sunbeams seaming up their light. In the distance, to the north, was the distinct *thump/thump/thump/thump* of helicopter rotors.

"If we're going to do it—and we are—now's the time," Kelly Dillard murmured, his tone devastatingly ruthless. "Hear those choppers? They'll land in another ten minutes."

"And we still have to get to the headquarters tent," Robert Follmer reminded the others, not that they had forgotten that grim fact.

"It will be our luck that Sidki, Aboussan, and the rest of them won't be in the tent," LaHann said absently.

"Let's get on with it," Camellion said in a businesslike voice. "If we fail, we can all sing '*O Drop Kick Me Jesus through the Goalpost of Life*.'"

A nylon cylindrical utility bag in his left hand, the Death Merchant walked lazily toward Frank Tiflorton and Elmore Fradenbach, who were still writing down their damage reports. They both glanced at Camellion and the other men when the Death Merchant stopped in front of Fradenbach, who smiled in a friendly manner. "I guess you men will be glad to get out of this hellhole and back to Amman," he commented, then turned and looked north. "The helicopters will be here shortly."

The first crucial moment had come. "Mr. Sidki wants to see us in the headquarters tent," Camellion said, deliberately sounding worried and looking apprehensive.

"Us? What for?" Frank Tiflorton appeared amazed.

"All I know is that Sidki sent a soldier to the motor home and told us to go to the headquarters tent. I assumed the soldier also told you," Camellion said. "The only reason I'm telling you now is because I saw both of you standing there as if you owned the hourglass of time."

Giving Camellion an annoyed look, Fradenbach dropped his cigarette and carefully ground it under his left heel. "I suppose we'll find out what it's all about when we get there." He glanced toward the green headquarters tent that had been erected a hundred feet southwest of the silver silo top domes.

A whimsical fate then pulled a dirty trick on Camellion. The instant Fradenbach finished speaking, Ami Sidki came out of the headquarters tent. Behind him were Amersi Karamesh, the two other Jordanian secret policemen, and Major Yosef Aboussan. The five turned and looked up at the sky, toward the three helicopters that could now be seen quite clearly in the morning sky.

"Let's go see what that damned Sidki wants," Camellion said authoritatively, afraid that Sidki and his group would disperse before he and Dillard and the other men, including Fradenback and Tiflorton, could reach the tent.

"That Sidki reminds me of a son of bitch in California," muttered Kelly Dillard. "Rance Galloway! That mammy whacker was so full of lies and hot air that every time he opened his mouth, the whole state rose two feet into the air."

Ami Sidki and the Jordanians with him watched curiously as the Death Merchant and the seven men approached the headquarters tent, Sidki standing hunched over, his hands thrust deeply into his coat pockets, his eyes narrow slits.

The Death Merchant marched straight up to the secret-police official, who said, "I see that you and the others are ready to get on the helicopter. They will land shortly." He smiled pleasantly. "I and my three associates will accompany you to Amman."

"Fine. I'm sure we'll enjoy your company," Camellion said pleasantly. Then, not giving Fradenbach and Tiflorton a chance to ask Ami Sidki why he wanted to see them, Camellion lowered his voice and said gravely, "Sahib Sidki, it's vital that we go into the tent. I must show you what I discovered. Believe me, its's extremely important."

"But I thought—" started Fradenbach. He looked from Camellion to Ami Sidki.

"Discovered?" echoed Sidki, his eyes narrowing even more. "What are you talking about?"

"I'll show you in the tent." Not giving Sidki an opportunity to question him further, the Death Merchant turned, walked quickly to the tent, brushed aside the flap, and went inside. Ami Sidki and everyone else had no choice but to follow, Robert

Follmer and Philip LaHann making sure they were the last to enter the large room-sized tent.

Inside the tent, Sidki frowned in annoyance at the Death Merchant, who had placed his nylon utility bag on one of the folding tables, had unzipped it, and was reaching into it with both hands.

"What is this all about?" demanded Sidki, his hands still jammed into his coat pockets, "this nonsense about a 'discovery'?"

He straightened up, alarm in his eyes, when Camellion's hands came out of the utility bag. In his right hand was a Beretta 93R machine pistol, a noise suppressor screwed onto the extra-long barrel.

The eyes of the four other Jordanians widened, expressions of astonishing crawling over their faces. They stood there, frozen with shock.

"It's about do what you're told and you won't die," Camellion said brutally. "Don't any of you try what you're thinking. You'll die. In fact, if need be, we'll all die."

"You're covered from behind—by us," Robert LaHann said in a low, pleasant voice. He and Follmer stood with drawn M-92SB Beretta pistols to which were attached silencers. In their left hands they held Israeli KG7 offensive hand grenades similar to the defused grenade that the Death Merchant held in his left hand.

"And by little old me," mocked Kelly Dillard, who was standing behind Ami Sidki and Zaid Quamiylin. He too carried an M-92SB Beretta and an Israeli grenade. "All of you keep your hands in sight, or I'll blow your Moslem heads off!"

"As I suspected—you're CIA!" spit out Ami Sidki. "You will never escape Al Mamlaka al Urduniya al Hashemiyah!"[2]

Sidki made his move—and committed suicide by doing so. His right hand, in his coat pocket, was wrapped around a .25 Bauer ACP autoloader. Thinking that he could fire the little pistol from inside his pocket, Sidki was moving the weapon to make its muzzle horizontal with Camellion's stomach when the Death Merchant, spotting the movement, fired the Beretta machine pistol that was set to a three-round burst.

Phyyttttttttttt whispered the silencer on the machine pistol. Sidki's lower jaw went slack. A look of total disbelief fell over his face and he staggered back. Two burn holes appeared in his coat, one on each side of a lapel. A third burn hole was born in his shirt, in the center of his chest.

[2]The official Arabic name of Jordan.

Dillard moved quickly out of the way, to his left, out of the way of the dead Sidki, who fell on his back, and jammed the muzzle of his Beretta into the small of Zaid Quamiylin's back, snarling in a whisper, "Freeze, or I'll shove two fingers up your nose and one up your butt and you'll die of suffocation."

"All of you—sit down! Now!" ordered the Death Merchant. He swung the Beretta machine pistol from a fearful Zaid Quamiylin to the equally frightened but cool Sakar Jalkuto and Amersi Karamesh, the two other Department 4 agents. Camellion was not concerned about Frank Tiflorton, Elmore Fradenbach, and Major Yosef Aboussan, not with Follmer and LaHann behind them and LaHann watching the opening of the tent, prepared to deal with anyone who might enter.

The four Jordanians, their eyes burning with hatred, pulled out folding chairs and sat down, placing their hands on the two folding tables.

"My God! What's going on here?" cried Frank Tiflorton, his voice shaking. He also pulled up a chair and sat down when Follmer jammed him in the back with a Beretta and motioned for him to sit.

"Camellion—you're crazy!" burst out Elmore Fradenbach, who remained standing, his eyes frantically scrutinizing Richard Camellion. "What—what do you think you are doing? If you and the others are with the Central Intelligence Agency, I—"

"There's no use keeping up the act," Camellion said, almost tenderly, to Fradenbach. "Your work here is finished. Ours isn't. But we have no choice but to leave. You no doubt will be decorated when we get back to Yerushalayim!"

"Jerusalem!" exploded Fradenbach. "What the devil are you talking about? I'm not going—"

"Stop it, *Chaver Binyomin*,"[3] Camellion said in Yiddish. "*Shemen zich in dein veiten haldz*."[4] He switched back to English when he saw that the Jordanians, knowing he had been speaking Yiddish, were regarding him with a greater hatred. "There isn't any need to pretend any longer, Binyomin," he said to a worried Fradenbach in a tone of confidential camaraderie. "Sooner or later, these Department 4 *shlubs*[5] would search your Caper on the pickup truck and find the transmitter. Even these Arab pigs know how to use a surveillance receiver."

[3] "Friend Benjamin."
[4] "You ought to be ashamed of yourself." Literally: "You should be ashamed down to the bottom of your throat."
[5] A jerk, a foolish and/or stupid person. Second rate. Inferior.

Fradenbach paled. A man who is a trained intelligence agent is equal to the most delicate of situations. But not always. Fradenbach knew he was neatly trapped—boxed in—damned if he did and damned if he didn't.

He stared at the Death Merchant with fierce eyes, his expression clearly conveying that he had gotten Camellion's subtle message: that it wasn't the Jordanians who might find the transmitter, but that Camellion and his men had already found it. Fradenbach wasn't a spy with Camellion's group. He was, however, an agent—for the KGB. That alone was enough to place him in front of a firing squad.

"Elmore, what's he talking about? What does he mean?" Frank Tiflorton sounded like a little boy asking why he couldn't go to the movies.

Fradenbach didn't answer.

The Death Merchant sneered at the Jordanians. "That idiot Sidki! Thinking we were the American CIA! You Jordanians should love the Americans! They have given you F-16 fighter planes and mobile Hawk missiles to use against us, against Israel."

"You Mossad bastard!" Amersi Karamesh, consumed with rage and hatred, could not contain himself. "You Jewish trash will never leave this solar station alive."

"If we don't, you won't either! None of us will!" the Death Merchant said, seizing the initiative. "All of us are going to get on one of those choppers, or"—he pulled the ring of the grenade in his left hand with his teeth—"we will all be blown apart together. Three grenades—each has a special three-second fuse—will very easily kill the twelve of us. Of do you think we're going to risk becoming victims of your special interrogation chambers in Amman. We of the Mivtzan Elohim prefer to take our enemies with us when we die."

The Death Merchant could hear the Super Frelons landing and knew that very soon either Captain Basi Hunada—Camellion had seen him inspecting one of the heavy-machine-gun emplacements—or Sergeant-Corporal Rif Jaffersi would be coming to the tent. No doubt, the Jordanian commandos and the American construction workers were wondering where Major Aboussan was.

"We are more than prepared to die and meet Jehovah," Kelly Dillard said, making his voice deliberately fanatical. "Are you Jordanian trash equally prepared to meet Allah?"

"This is crazy!" Frank Tiflorton began rubbing his hands together, an idiosyncrasy of his indicating extreme tension.

"Camellion! Y-You and the others are American engineers! You can't be I-Israelis. You came from the United States and-and—"

"Shut up, you American fool!" ordered the Death Merchant, feeling sorry for the distraught man. "It took precise timing to intercept the real engineers after they landed at Beirut. As you now know, we succeeded. We had passports and visas already prepared with our own photographs. The technical data, the various graphs and charts we took from the real engineers made the deception complete."

Tiflorton stared at Camellion for a moment. "That explains why you stalled about going over technical material in the head-quarters building," he said angrily. "Goddamn you murderous Jews! What did you do with the real engineers?" Without think-ing, he started to get up from the folding chair.

"Unless you're growing like a wild weed—sit down!" warned the Death Merchant. "The American engineers are dead." His bright blue eyes darted first to Sakar Jalkuto and Amersi Karamesh, then to a frozen-faced Major Yosef Aboussan, who was seated to the right of Tiflorton. "Dead—like all of us are going to be. Either the Jordanians cooperate, or all of us die."

Camellion noticed how Jalkuto, Karamesh, and Quamiylin kept their eyes fastened to the grenade in his left hand, afraid that he might release the pressure on the lever—*Good! They're afraid! I'd be scared one-third stiff if they weren't!*

"We're getting company," Phil LaHann said worriedly. "It's that frog-faced Captain Hunada and three soldiers. What's the play?"

"Holster your weapons," Camellion said earnestly. "Keep the grenades in your jacket pockets. The rest is up to our Arab 'friends.' At even a hint that they might try to grab us, explode the grenades. At the same time, I'll use the remote-control device to explode the five-pound block of RDX in my bag."

A gamble! A desperate game of chance. The risk, however, was necessary. The grenades were duds and there wasn't any RDX in his bag. Camellion had one factor in his favor: the fact that all men (except philosophers and thanatologists) fear death. The Jordanians were not cowards; neither were they suicidal. No more or less than men of other creeds and cultures did they look forward to the moment that would be a color out of space and a shadow out of time—to That Moment when the Cosmic Lord of Death would sweep them into another dimension.

Camellion had analyzed the possibility of marching the Jordanians to one of the helicopters with weapons drawn, in which case the soldiers and the American construction workers would realize that Camellion & Company were enemies. The Death Merchant had decided against such an "open" tactic. One of the Fourth commandos might be trigger-happy or, just as likely, a Moslem fanatic.

Kelly Dillard, standing against the west wall of the tent, said matter-of-factly, "We can't make the corpse of Sidki invisible. I guess we must assume the soldiers and Hunada are blind and won't see the body." Like Follmer and LaHann, he still had his Beretta out, the muzzle of the noise suppressor only several feet from the head of Zaid Quamiylin.

"I'll use black magic," Camellion said, a mocking lilt in his voice. He warned the Jordanians already inside the tent, "If one of you as much as breathes heavily, I'll turn him into an instant ghost."

By then, Captain Basi Hunada and the three commandos had reached the headquarters tent. Holding the Beretta autoloader behind his back, Phil LaHann pushed aside the tent flap and the four men entered. Lahann was letting the flap fall back into place and Captain Hunada was getting his first—and last—glimpse of Ami Sidki's body when Camellion said calmly in Hebrew, "Stiff all four of them."

Massacre! Hunada and the three commandos never fully comprehended what was happening. They died too quickly, before their conscious minds could fully operate all thought circuits. The noise suppressors on the Berettas of LaHann and Follmer spit in a loud whisper and 9mm Luger/Parabellum slugs banged into the backs of Captain Basi Hunada and the three fourth commandos. Within moments, Life had been turned into Death[6] and there were three more cold cuts on the ground inside the tent.

A low moan came from one of the commandos that LaHann had whacked out. "I must be getting rusty," LaHann said almost angrily. He stooped and fired another round into the head of the still alive Jordanian. The moaning stopped, the left leg of the man jerked, and he was dead.

One huge mass of detestation, almost trembling in their rage and hatred, Major Yosef Aboussan and the three Department-4 secret police officers were helpless. They knew that they couldn't prove anything, to either themselves or Allah, by committing suicide; and they had no doubt that if they made a sudden move,

[6]A matter of relativity, since there isn't any "death." There is only a change of consciousness.

the tall, lean man with the strange-looking blue eyes would kill them. The man Camellion killed with an expertness that surely was a gift of Shaitan the Evil One.[7]

"In a moment we leave," Camellion said emotionlessly. "Phil, can you see where the choppers landed?"

"A couple of hundred feet from here, to the north of the work-and-assembly shed," LaHann replied, peeking through the tent. "We'd better get the lead out before the rest of them think something is wrong."

"Keep them covered," Camellion said, speaking very rapidly. He shoved the Beretta machine pistol into the utility bag and, all the while holding the dummy grenade in his left hand, reached into his right coat pocket with his right hand, took out the Merix remote-control detonator, switched it on, and very carefully returned the device to his pocket. He pulled his right hand from the coat pocket, slipped it through the two straps of the bag, then, supporting the bag on his wrist, shoved his hand back into the right coat pocket.

"Now, you Moslem idiots, let's see if you don't mind being blown to little bits and pieces. When this five-pound block of explosive goes, so do we. They might find a fingernail or two; that's about all." Camellion further taunted the Jordanians with, "Here's your chance to prove *'Al ain bel sin al sen bel sen'!*[8] Now either walk to the nearest chopper or die. I'll give you two seconds to decide. One! Two!"

"WAIT!" The word leaped from Major Yosef Aboussan's mouth, his fright very apparent. "We'll go to the helicopter— and may your stinking Jew God damn you to hell!"

"If and when He does, you'll be there too, major—on my lap," the Death Merchant hissed. "Here's how we'll do it. You go first, major. Karamesh, to his left; Quamiylin, to the major's right. Mr. D. and F. will follow. Then Tiflorton and Fradenbach. Mr. L., you walk to their right. I and Jalkuto will walk behind them. Mr. N and Mr. G., you two walk behind me. And remember, one wrong move—try to make any kind of warning signal, and we'll all go to hell together—instantly. Bob, take the major's Browning out of its holster and unload it; then shove it back in the holster."

They left the tent in the order that had been demanded by the

---

[7] Arabic for the Devil/Lucifer/Satan.

[8] Arabic—"An eye for an eye, a tooth for a tooth." The Islamic vow of revenge.

Death Merchant, the group moving at a slow pace until Camellion whispered, "Faster! I won't say it again."

Most of the soldiers, unaware of the true circumstances, went about their duties, merely glancing at Major Yosef Aboussan and the men behind him. The danger now was that some soldier might stop him for clarification of some order.

The American construction workers were still estimating the damage done by the Israeli gunship. Like the Jordanian soldiers, they, too, knew that the "five engineers" and Camellion, their supervisor, would be returning to Amman. The Americans didn't think anything was wrong. The group was merely going to one of the choppers.

I think we'll make it! It wasn't that Camellion had staked everything on his bluffing the Jordanians. Shucks, a really good poker player always had a few good cards stashed, never folding until he had to. If the Jordanians hadn't fallen for his we'll-all-die-together act, he merely would have terminated them. He and the other men would have then left the tent and ambled to the choppers, just as they were doing right now—*Only your odds of survival would have decreased by a factor of 70.3!*

This whole damn business is similar to abstract art—a product of the untalented, sold by the unprincipled to the utterly bewildered. But Grojean does have talent for intrigue. Ha! We're still the unprincipled, and the Jordies are more than bewildered! They're angry and afraid. Join the club, boys. So am I.

The Death Merchant wasn't enthused over how the Super Frelons were parked. Indeed not. Two of the birds were resting fifty feet to the north of the work/assembly shop shaped like one-half of a swastika. The third bird was sixty feet to the west of the building. The pilots had shut down two of the Super Frelons and their big rotors were not moving. The rotor of the third chopper was in 5th-idle, the pilot and copilot standing outside the craft, in front of the nose, smoking cigarettes. The two other pilots and two copilots were not in sight, nor were the gunners of the first two ships. Each Super Frelon had a British L7A1 belt-fed heavy machine gun mounted on a ring swivel, on both the port and the starboard sides. That was the rub. Although the gunners had left the first two birds, two Jordanians were at the L7s in the last chopper, the one whose rotor was slowly revolving. Camellion wasn't worried about their swinging the heavies to him and his group if trouble started. The gunners couldn't: the azimuth range of the swivel would not permit it, the angle too steep. The second rub was that Camellion and his people and the Jordanians had to move between the first two choppers in order to reach the third bird, the craft that was obviously waiting for them.

Parrot poop! We can't turn back. Let's hope none of these Jordanians get crazy-brave or stupid-foolish. What the hell! This still beats being in L.A. or New York City, where rats crawl over babies and all civilization has stopped. Crazy-brave? I don't think they will!

With Major Aboussan in the lead, the group started moving between the first two helicopters. For the barest fraction of a micromoment, Sakar Jalkuto, to Camellion's right, hesitated. Then he moved ahead with the rest of the men.

Camellion was only three-fourths right. The secret policemen kept their mouths shut. Major Yosef Aboussan didn't. His pride and love of nation overpowered common sense and the urge for survival and he suddenly dove to the right, shouting in Arabic at the pilot and the copilot of the helicopter ahead, "Stop them! They're Israeli Wrath of God agents!"

God Save the White Sox and damn the Mohawks if there are any left!

Knowing that the boiling fat had spilled over into the hot, roaring fire, the Jordanians and the Americans reacted, the latter group including Frank Tiflorton and Elmore Fradenbach.

Dillard, Follmer, and LaHann, having expected the worst kind of trouble (short of having hemorrhoids in Sydney, Australia) were not caught with their reflexes and attention span napping. The three Company men were almost as fast as the Merchant of Death who instantly—as his left hand dropped the defused grenade and streaked to the S.A. .45 Enforcer pistol in his right shoulder holster—spun to his right and executed a low front snap kick that landed where he wanted it to land. The toe of his foot hit the testicles of Salkar Jalkuto like a battering ram, the terrible blow stopping Jalkuto, who had turned to his left, with the intention of pulling Camellion's right hand from his coat pocket.

"OHOHOHOHOHOHOHOH!" Jalkuto looked like a man who had just been impaled on a white-hot poker. He mouth formed an *O*. His eyes rolled around in his head like two black marbles while his hands tried to reach his crushed dingle dangles between his legs. He failed. The agony was too great, raw pain that was excruciating. Only half conscious, the D-4 agent sank to his knees. He hadn't even started to fold by the time Camellion had pulled the Enforcer and a finger on his right hand was pressing the button of the Merix remote-control detonator.

During those few seconds, the three CIA men went into action. LaHann wasn't too concerned about Frank Tiflorton, who

92

was slow moving and out of condition. Tiflorton would do well to run a fourth of a block without losing breath. Not so with Fradenbach, who was a karate expert—and now he proved faster than LaHann. LaHann's Beretta was only halfway out of the shoulder holster as Fradenbach spun and tried a vicious right-legged spin kick, which he intended to follow with a two-handed *Shuto* chop that would have shattered LaHann's collarbone if the twin knifehands had landed. They didn't! Neither did Fradenbach's right foot make contact with LaHann's groin. The CIA man, his right hand still inside his jacket, arched himself back, stumbled, and went down on one knee. In that micromoment, Fradenbach had him cold. One expertly delivered kick could kill Phil LaHann. It never came.

LaHann couldn't believe what happened next. Before Fradenbach could even begin to get another maneuver going, Frank Tiflorton came up behind Fradenbach, threw his right forearm across the front of Fradenbach's neck, pulled back and jabbed a knee forcefully into the small of the astonished man's back. Fradenbach had been caught completely off guard and for a few seconds was helpless—long enough for LaHann to finish pulling his 9mm Beretta and deliver a left roundhouse heel kick to Fradenbach's right kneecap. With a loud yell, Fradenbach sagged and, when Tiflorton released him, went down, his kneecap shattered.

Tiflorton was starting to say, "I'm with you guys. I know you're Company men!" But all LaHann heard him say was "I'm—" The rest of the words lost in the thunderous *BLAMMMMMMM* of the two-pound block of PETN in the motor home, a blast that sent parts of the long, wide vehicle rocketing for a hundred and fifty feet, the left front wheel and tire coming down and hitting the ground only four feet south of the tail rotor of the Super Frelon whose main six-bladed rotor was turning. The rim and tire bounced over the tail rotor and kept right on going.

The waves of concussion from the exploded PETN were still expanding and parts and pieces of the demolished motor home were still falling as Kelly Dillard's M-92SB Beretta roared and 9mm (9.355″) 125-gr. hollow-pointed slugs sliced into Major Yosef Aboussan, who was trying to get through the portside opening of the first chopper parked to the north. One HP bullet caught Aboussan in the left side, just above his Sam Browne belt. Going in sideways, the bullet bored a bloody tunnel through his pancreas and his stomach and made its exit. Two more of Dillard's 9mm projectiles popped Aboussan high in the left side, going through his lungs and lodging against his ribs on the right side.

The dying dummy was still jerking like a tap-dancing frog on a hot plate at the same time that Robert Follmer snuffed Amersi Karamesh and Zaid Quamiylin. Of the two Jordanian secret-police agents, Karamesh was the faster. He was turning around to make a grab for Follmer, so he caught Follmer's first bullet in the left side of the chest. He caught another slug in the gut coinstantaneously with Follmer's delivering a front snap kick to Zaid Quamiylin, aiming for the coccyx. Follmer missed the mark. His heel made contact five inches higher. Snap! But no pop and crackle! His back broken, Quamiylin gave a short scream and started to wilt, all to the tune of the Death Merchant's Enforcer autoloader.

A mere twelve seconds had passed since the now dead Major Aboussan had shouted the warning. The monstrous blast of the motor home's blowing itself to rubble had confused the Jordanian commandos and the rest of the Americans, neither group having the slightest idea of what was really happening, except six Commandos who happened to be passing the starboard side of the first chopper to the north.

Still trying to recover from surprise, the pilot and the copilot, standing in front of the cockpit of the third chopper, had as much chance to live as an Israeli surrounded by Black Septemberists.[9] The gunner on the port side was in the same fix. Already in the Valley of the Shadows, Nitzan Assifa was sticking his head out the opening to see what was happening. He never found out. One of Camellion's 200-gr. HP .45 slugs struck him in the forehead, just above the bridge of the nose. Assifa fell back against Jamil Hawatmeh, the starboard gunner, who was unstrapping a West German Walther MPK/MPL submachine gun from the round wall of the helicopter.

Meanwhile, the six commandos who had been passing the starboard side of the first Super Frelon to the north made the

[9]Called "Black September" after the events of September, 1970, when King Hussein began his stern measures against the fedayeen—*fada'iyin,* from the Arab verb *fada,* meaning "to redeem," or "to sacrifice," particularly for a cause that is a religious one.

Black September is the special murder organization of the Palestine Liberation Organization—the PLO—and Fatah. Fatah is the Arabic word for "conquest." It is an acronym in reverse of the initial letters of the PLO—*Harakat at-Tahrir al-Filistini.* In short, "conquest" of Israel and a complete restoration of all Israeli land to the Palestinians. There can never be peace between the Israelis and the Arab states.

mistake of rushing around the front of the chopper—straight into the slugs from the Death Merchant, who had drawn his other S.A. Enforcer and had pulled the Beretta machine pistol from his kit bag. Enforcer and MP roared, 9mm and .45 slugs chopping into the Jordanians, of whom only two were able to get off shots from their Browning autoloaders. Both slugs missed Camellion and the two Jesuits. Fathers Norton and Gatdula, while having the faith of the prophets in God Almighty, also had earthly common sense. They had fallen flat to the ground and were saying Hail Marys—a fitting benediction for the six Jordanians, four of whom were tugging at their Brownings in their flap-over holsters as they died. The two who had managed to get off rounds fell back riddled with 9mm machine pistol and .45 Beretta hard lead core metal in their bodies.

"Get up and follow me," Camellion said to the priests. He then glanced at LaHann, who had just slammed the side of his Beretta against Fradenbach's head, and at Frank Tiflorton, who said quickly, "I'm on your side. I'm positive you're not Israeli agents."

Camellion didn't have time to ask Tiflorton how he knew—time for that later. Instead, he yelled at Dillard and Follmer—who had by now let their kit bags slip from their wrists and had pulled Mini-Uzis from the bags—"Watch both sides, and be careful of the machine gunner on the starboard side." Camellion then said to LaHann, who was throwing off the safety of his own Mini-UZI, "Phil, you and Frank—" Camellion turned and looked at the two nervous Jesuits. "You two can carry Fradenbach to the plane. Hurry it up. I need Phil's firepower."

The two Jesuits quickly moved around the Death Merchant, who shoved a new magazine into the Beretta machine pistol.

Tiflorton said eagerly, "Give me a weapon and I—"

"Shut up," warned the Death Merchant. "Make a wrong move and you'll die. Keep in front of us and get to the chopper."

Jamil Hawatmeh, the starboard gunner in the third chopper, was not a stupid man. He wasn't as sharp in the brain department as Kelly Dillard and Robert Follmer either, or he would have remembered that the bottom of the Super Frelon—resting on a tricycle landing gear, one wheel in front, two in the rear—was almost three feet above the ground and that his lower legs could be seen by another person, especially if that person were lying on the ground. That's exactly what Robert Follmer was doing as Kelly Dillard covered him and watched for any Jordanians who might approach.

Hawatmeh figured he'd sneak up the starboard side and open fire by the side of the nose, with a sweeping motion. The Walther MPK/MPL SMG would cut the Americans apart. As careful as a cow chewing a cud of cactus, he jumped from the starboard opening and started to move toward the nose.

Lying on his stomach, Follmer watched Hawatmeh take a few steps, and then pulled the trigger of the Mini-Uzi, the little weapon chattering. Two 9mm FMJ slugs almost tore off Hawatmeh's left foot at the ankle, the foot turning one way and a screaming Hawatmeh another as the third bullet of the three-round burst broke his right ankle. The commando crashed to the hard ground.

Follmer grinned. Thinking that Hawatmeh was about as efficient as the state of California's "Department of Justice," Follmer fired another three-round burst. One slug stung Hawatmeh in the upper lip, tore through his throat, and took off into space through the back of his neck. The second bullet stabbed him in the chest, ripped through his esophagus, and lodged against his backbone. The third caught him in the stomach and buried itself in a back rib.

"Hurry it up!" urged the Death Merchant sternly. The Enforcer and the Beretta machine pistol in his hands, he hurried past the pilot and the copilot he had snuffed with the .45 Enforcer, prodded Frank Tiflorton with the barrel of the Beretta MP; glanced to his right, and growled at the solar-power engineer, "Wait right here and help Norton and Gatdula when they get here."

Camellion jumped through the portside opening of the helicopter, following LaHann, who went straight to the British L7A1 heavy machine gun mounted in the opening on the starboard side. He glanced down at the dead Nitzan Assifa and felt a cold chill slide down his spine. *Time is running out for us!* Only four minutes had passed, but the exploded motor home wouldn't keep the Jordanian commandos confused forever. Very quickly they would figure out what was happening and do something about it—*Like concentrating their firepower on this chopper!*

He glanced out the opening and saw that Kelly Dillard was only seconds from jumping into the chopper through the port doorway and that the two Jesuits, huffing and puffing from carrying the unconscious Fradenbach, were moving faster than the Death Merchant had anticipated—*It must be all their prayers and clean living!* Behind the two Jesuits was Robert Follmer, shoving a full magazine into a Beretta machine pistol. In his right hand was a Mini-Uzi. He finished reloading the MP none too soon. Five Jordanian commandos came around the front of the first Super Frelon parked to the north, two of the men raising 9mm Browning autoloaders, the other three swinging up Belgian FN 50-41 automatic rifles.

DLDLDLDLDLDLDLDLDLDLDLDLDL-PHYTTTTTTTTTTTTT—
the Mini-Uzi and the silenced Beretta sang their song of destruction, the 9mm projectiles raining like metal hail all over the Jordanians, ripping them across the middle and making the doomed men dance and jerk in a fandango of death. Only one commando got off a stream of FN 5.62 × 51mm slugs (the same as a .38 Winchester)—unintentionally. Dying, he was falling backward, reflex pulling his finger against the trigger—and whoever heard of killing clouds? Or shooting down the sky?

Dillard leaped through the portside opening and headed straight for the cockpit of the big Super Frelon, muttering something about "a piss-poor way to spend a day," while the Death Merchant watched the two Jesuit priests and Frank Tiflorton shove Fradenbach into the chopper, and then get in themselves, followed by Robert Follmer.

The three 1,630 h.p. Turboméca Turmo IIIC turboshafts began roaring and the main rotor of the chopper began to spin faster and still faster.

Camellion motioned with the Beretta machine pistol to the Jesuits, Follmer, and Tiflorton. "Drag Fradenbach to the stern and secure him. Get down on the floor and hang on. For all I know, Kelly might tip us over. Bob, if Tiflorton gets cute—kill him!"

"Goddamn it, Camellion!" raged Tiflorton, "I said I'm on your side. I know you men aren't Mossad or Wrath of God killers."

"We'll take it up later," Camellion said bitterly. "Right now, you could be on the side of Fradenbach for all I know."

As the men dragged Fradenbach to the stern, the Death Merchant holstered the .45 Enforcer and shoved the machine pistol into his belt. He was pulling back the cocking knob of the port L7A1 heavy MG when Dillard pulled in pitch and the large helicopter started climbing the steps of the sky, the craft swinging slightly to port.

Camellion wasn't ready with his MG, but Phil LaHann was more than prepared with his. He fired at the second chopper—the one parked to the north—when the craft in which he was a passenger was at an altitude of eighty feet and rising rapidly. More than a hundred 7.62mm spire-pointed projectiles swept all over the enemy craft. Getting ready for the pursuit, the pilot, copilot, and the two gunners were torn into blood-tinged messes of chunks of flesh and torn uniforms. A split second later the chopper exploded into a bright ball of brilliant fire, the blast disintegrating the big bird.

Fortunately for the Death Merchant and his people, the Jordanians at the heavy machine guns on the perimeter of the solar station had not had the time to swing their weapons inward. It wouldn't have made any difference—not now—if they had. The machine guns could not be raised at a high enough altitude to fire at Camellion's bird. Nonetheless, an enemy who is dead today can't fire at you tomorrow. The Death Merchant raked the machine-gun nest to the south, his wave of metal death washing all over the Jordanians and throwing up dirt and rocks around the corpses.

Camellion's Super Frelon, at 400 feet now and still climbing, was far from safe. There was always the possibility that he and his men might meet one or more Jordanian patrol choppers before their own craft crossed the Jordan/Saudi Arabia border, much less made its way to At-Turayf. It was the Now that mattered. Any number of Jordanians were firing at the Super Frelon with assault rifles and submachine guns, and there were numerous chilling high-pitched *zingssssss* as enemy projectiles struck nonvital parts of the chopper and ricocheted. All it would take was one bullet in the right place to bring the big helicopter crashing to the ground; and should the main rotor, or the tail rotor, be hit in a vital spot, the bird would go down like a rock.

The second enemy Super Frelon (to the north of the work/assembly shop shaped like half a swastika) was at an altitude of 161 feet when Phil LaHann—now able to zero in on the bird because Dillard was still swinging the chopper to port—raked it from end to end with a tornado of slugs. There was a thundering kind of *BEROOOMMMMM*, a big, blossoming ball of bright fire, and parts of the chopper were raining all over the sky, a downpour of parts that would fall over a 200-foot area.

Zingggggg! An enemy 7.62mm, fired from an FN-FALO light machine gun, had stabbed through the flooring on the starboard side and had glanced off a portside handhold, only five feet above Father Gatdula's head. Shooting up at an angle, the flattened-out blob of metal sped through the portside opening, narrowly missing the Death Merchant.

ZingggggggGGGGGGGGG! Another FN-FALO LMG slug struck one of the blades of the main rotor, the sound made extra sharp and loud by the rotation of the rotor. Luck remained on the Death Merchant's side. Fortune did because the chopper was almost 1,000 feet high and 1,200 feet to the south of its original position. The majority of the bullet's power had been spent. Its power was weakened further by the powerful downdraft of the 62-foot six-bladed rotor. The total result of the two combined factors was that the projectile was only an annoyance, similar to a flea flying into the prop of a propeller-driven aircraft.

The same Jordanian firing the FN-FALO LMG got lucky with Philip LaHann, although the commando would never know it. Three more 7.62 × 51mm NATO slugs cut upward through the lower part of the craft to starboard. One ripped through the floor and, its force almost spent, half buried itself in one of the wooden slats running horizontally across the ceiling. The second projectile struck under the barrel of the L7A1 machine gun, toward the center of its length, the impact knocking the barrel sharply upward while the front section of the weapon went downward. The slug glanced off as a third projectile cut through the floor, shot straight up, and ripped into the stomach of LaHann, who was bending over to raise the weapon to its locking position. The slug came to a halt after it had cut through one side of the common iliac artery.

"OHhh!" Realist that he was, LaHann knew that the Cosmic Lord of Death had gently tapped him on the shoulder. An icy wind blew against his soul and there was a horrid howling in his mind. In an instant, confused images began to broaden in his brain and he felt that he was an actor in some quick-change theater playing any number of roles, a mummer consumed first with horror and mostrousness, then with fantastic beauty, with a splendor that filled him with ecstasy. Very suddenly his entire universe was one large vastness, out of space and out of time, a titanic immensity free of all desire and volition. There was no regret. There was no fear. There was only an unbelievable peace and a very soft, velvety blackness.

During that eye blink in time, neither the Death Merchant—who was securing the port machine gun—nor anyone else saw Phil LaHann take the fatal bullet. It was Father Bernard Norton (who had been silently praying) who saw the unconscious and dying LaHann—who had not had time to secure the gunners' straps—pitch forward, a river of red running out of his mouth.

"Oh, my God!" Norton's high voice of alarm alerted the other men, except Camellion, who could hear only the savage rush of wind. The Death Merchant then turned and, with the other men, was in time to see the body of LaHann fall through the starboard opening. In an instant he was gone.

The Death Merchant's mouth became a tight line and he thought of a line by Vergil—*Deus nobis haec otia fecit. . . .*[10]

Knowing that the Super Frelon was now beyond the range of Jordanian guns, Kelly Dillard pointed the chopper south and continued to climb into the sky

He looked carefully at the instrument panel.

He didn't like what he saw!

The needle on the transmission oil temperature indicator was slowly dropping. Dillard felt like a man who had crawled ten miles across a burning desert, but who had collapsed ten feet from the pitcher of ice water. Saudi Arabia, at the closest border point, was still forty-seven miles away. . . .

[10]"A god has wrought for us this repose; a deity has conferred these comforts upon us. . . ."

CHAPTER SEVEN

Tel Aviv–Yafo.
1600 hours.

"A good lie always finds more believers than a bad truth," General Yigel Bar-Levinsky said in guarded tones. Dressed in civilian clothes, he pulled a cigarette case from his right inner coat pocket, peered for a moment at Isser Ben Zur, and sat down heavily in the armchair. "It's been over a week, and the Jordanians haven't leaked anything to the world's press about their victory over us near Ra's an Naqb." His thin face broke out in a satisfied grin. "Believe me, Issar. Amman isn't going to reveal the secret. It would be a 'bad truth' and the world at large would never believe that the Jordanians, without help, could defeat us in any battle."

Sitting by the modular desk, Isser Ben Zur, the chief of Mivtzan Elohim, was not so sure, his doubt reflected in his gloomy expression.

"We would have won the battle if Major Mosshin had been given the three helicopters we requested," he said irritably. "Damn Begin! I tell you, Yigel. He has to go! He's like a *yungatsh*.[1] There's no reasoning with him. He's already severely wounded our relations with the Americans and is convinced that the scrolls are a CIA plot, put together with the help of the Jordanians, supposedly to embarrass the land of Israel." He lowered his voice. "I'm convinced that Menachem Begin has become a *Malech-hamovess*[2] for all of us!"

Almost six feet tall and slim, Bar-Levinsky was fifty nine years old, had a deeply lined face, enormous ears, stone gray eyes, and fingers stained from tobacco. Years of living in a kibbutz had made his skin look like brown leather.

Managing to escape from the Soviet Union in 1952, he had

---

[1] A street urchin and/or street Arab.
[2] Angel of Death (of the male gender). Sarcastically, a bad husband.

learned Hebrew very quickly; yet he had never lost his Russian accent. His fellow *kibbutznikim* had regarded him as an overly serious, stern personality, and called him "Stakhanovitch," an inference to Alexei Stakhanov, the Russian coal miner, whose name the Soviet propaganda writers had made synonymous with high productivity. Thirty years after arriving in Palestine, Yigel Bar-Levinsky, who was a genius at intrigue, was the *memuneh* —the "Big Boss"—of the Mossad, having inherited the position from Isser Harel,[3] who had resigned after he had gone against Premier Ben-Gurion's wishes to assassinate German scientists working for the Egyptians.

"We mustn't let impatience overcome our common sense," Bar-Levinsky said with his usual briskness. He exhaled cigarette smoke while toying with a BIC lighter. "Begin will eventually topple himself. He doesn't need any help from us." His frigid gray eyes locked with the hard gaze of Isser Ben Zur. "After all, Isser, how would it look if the PLO or some assassin of another Arab group 'assassinated' Begin? What would the world then think of our security methods?"

A look of cool appraisal came into Isser Ben Zur's brown eyes.

"I talked to Eli yesterday and he's still enraged over Begin's disregarding his intelligence estimates of the situation at the Jordanian solar station the Americans are building. I—"

"Were building!" Bar-Levinsky said significantly.

"All right. *Were* building. Of course, I didn't ask Eli about his secret meeting with you, earlier in the morning. I did tell him that he shouldn't have been surprised over Begin's refusing to listen. We all know what Begin thinks of Arabs."

"How well we know," replied Bar-Levinsky in disgust, the side part of his mind thinking of Colonel Eli Lodtz, the director of the Sheruth Modiin. Lodtz would have liked to incorporate the Mossad into his military intelligence division. For that reason, Bar-Levinsky had to be very careful in his dealings with him. However, the two Israeli intelligence chiefs were in agreement that Menachem Begin had to go. The Hitler-like tactics of the pinched-faced little bastard were a danger to all the Israelis.

Continued Bar-Levinsky, still playing with the BIC lighter,

---

[3]Known as Isser "the little"—he was only four feet eight inches tall—it was Isser Harel who shaped the Mossad in its formative years. An austere man in his habits, he had only one flaw: he loved power. His real trouble was that he viewed himself as vice-premier of Israel.

"For the past year, I've been trying to tell our exalted prime minister—the son of a bitch thinks he's the second Moses!—that Hussein's army[4] is the best-trained Arab force in the Middle East. He refuses to listen, insisting that the average Jordanian soldier is no better trained that the Egyptian fighting man. He even refuses to consider the strong position that sawed-off little runt Hussein has in this area, particularly in achieving autonomy for the 850,000 Palestinians living on the occupied West Bank." His expression grew more serious and he flicked ash from his cigarette. "Begin is as stupid as Arafat. They're both cut from the same cloth of irrational determinism—don't you agree?"

Isser Ben Zur disagreed, but he didn't say so. He did treat Bar-Levinsky to a quick nod of appreciation, his hazel eyes-filled with deep concern. "Eli did agree on our plan regarding the Scrolls, didn't he? He had to commit himself one way or another during your meeting with him."

Bar-Levinsky's wiredrawn face grew thoughtful as he studied Isser Ben Zur, who was a Sabra—one born in Palestine. A muscular man in his late forties, of medium height, he had a mild-looking face and a head topped by a thick shock of dark hair, infiltrated by streaks of gray. He always had a quiet manner that carried him unhurriedly toward his goal, usually a bit quicker than the next man.

When people spoke about Bar-Levinsky they said that, if he had stayed in the Soviet Union, he would have become head of the KGB!

When people spoke about Ben Zur, they said that when he looked at you, you felt as if you were being measured for a coffin!

"Lodtz agreed in principle," Bar-Levinsky said soberly. "He didn't say he would help, but he will commit himself. I'm sure of it. The fact that he even conceded—especially to me—that Begin is a clear-cut danger to our nation means that he's with us."

"Then we're almost home free." Ben Zur smiled with satisfaction. "We're helpless without Colonel Lodtz's assistance. Only he can talk General Sharon into using those two special commando groups."

Bar-Levinsky's voice was cool and decisive. "Remember what

[4]Known as the Arab Legion—60,000 strong. The Jordanian air force numbers 7,340 men. However, the Jordanians are not a match for the well-trained Israelis, who are just as fanatical. The Israelis have to be. If they are pushed out of Israel—where can they go?

I said about impatience. All the military brass is against Begin, all except General Azzar. He's another fool who thinks he's living in Old Testament times.

"Fortunately for us, we don't need him."

"It's Lodtz we need," Yigel Bar-Levinsky said. "He will have to convince General Sharon of the immense historical value of the scrolls penned by Judas and that they are probably in a cave in the Arqā Mountains."

"I still find it difficult to believe that Ghassan Nazzal lied to us." Ben Zur's eyebrows weaved into a frown as he looked at Bar-Levinsky. "We really don't know that he did."

"Yes, but we will, if and when the CIA and their mercenaries fly from Saudi Arabia to the Arqā Mountains," Bar-Levinsky said quickly, his smile barely discernible behind his thick bush of a mustache. "I have our sensor station in Yotvata monitoring all air traffic from northern Arabia. With the new microwave pickups, we'll know the second a helicopter fleet crosses the Arabian-Jordanian border."

Ben Zur was silent, pondering all the possibilities.

"Yes, the Americans will have to have troop and gunship helicopters," he said at length. "But only if we're right, only if the Americans fly from Arabia.

"What do you mean 'if'?" snapped Bar-Levinsky arrogantly. "I've been in this business too long not to look for the rats when the fresh cheese is out in the open. The six Americans that flew from Amman to the solar station were no more sun-power specialists than I'm the Pope! They went to the station to snoop around and to throw us off track."

"There's the possibility we could be wrong," Ben Zur said decisively, determined not to let General Bar-Levinsky overpower him verbally.

Bar-Levinsky made an angry motion with his left hand. "Sure! There's also the possibility that Jesus Christ will return in something the Christians call 'the Second Coming'! You'll be saying next that Mahmoud Khalil doesn't exist, that Ghassan Nazzal lied about him! Well, we know that he's a real Arab. He's in our records as a protester in the Golan Heights."

"You won't get an argument from me about Khalil," conceded Ben Zur. "He's flesh and blood—and invisible!"

"We can make an educated guess where he is. The Americans have him—the CIA in the American Embassy in Amman." Fiercely, General Bar-Levinsky crushed out his stub of a cigarette that had burned almost down to the filter. "Now, you know that the Company isn't naive enough to go poking around in the

Arqā Mountains without knowing where to look. They'll have Khalil with them. He'll take them right to the scrolls—and we'll be right behind the CIA and its mercs! Granted, it will take some timing, but the operation can be pulled off."

"I have just one question." Ben Zur was brutally blunt. "Have you thought of any tactic by which all of us can protect ourselves from Begin and the parliament should General Sharon and his commandos fail. Or is my question ridiculous?"

"We, or Sharon or Lodtz, won't be able to offer any rationale, any excuse, to Begin and parliament should Sharon fail to get the scrolls," General Bar-Levinsky said in admonitory tones, adding harshly, "Failure means that you and I will be resigning. Can you imagine yourself resigning as head of the Wrath of God?"

Isser Ben Zur couldn't. . . .

CHAPTER EIGHT

The Death Merchant, dressed in camo fatigues, garrison boots, and a white Arab *ghutra*,[1] stood in the opening of the big tent and watched the three commanders of the *Abu Jihad Falaj' i*[2] and their dozen guards approach the tent in which Camellion and the other members of his party had been waiting for two and a half days. Camellion had presented his master plan to Hajj[3] Auda bin Bahadu, and for two and a half days, Crown Prince Abdullah ibn-Abdul Aziz, third in succession to the throne of al-Mamlak al-'Arabiya as-Sa'udiya[4] and the legal commander of the special Arabian commando group, had been trying to make up his mind, analyzing Camellion's proposal—all from the comfort of his palace in Riyadh, the capital. During this time, Camellion and his people had nothing to do but cool their heels at the main training camp of the *Abu Jihad Falaj' i*, six miles east of Hā'ìl, in northcentral Arabia.

It was pleasant enough at the camp, except when one noticed the three rows of barbed-wire fencing around the complex. Otherwise there were flowers, jasmine, and honeysuckle, roses, pinks, and primulas that dotted the camp. In the distance, to the northwest, were the Jabal Ba'Yill'il, a range whose peaks were high and steep and pronounced, many rising to gigantic pinnacles that poked upward into blue-white-purple clouds of mist. Ordinarily there weren't any clouds around the summits, but it had rained during the night and by the middle of the afternoon clouds were again threatening to pour more water on the sands. A good thing too. Shortly, the rainy season, in this part of the

---

[1] A headdress. It differs from the *kaffiyeh* in that it is looser.

[2] Translated as "Father Holy War." *Abu*: Arabic for "father." *Jihad* is Arabic for "Holy War." Fully translated: "Father Holy War Unit (or command)."

[3] *Hajj* is not a name. It is the title given to those who have made the pilgrimage to Mecca.

[4] The full Arabic name of Saudi Arabia.

Arabian peninsula, would end, and the sands would become dry, then hot, and remain that way for many months.

Between the training camp and the mountains was the desert, the sands golden in color, yet shimmering with blues and purples as the sand dunes neared the Jabal Ba'Yill'il, twenty seven kilometers away.

To the north the desert merged with wide stretches of partial grazing land. On the plain the sand mingled with rocks and patches of soil and scrub grass. It was a land of silence, a land in which wind-polished fragments of granite, jasper, and porphyry formed twisted mosaics in the hard sand. In the sand would be tracks of gerbils and gerboas.

For several moments, the Death Merchant studied the all-green Robertson Executive Jet—parked on the runway outside the complex—that had brought Colonel Bahadu and his two aides from Riyadh. Camellion frowned. That was one of the prime weaknesses of the Saudi defense system: the men who made the decisions were all members of the royal family and were not necessarily trained in military tactics.

A good example was Prince Abdullah ibn-Abdul Aziz, the commander of SANG, the Saudian Arabian National Guard, to which the Father Holy War Unit belonged. SANG was the traditional guard to the royal family and consisted of 26,000 Bedouin tribesmen who were stationed in battalion-sized formations throughout the kingdom.

Originally, SANG fighters had been trained by the British; the results had been disappointing. SANG would have lost a battle fighting Hottentots! Uncle Sam had then taken over, with the Vinnell Corporation of Alhambra, California, being awarded a contract to reorganize, reequip, and retrain four SANG battalions into light cavalry units, so that the present battalions were structured as Combined Arms Battalions (CABs), completely motorized tactical combat units very similar to U.S. Army cavalry squadrons.

The Vinnell Corporation people had not trained the *Abu Jihad* commandos. U.S. Special Forces Green Beret officers had attended to that task. Nonetheless, the *Abu Jihad* commandos were still untried. They had never proved themselves against a foreign enemy, nor even, for that matter, against homegrown fanatics.

At least they have to be better than the Arabian National Guardsmen. *They couldn't be worse!*

The regular SANG fighters were basically undisciplined, fanatically religious, and so lazy they had to think twice about brushing away a fly. They did have a fierce pride—*what Bedu hasn't!*—but egotism can never overcome lack of training.

Camellion turned to the men who were sitting on camp chairs. "Here they come—flowing robes and all. Better get up front with me, Macke. You know the protocol. As for the rest of you, don't forget to stand up when they enter the tent. Let's not have them think we're barbarians, even if we are."

"And proud of it!" said Kelly Dillard. "It beats walking around in nightgowns."

"Has Colonel Bahadu got his pet rat with him?" chuckled Wesley Ritter, one of the CIA men who had been at At-Turayf and was part of Green Gables.

Terry Macke, the Green Beret officer, took a position beside the Death Merchant and waited for the three approaching Saudis. Finally, the forward group of guards parted and Colonel Bahadu, Major Muhammad al-Staiyun, and Captain Falih Bin Majid walked up to Camellion and Macke. Behind the three officers came a commando carrying a solid gold eighteen-inch square cage. A present from Crown Prince Abdullah ibn-Abdul Aziz to Colonel Bahadu, the cage contained a white and brown rat of the domesticated variety.

Camellion and Macke raised their right hands and said in unison, "*Salam alaikum.*"

The three Arab commando chiefs returned the greeting with the standard reply, "*Alaikum as salam.*"

The Death Merchant turned to one side and brushed aside the tent flap. "Gentlemen, please enter and be seated."

The three commanders of *Abu Jihad Falaj'i* entered the tent, the commando with the caged rat following them.

Amenities had to be observed. More "*Salam alaikum*(s)" and "*Alaikum as salam*(s)." Coffee—thick, made the Arab way—was poured, dates, with cheese, and small square sugar cakes placed on a long table in the center of the tent. The Death Merchant knew that in due time Hajj Auda bin Bahadu would get around to saying whether Prince Aziz had said yes or no to Camellion's proposal. Colonel Bahadu did, ten minutes later as he sat drinking coffee, the white rat and cage on a stand on his left. For a reason known only to Bahadu, he had named the rat "Saturn."

Bahadu's dark eyes first captured Camellion; then they swung to Macke and Wesley Ritter, the later of whom was one of the CIA specialists within Green Gables.

"Gentlemen," began Bahadu, his Royal Excellency, Prince Abdullah ibn-Abdul Aziz, has decided that Sahib Camellion's plan is worthy of consideration."

Kelly Dillard opened his mouth, then snapped it shut when he remembered that one does not negotiate with Arabs in the knock-down-and-drag-out American way.

"Colonel Bahadu, 'worthy of consideration' could imply that His Excellency, Crown Prince Abdullah ibn-Abdul Aziz, has not yet made a decision," the Death Merchant said diplomatically. He turned and put his cup and saucer on the table next to which he was sitting.

Colonel Bahadu smiled and glanced down at Saturn, who was washing his face with his pink, handlike paws.

"Sahib Camellion, His Excellency, Crown Prince Abdullah ibn-Abdul Aziz, believes that your plan regarding Jordan can succeed. His Excellency, Crown Prince Abdullah ibn-Abdul Aziz, has instructed me to work closely with you in implementing the plan, which you have designated Operation Clover. His Excellency, Crown Prince Abdullah ibn-Abdul Aziz, has the assurance of certain officials within an agency of the United States government that you are an expert in such clandestine matters. In conclusion, I"—he motioned to the two other Arabian officers—"and Major Hajj Muhammad al-Staiyun and Captain Hajj Falih Bin Majid are placing the *Abu Jihad Falaj'i* at your disposal."

Colonel Bahadu was dressed in a white *throb,* a shapeless robe, and wearing the all green *kaffiyeh* that was the trademark of the Father Holy War legion. Other than the way he was dressed (and his features), any resemblance to his being an Arab national was ridiculous. Educated at Harvard, he sounded more American than Arabic. Even some of his gestures were subtly American—easily recognized by the Death Merchant and the other men, except the two Jesuits, all of whom had traveled widely and were at home in any number of cultures.

"How do we proceed, Sahib Camellion?" asked Major Hajj Muhammad al-Staiyun in cautious tones. A solidly built individual, on the downhill side of thirty-four, he had a square face, a long, straight nose, and was dressed in a pale blue *throb* and an emerald green[5] *kaffiyeh*.

"How many men will we need for the operation?" In contrast

---

[5] The color of the Saudian Arabian flag. On the flag is written, in Arabic script, "*There is no God but Allah and Mohammed is his prophet.*" Beneath the script is a white saber.

to Staiyun and Bahadu, Captain Hajj[6] Falih Bin Majid was tall for an Arab, almost an even six feet. Although on the lean side, he wasn't thin. His black hair was rather long, his eyes flecked with gold, his dark eyebrows, over intelligent black eyes, very thin.

"We'll need a hundred of your commandos," started the Death Merchant, "plus six troop-carrying and a half a dozen gunship choppers."

Kelly Dillard said quickly, "General Bahadu, our people managed to smuggle Mahmoud Khalil out of Jordan a week ago. He was taken to a U.S. aircraft carrier in the Mediterranean and from there flown to one of our subs cruising in the Indian Ocean. We can have that sand—we can have Khalil here within four to five days, six at the most, as soon as you obtain clearance from Ar-Riyad[7] to bring him into the country."

"Sahib Dillard, we already have that clearance," Major al-Staiyun said in a businesslike voice.

Smiling, as if enjoying a private joke, Colonel Bahadu looked at the Death Merchant. "Tell me, Camellion—are you sure that Khalil "—he chuckled—"the sand crab, knows the exact location of the scrolls." He answered his own question. "Of course, you and your people are. So it seems that whether or not he can do it—if his memory is still good—is the question."

"It's a risk," admitted Camellion. "Khalil does believe that if he doesn't lead us to the scrolls, he'll be executed. I'm sure he will not deliberately lie to us. He wouldn't have any reason to."

"Our people in Amman have assured us that Mahmoud Khalil does remember the location of the cave," Wesley Ritter said in an even voice.

Said the Death Merchant, looking steadily at Colonel Bahadu, "As to the time factor—I presume you can have the twelve choppers here and pick out the hundred commandos within two weeks?"

Opening the door of the gold cage, which he had taken from the stand and placed in his lap, Colonel Bahadu responded promptly. "Three days at maximum. The helicopters will be flown from the vicinity of Ar-Riyad. The best units of the *Abu Jihad Falaj'i* are already here, right at this base. We won't have

---

[6]Above the rank of noncom, all officers in SANG have made the journey to Mecca. All have the title of *Hajj*—another weakness of the Saudi defense system: putting religion ahead of common sense.

[7]Riyadh, the capital of Saudi Arabia.

a problem in choosing the hundred best men. Allah keeps careful books. So do we—the records of each man.''

Harlon Moore, the other Green Gables CIA man, thrust out his big jaw and looked questioningly at Colonel Bahadu. ''Colonel—correct me if I'm wrong. But you sound as if we could leave in three or four days, at least as soon as we fly in Mahmoud Khalil. Why, it will take a week, if not longer, for other units of SANG to get set to fake an attack on Jordan from the north, where the border of your nation is close to the borders of Jordan and Iraq.'' Moore's gaze swung to the Death Merchant. ''It was my understanding that the fake attack would be coordinated with our actual sweep into the Jabal Arqā.''

Camellion leaned back in his chair, crossed his long legs, and watched Saturn, who was crawling around on Colonel Bahadu's right shoulder, his little pink nose sniffing the air.

''I was going to say the same thing, colonel,'' Camellion said, the barest flicker of doubt crossing his lean face.

Bahadu turned his head, placed his chin on his right shoulder, and tried to get Saturn's attention. Ignoring him, the rat continued to furiously sniff the air.

''I'm afraid that part of Operation Clove has been dropped, Mr. Camellion,'' Bahadu said, still looking at the rat. ''His Excellency, Crown Prince Abdulah ibn-Abdul Aziz, has decided that the fake attack on Jordan is too dangerous.'' Very quickly, Bahadu turned his head, his eyes sweeping over the Death Merchant and the rest of the men, including the two Jesuit priests who, upon their arrival in Arabia, had been instantly ''blessed'' with a ''miracle.'' They had become CIA men and had been posing that way for nine days.

Continued Colonel Bahadu, ''It must be kept in mind that while we are willing to help you obtain the scrolls—and taking a great risk in doing so, I might add—we cannot and will not participate in any operation that might trigger a war between Iraq and Jordan.''

''Al Jumhouriya al 'Iraqia has already been greatly weakened in its war with Keshvaré Shahanshahiyé Irân,''[8] said Captain Falih Bin Majid firmly, using the Arabic names of Iraq and Iran. For al Jumhouriya al 'Iraqia to war with Al Mamlaka al Urduniya

[8]It should be noted that the Iranians, being Persian, are not Arabs as such. They are not Semitic. Arabic is spoken and the religion is Islam because the Arabs conquered and controlled Iran for hundreds of years.

al Hashemiya—the nation you *Nasranis*[9] refer to as Jordan—would weaken both nations. Such a tragedy would be an enormous blessing to the Israelis; and it is they who are the real enemy."

Pointed out Major al-Staiyun, "A conflict between Al Mamlaka al Urduniya al Hashemiyah and al Jumhouriya al 'Iraqia would give the Israelis the chance to invade al-Jumhouriya al-Lubnaniya— or Lebanon. The Israelis could even declare war against Jordan and Iraq."

"Or against Arabia," Colonel Bahadu said severely. "Begin is like Hitler, both clever and crazy. Think about it, gentlemen. As we view the overall situation, it's Prime Minister Begin of Israel who poses the biggest danger to peace in the Middle East."

"We dare not risk Al Mamlaka al Urduniya al Hashemiyah being weakened by war, especially a bloodbath with another Arab nation," Major al-Staiyun said politely but firmly. "There can be no solution to the Palestinian problem without King Hussein assuming a major role. We can assure you Americans that Hussein is not going to change his mind about the Camp David Accords. He will never approve of any so-called peace plan that favors the Israeli dogs, whose only real talents are stealing the lands of their neighbors and manipulating the world's press."

"Colonel, before too long, Jordan might just be in a war anyhow—with Iran!" said Wesley Ritter, who was wiping his dark glasses. "For months, King Hussein has been threatening to send a 2,500-man volunteer 'Yarmuk force'[10] to fight on the side of Iraq in the Persian Gulf war with Iran. He's taking an enormous risk. If he does lead such a force—and he's told the foreign press more than once that he would—Iran could easily bomb Amman and Syria could start planting bombs around Amman, as it has in the past. That could easily degenerate into full-scale war."

"War is war and dead is dead, no matter who starts the killing process," Harlon Moore said in his most persuasive voice. "Our counterfeit attack against Jordan would simply involve a lot of firing at the Jordie camel patrols in the northeast quadrant. Your men would naturally miss. None of the Jordanian soldiers would be hurt. To place the blame on Iraq, several of our scout cars would fly the Iraqi flag. By the time an enraged Amman con-

[9]Christians.
[10]After an Arab battle against the Crusaders.

tacted Baghdad and the Iraqi government denied the charge and pointed a finger at you Saudis, we——''

"And who in his right mind would believe the Saudis would deliberately attack another nation?" offered Terry Macke in a loud voice. "Why, you Saudis are known for your evenhandedness with your Arab neighbors!"

"By the time the—let's call it a misunderstanding—was straightened out, we would have been in and out of the Arqā Mountains," finished Harlon Moore.

The expressions on the faces of Captain Falih Bin Majid and Major Muhammad al-Staiyun didn't change. If anything, the harshness deepened, becoming more fixed.

Colonel Bahadu gave Moore a quick, amused smile and lifted Saturn from his right shoulder and placed the rodent on his left shoulder. "Ah, Sahib Moore, you seem to have all the answers."

Wesley Ritter jumped into the act of convincing with both feet.

"The only thing the Saudi government would have to do would be to refute the Iraqi charge that it was the Arabians who fired on the camel patrols," he said enthusiastically. "The real truth will never be known."

"That is precisely why we Saudis have no intention of lending our people and equipment to such a venture," Colonel Bahadu said rigorously. He was no longer smiling. "Why should we even have to deny any charge to our Arab neighbors? We shouldn't. We're not going to. You Americans expect too much and demand more than we are prepared to pay. Honor cannot be bought, Mr. Ritter."

Camellion glanced sympathetically at Ritter. He felt sorry for Moore and Macke too. He knew exactly what all three were trying to accomplish and knew they would fail.

The Saudis say what they mean and they mean what they say. *God could change their minds, but Moore and Macke and Ritter aren't even in the "angel" class. Neither am I. . . .*

The Death Merchant felt particularly sorry for Terry Macke, who had held the rank of Lieutenant Colonel in the Green Berets. The decision of the Arabian brass not to fake an attack from Iraq had to be particularly discouraging for Macke, who viewed the world from the standpoint of a field commander.

The tall, beefy Macke, with his short hair and short beard, had been among the impressive military talent of U.S. Army veterans the Vinnell Corporation had imported to Arabia. In 1981, he had been placed in charge of the thirty-one advisory teams, each of which resembled a Special Forces team, with each American specializing in a particular military skill. The previous commander had returned to the United States to train mercs who would work for the CIA.

Camellion smiled to himself. Macke was too thick-skinned and too practical to be either embarrassed or annoyed by Colonel Bahadu's admonitory tone. Moore and Ritter were equally tough. They knew the world for what it really was—an ulcer in the stomach of the Creator—a severe headache in the minds of all gods . . .

Camellion admitted to himself that he had to give credit to Fathers Bernard Norton and Victorio Gatdula. All these days they had behaved admirably and were not ill at ease around the CIA men (whom the two Jesuits considered murderers) and the Saudi commandos, who were fierce Moslems.

Even when Kelly Dillard was fighting the controls of the Super Frelon and the big helicopter was going down at an angle, only eight miles inside the Saudi border, the two Jesuits had remained as calm as a pane of glass.

Later, Father Norton had remarked to Camellion, "One should always be prepared to die and stand before God. After all, Life is but a short journey to Death."

How well I know it! Reluctantly, the Death Merchant found himself admiring the two Jesuits for their principles, even if he did disagree with many of their doctrines and teachings.

Everyone thinks of changing the world, but no one thinks of changing himself! Those two did! They first became priests to change themselves! Quiet fanatics! Like many of the old Nazis and a lot of today's commies!

Harlon Moore was not a man who gave up easily. He folded his arms and said to Colonel Bahadu, "Well, colonel, it's like Ritter said. There might be a war anyway, if King Hussein leads a small force against Iran. As for the fake attack we would undertake, I hardly think Hussein would declare war against Arabia or Iraq over a 'misunderstanding' over the border, a mere shooting."

Colonel Bahadu, returning Saturn to his cage, responded in good old Americanese, "Look, buster! You're not selling vacuum cleaners from door to door. You had better learn to take no for a definite answer, or you'll start reminding me of a joe I once met in the States. He didn't have the sense God gives ducks. He answered every question I asked him."

Bahadu might as well have been trying to insult a Reformed Druid who had graduated from Adolf Hitler High School! Moore,

114

who secretly considered Arabs inferior, didn't feel the least bit humiliated.

He raised his head as though sniffing for gas in the air. "I only hope that King Hussein doesn't mean what he's been saying . . ."

The three commando officers smiled, Captain Falih Bin Majid saying with frank amusement, "There is a vast difference between what King Hussein says to Westerners and what he says to other Arabs. To us, he is not merely making wind like a camel."

"In short, boys"—Colonel Bahadu was bursting with amiability—"King Hussein is feeding the West a lot of bull, merely building up his image—and no doubt his own ego—with the Western press. That little twerp isn't about to lead any force into Iran. He's much too clever, much too cautious."

Seeing how Kelly Dillard's jaw muscles were working and afraid that the blunt-speaking agent would open his big mouth and complicate the situation even more, the Death Merchant changed the subject.

"Colonel, I'm sure you realize that we'll run more than the risk of having the Jordanians in our laps, depending on our luck and how efficient their listening posts are. Department 4 only knows there is something of value out there. The Mossad believes that the scrolls are hidden in the Hārun Mountains. Sooner or later the Israelis will use some logic and consider the Arqā Mountains as a possibility."

"The *Abu Jihad Falaj'i* is more than anxious to prove itself against the Israelis. We will be wearing Jordanian uniforms of the Ninth Paratroopers, and we will not carry anything that can identify us as Saudis," Major Muhammad al-Staiyun coolly. "The helicopters—what is the term? Yes, they will be sanitized."

Wesley Ritter shifted his weight in his chair and loudly cleared his throat for attention.

"This is one for the books!" he said in disgust. "We're going into Jordan, dressed in Jordanian uniforms, and maybe fight Israelis as well as the Jordies!" His bitter gaze knifed into Colonel Bahadu. "After we tangle with the Jew-boys—if we do—where's the guarantee that the Israelis won't declare war on Jordan. A war between Jordan and Iraq would be a stalemate. The Israelis would slaughter them."

Camellion slapped Ritter with a fierce look—clearly irritated with Green Gables' persistence. "Quit talking like a fool!" he said hotly. "You know better! The last thing the Israelis want would be the world to know they invaded Jordanian soil. Besides, if we run into any 'King David' jokers, I don't intend for a single one to get back to the 'Promised Land!' You dig, Jack?''

Ritter "dug," and so did the three Saudis—smiling in approval.

Pleased with the Death Merchant's words, Colonel Bahadu studied Camellion for a moment. "What does your HUMINT[11] intelligence reveal of Mossad plans? We cannot hold back from each other, Camellion.''

Camellion smiled a crooked smile. *HUMINT! Not bad for a nonintelligence agent. Bahadu is a clever man. Uh huh—as cunning as a man who complains to his wife that his secretary doesn't understand him!*

The Death Merchant had no intention of telling Bahadu the secret that Roy Anderson, the chief of the Amman station, had divulged: that the Company had an informer in Sheruth Modiin, Israeli Military Intelligence. It might not even matter that the Company had a man in place. Only on rare occasions did the Sheruth Modiin work hand-in-glove with the Mossad, and never with Wrath of God personnel. It was even possible that the Sheruth Modiin wasn't even aware that the Judas Scrolls existed.

There had been a good deal of discussion among Camellion and the CIA experts on the subject, because of the Israeli armored column that had attacked the solar-power station. The attack unit had been a part of the Israeli army; therefore, either the Sheruth Modiin knew about the attack—and the scrolls—and had given its permission, or else the Mossad had used a tiny particle of the Israeli army without the knowledge of Israeli Military Intelligence. A third possibility was that (A) the Mossad had contacted the Sheruth Modiin immediately upon hearing the fantastic tale from Ghassan Nazzal or (B) had informed the Sheruth later. Assumptions! Either could be correct.

"Our HUMINT intelligence tells us nothing about Mossad plans—for that matter, about the plans of the Sheruth Modiin either," Camellion answered Colonel Bahadu's question. "But"— he emphasized the *but*—"our IMINT intelligence, both satellites and Spytech planes, reveal that during the past six weeks the Israelis have been operating a longitudinal high-wave-density sensor station at Yotvata at the extreme end of southern Israel. The second we cross into Jordan, the Israelis will know it; and they'll know we're choppers!''

[11]Intelligence gathered by human beings, by agents, informers etc., as against IMINT intelligence—photographs by spy planes and satellites.

116

"I offered the solution to the problem at Yotvata days ago," chimed in Kelly Dillard, his voice low and strained. "Hell, that station is only sixty klicks from the Saudi border. We could blow that tracking station all over the sands—and Terry agrees with me!"

"Two jet fighters could do the job easily," spoke up Macke with new enthusiasm. "There are nine dishes at the station. Knock out only one dish, and the whole station is rendered inoperable. One dish is mounted on a hundred-foot tower. A rocket could get that one easily."

The three Saudis nodded thoughtfully.

"We've known about the station at Yotvata for the past month," commented Captain Hajj Falih Bin Majid, about whom there was a honed awareness. "It can monitor all our northern air traffic—thanks to the technology the Israelis have received from the United States."

Robert Follmer's eyes flashed angrily. "This time you're wrong!" He leaned forward and looked daggers at Captain Majid. "It was West German technology that enabled the Israelis to erect the station at Yotvata."

Captain Majid made an indifferent gesture with his shoulders. "Wrong this time but correct a dozen times before," he said. "You Americans are also giving military aid to Jordan."

"And to Saudi Arabia," responded Follmer evenly. "Certainly Jordan is not your enemy. Your causes walk hand in hand."

"That is also true," agreed Falih Bin Majid. "True and mystifying. It seems that American policy is to help enemies as well as friends."

Harlon Moore beat Follmer to the counterattack. "Whose enemies? The enemies of the United States are not necessarily the enemies of Saudi Arabia and vice versa. Our main objective is to preserve peace in the Middle East."

"Gentlemen, this is not a political discussion!" The Death Merchant cut in sharply. "I suggest we stick to the subject and stop the political philosophizing.

"Mr. Camellion is correct," seconded Colonel Bahadu, frowning at Follmer and Moore. Then he turned in his chair and let Captain Majid have a warning look, after which he turned and very seriously inspected Camellion.

"How close can the station at Yotvata monitor us? By that I mean, How close can they pinpoint our position after we put down in the Arqā Mountains?"

Camellion's words were bad news. "Within a one-mile radius. On the assumption that the Mossad—and the Sheruth Modiin—do suspect the scrolls are in the Jabal Arqā and intend to follow us there, they could easily find us with infrared night-sight devices and other equipment, such as heat sensors."

"He's saying that even if we do knock out the monitor station," said Robert Follmer, "the Israelis can still find us, if they suspect we're in the Arqā Mountains."

Inquired Major al-Staiyun, "Is it possible to somehow jam the station, or to sneak in low, using the method that an airplane would use to foil radar?"

"No, not in this case," Camellion said flatly.

"And we can't get in and out fast enough to avoid the Israelis," added Terry Macke gloomily, "if Camellion is right—if the Israelis are expecting us to go to the Arqā Mountains."

"Well, Camellion, what is your solution to the problem?" Colonel Bahadu gave the Death Merchant a long, earnest look. "The problem must be faced and resolved. Dillard could be correct about bombing the station. Have you considered that option?"

Camellion gave a low laugh. "No one has given me a chance to say that Dillard and Macke were wrong. They're halfway right. We could easily destroy the station, but it wouldn't stop the Israelis from locating us if they guessed we were headed for the Arqā Mountains. You don't exactly hide twelve helicopters under a ledge."

A look of puzzlement crossed the face of Colonel Auda bin Bahadu, who, for a Saudi, had very light skin. His intense eyes bored into Camellion.

"Suppose the tracking station was destroyed before we took off from our land, or say ten minutes before we crossed the border and entered Jordan?"

"Well, if the station is destroyed before we take off, then it's obvious the Israelis can't track us," Camellion explained in a brisk manner. "We still won't be out of the woods. Destroying the station could be the tip-off to the Israelis that we're about to pick the turnip greens, in which—"

"I beg your pardon! 'Pick the turnip greens'?" Hajj Muhammad al-Staiyun was in need of enlightenment.

"A warning to the Israelis that we are moving into Jordan," explained the Death Merchant, "on the condition that they suspect that's what we're going to do. In that case, Israeli war planes would take off and find us in the Arqā Mountains." Anticipating Colonel Bahadu's next question, Camellion gave him the answer in advance. "You're wondering about the efficiency of the station's tracking us once we're in the air. How fast can we be picked up. The answer is, within a radius of sixty miles—that's ninety-six kilometers—of the Arqā Mountains.''

A calculating flame began burning in Colonel Bahadu's eyes.

"It would seem that the real question is whether the Israelis could find us faster after we destroyed the tracking station, or get to us slower if we let them discover us after we are airborne!"

"Take your choice." Camellion made a motion with his left hand. "It's as broad as it's long. For that reason, I don't believe we should risk the lives of the two Saudi pilots who would have to do the job. The defense at the tracking station will almost surely include ground-to-air missiles.''

Colonel Bahadu motioned to the soldier whose job it was to carry Saturn. The commando stepped forward, picked up the gold cage, then resumed his position, standing to one side, as straight and expressionless as a statue. Colonel Bahadu and the two other officers stood up. The Death Merchant and the rest of the men got to their feet.

"We'll fly to Ar-Riyad at once," Bahadu said to Camellion, "and give our report to Crown Prince Aziz. We will return Thursday, two days from now, and bring the helicopters and their crews with us. In the meantime, you can radio specifics, in supplies and weapons. We will have more than enough time, since it will take almost a week for your people to fly Mahmoud Khalil to this base.''

"He'll be on his way within several days," the Death Merchant said. "You'll arrange for an escort once his plane reaches the Arabian coast?''

"There will be no problem," Bahadu said "One more thing. I presume we will fly into Jordan at night?''

"We can't," Camellion replied unctuously. "Khalil will be nervous without our putting a damper of darkness on his memory. I estimate we'll be landing at about 1400 hours.''

Colonel Hajj Auda bin Bahadu smiled faintly at the expressionless Death Merchant. "In bright sunlight!" He sighed deeply. "I am only an average man, but I work at it harder than the average man. I think all of us will have to work doubly hard on this operation.''

Camellion said simply, "I'm sorry I couldn't give you a better answer. Look at it this way: answers that sound good aren't necessarily good, sound answers.''

"May Allah help us!" Captain Falih Bin Majid shook his head.

119

"Uh huh. Our *Nasrani* god had better throw in a lot of help too," Camellion said with a straight face.

Harlon Moore, whose only god was the Central Intelligence Agency, snickered, "Hopefully, the Israeli Jehovah will be taking a long nap, or be away on some cosmic vacation."

They stood in front of the tent watching the Robertson Executive Jet lift smoothly off from the runway and start its climb into the sky thick with clouds. The plane turned, starting on a southeast heading that would take it to Riyadh.

Philosophized Kelly Dillard, "I hope they can fight better than they talk." He continued to watch the jet grow small in the distance.

"I'll buy that," conceded Wesley Ritter, taking off his silver-mirrored sunglasses. "Personally, I'd rather have Mad Mike Quinlan and his maniacs.[12] backing me up than these Saudi jokers who are still living in the dark ages of religion."

"It's all relative," Camellion said with a tiny laugh. "The Arabs consider Christianity a disgrace—and the Hindus hate the Moslems. Half the wars in recorded history have been started over the 'one true god.'"

Ritter and Dillard gave a final look at the airplane, now a dot in the cloudy distance, after which they started back with the rest of the group, to the rear of which were Camellion and Father Bernard Norton.

After several steps, Father Norton paused, reached out with his right hand, and touched the Death Merchant on the shoulder.

"Camellion, listen to me," he began in a low, urgent voice. "All the killing that has been done—and there will be many many more deaths in the days to come."

The Death Merchant stopped and turned to Father Norton. Whom does he think he's fooling? "You're whistlin' Dixie the hard way, Norton. I could cancel Operation Clover, but I'm not going to. I have a job to do."

"Surely the security of the United States does not rest on our finding the Judas Scrolls?" There was a heavy pleading quality in Father Norton's voice, a desperateness in his eyes. "Or—are you doing this solely for money? I can't believe that of you!"

"You had better!" Camellion was brutally blunt. "One hundred thousand American dollars can give me a lot of security.

---

[12]See Death Merchant #49, *The Night of the Peacock*, and #51, *The Inca File*.

Don't con me, laddie! What's the real reason why you don't want the scrolls found?''

"There are some things the world is better off not knowing!"

"What makes you think that the world will ever know—unless the scrolls fall into the hands of the Israelis?"

The Death Merchant started back to the tent. Father Norton followed.

CHAPTER NINE

Operation Clover was both airborne and under way, a twelve-craft armada that filled the sky with a roaring similar to a score of express trains all running on the same track. Flying at only 3,000 feet, the six Boeing-Vertol 113 troop carriers bored north-west in a "wild geese" formation, or wedge.

The command chopper was at the point. Other than the regulars of the Saudi commando, the big bird contained Colonel Auda bin Bahadu, the Death Merchant and the Company men, Terry Macke, and the two Jesuit priests. Like the others, Father Norton and Father Gatdula were dressed in brown poplin camo fatigues (Angolan pattern) and tropical combat boots. They also wore bulletproof vests of the executive type; and while they had firmly refused to carry weapons, Camellion had forced them to accept 9mm Beretta pistols and SIG M542 assault rifles—the same kinds of weapons that, along with Colt CAR-15 subma-chine guns, were carried by the Father Holy War commandos.

The Death Merchant had pointed out to the priests that they didn't have a choice, not unless they wanted the Arabians to become suspicious.

"You either carry the weapons, or the Vatican will get a report about you two that will keep you in the doghouse for years," Camellion had said coldly.

"We won't use them!" Father Gatdula had warned Camellion savagely. "We did not come to Jordan to kill fellow human beings."

Camellion had shrugged. "Fight or die—if it comes to that. I couldn't care less. After all, you're not along to wet the rocks with holy water."

Major Muhammad al-Staiyun and Captain Falih Bin Majid were in the carrier choppers directly behind, and to each side of the command ship. With Captain Majid and Major al-Staiyun—other than rank and file commandos—were six noncoms who held the rank equivalent to sergeant major in the British Army. All six were also mullahs, or Islamic priests, whom the Bedoui commandos feared and respected. It was these mullah/noncoms who maintained discipline, and had prompted the cynical Kelly Dillard to remark that "It's a screwball outfit that has to depend on 'priests' to maintain discipline."

"Who gives a damn about discipline," Harlon Moore had remarked, "provided they have the training, don't panic, and can fight."

During the previous six days, everything had gone smoothly, had been on schedule. However, Camellion, because he had not trusted the Saudi pilots, had made one change: he had arranged for Americans from the Vinnell Corporation's personnel to fly nine of the choppers. There hadn't been enough American pilots to go around; consequently, three pilots were Saudis. One of them flew a Boeing-Vertol troop carrier, the other two two of the Sikorsky (SH-3) Sea King gunships.

Only five of the Boeing-Vertols carried troops; the sixth was crammed with Tiger surface-to-air-missiles and their launchers, Viper and Stinger missiles that could be used against armor and ground personnel, and U.S. M-67 90mm recoilless rifles.

Armed with port and starboard .30 caliber T66 heavy machine guns, each Boeing-Vertol 113 was camouflaged, without any markings, and was so sanitized that even the tiny nameplates on the Rolls-Royce Gnome turboshaft engines had been removed.

Three of the Sikorsky gunships flew 500 feet above the "wild geese" formation, the other three SH-3s 400 feet below. All six gunships were camouflaged and sanitized. All six were pure poison. On the sides of each SH-3 were pods containing XM31 20mm cannons. Farther out, both to port and starboard, was another pod, this "hog" filled with forty-eight 2.75-inch HE rockets, which could be fired in any combination or all at once. The port and starboard openings were filled with M-134 miniguns on Sagami mounts. On the nose of each gunship was an M-5 40mm grenade launcher; behind the launcher, farther down on the bottom hull, was a GAU-8 Avenger seven-barreled electric 30-mm cannon.

Terry Macke had very accurately described each gunship, saying that each Sikorsky Sea King was nothing but ". . . a mess of weapons built around an airframe and two General Electric turboshafts."

Five air miles from crossing the Saudi border, the pilots of the twelve choppers turned on their radar and, with the port and the starboard gunners already in position, lost altitude, the three SH-3 gunships below the troop-carrying Boeing-Vertols going down to a mere 200 feet. Still in a perfect V-formation, the Boeing-Vertols dropped until they were only 400 feet above the floor of the desert, while the three SH-3 gunships, still above the troop-carrying choppers, lowered to 600 feet—and Allah help any Jordanian patrol spotted by the three lower SH-3s. However, the tactic was not employed to look for Jordanians, but to fool Jordanian radar and to make the job of the Israeli technicians at the Yotvata tracking station more difficult.

Above, the clouds had parted in places, permitting the sun to flow through. In other places there was only clear, cobalt sky, empty except for high-flung wisps of cirrus. Below, the desert rushed by, a fast-moving, variegated picture of various browns, even the long dunes vanishing to the rear with such rapidity that one didn't have time to see fully their general outlines—a brief blur and the dunes were gone.

The mosaic of color was forever changing. At times the sands were brick red; other times, honey colored, or even coppery. There were wide patches of ash white gypsum, and plains that were tawny. Twice there were brief glimpses of Bedu camel caravans. First, a thin, crooked line in the distance; then all too quickly the choppers were upon the caravan. A single second of seeing tiny men and tiny camels, the men looking upward in awe and confusion. A micromoment. That was all. By then, men and animals had vanished far to the rear of the helicopter fleet, and there were new sights in front of the choppers.

All the men were uneasy, all except the Death Merchant, who didn't give a damn. Who knew that what had to be would be, who realized that he had done this before and would do it again—the same motions, but new kills, like a motion picture that was run over and over, but spliced each time, with tiny pieces of film added, before the reels were started in motion. Before, right now—*And I'll do it again!*—not necessarily in a helicopter, nor even in this present century. Just the same, he had been on this desert, in another time, in another era, in another life—on another merry-go-round of Death.

The most terrified of all was Mahmoud Khalil, who, with his ill-proportioned features and weak chin, looked ridiculously out of place in Jordanian army fatigues, Jordanian army boots, and a Jordanian riot helmet. The fatigues were a size too big. They had to be, to accommodate the American-made M-14 armored vest/shield made of DuPont Kevlar.

Khalil was a very important man! He was the goose that knew where the Great Golden Egg was hidden. Only he could take them to the right cave.

Roy Anderson and his CIA staff at the Amman station had done their work well. With Mahmoud Khalil, Anderson and his people had pored over all the maps available of the Jabal Arqā, the maps ranging from 1:80,000 scale to the 1:1,200,000 scale.

It was Marie Dine, the Station's girl Friday, who had gotten an idea to build a topographical map of the Arqā Mountains. It was this type of map, which allowed Khalil to see the mountains in three dimensions, that jarred free his memory. The difficulty had been the lines, the swirls, and squiggles on ordinary maps. Another difficulty was that he had hidden the scrolls while on the ground. Looking at the mountains as they would appear from the air was an entirely new perspective, which confused him. He had, however, upon seeing the topographical map that filled half a room, recalled the Das'ayid'a Shaitan, the Tongue of the Devil, a jagged 500-foot pinnacle on the southwest edge of the Jabal Arqā.

From that moment on, once he had recalled the Tongue of the Devil, the process of memory had become a matter of step-by-step recall. Southeast of the Tongue was a long incline of scree and large rocks that, over hundreds of years, had tumbled from above. A few hundred feet up the slope was a twisting, tortuous trail that rose and dipped and moved to the north, then to the southeast. All along the route were hundreds of caves, some so small that one had to get on his hands and knees to enter. Other caves were large enough to drive a tank through. To investigate each cave throughly and completely (suppose the scrolls had been buried or hidden under "tumbled" rock?) would have taken a year.

Had Khalil marked the entrance of the cave, or had he fixed landmarks in his mind? Once the river of memory had begun to flow, the words poured excitely from his mouth—a mixture of English and Arabic.

The cave had a square-looking entrance, and there was a single Kermes oak growing to the left of the cave mouth.

"I remember!" Khalil had cried, jumping to his feet. "The cave *wa'il'i uq-ari'll midaqui oshkeh-jaz'match ailoq'il'l unni'afi!*"

The cave was under a long granite edge that poked outward like a giant, flattened penis!

"*Madham hia'qll-rek!*" Khalil was positive, absolutely certain. "*Rahmat Ullahi so'wat i'll-tag'll!*" Allah's mercy had been bountiful.

The fleet of helicopters went down another thirty meters as they streaked in a northwest direction over the Jordanian plains and deserts, at times their tricycle landing gear seemingly about to touch the summits of the low hills.

The Sikorsky gunships below the B-V troop carriers did not bother with the camel caravans they saw. It was a far different matter when they spotted a motorized column of Jordanian armor sixteen klicks east of Bi'anann—a Hubler armored car, a DCB scout car, a command APC with raised superstructure, a TOW missile carrier, and three armored infantry carriers.

The seven enemy vehicles didn't have time to break the line and scatter—not that it would have done them any good. It would only have taken longer to destroy them. Two of the Sikorsky gunships revved down and opened fire, their GAU-8 Avenger cannons roaring.

The linkless ammo belts of the Avender cannons were loaded "Dutch" style, every other shell being an API, an armor piercing incendiary. The other shells were HEIs, high explosive incendiaries. The Jordanian vehicles literally exploded from the impact of the 30mm shells. It took less than a minute to destroy the vehicles, since the pods could rotate the cannons in any direction but up.

The dozen eggbeaters moved northwest, leaving behind them wrecked vehicles that burned and gave off oily black smoke— hot metal that had become the mausoleums of 134 corpses. Destroying the Jordanian army column had been a vital must. Even so, the commander might still have gotten off a warning radio message. A risk! A cross that the men of Operation Clover would have to bear.

Just so the cross didn't become a bloody crucifixion in the Jabal Arqā!

Since an exact course had been plotted, the pilots had a definite destination and would land immediately once they reached Section 16 of the Arqā Mountains. All the maps revealed that southwest of the Tongue of the Devil was a plain not quite a mile wide and slightly over three-fourths of a mile long—more than ample room for the helicopters. North of the plain were enormous boulders, so colossal they could be considered small hills. South of the open area, which was fairly level, although dotted with rocks, were the foothills of mountains whose slopes were partially covered with Aleppo oak and pine, plus tangled scrub. West of the small plain, where the helicopters would put down, were low, rocky hills, the highest of which was not quite a hundred feet. Beyond these hills, to the west, was a mammoth plain of level rock. Some of the plain was covered with sand, or with pebbly rocks the size of marbles. Over all of it was blown *ar'ill-i'-uk'l*, the Jordanian version of tumbleweed.

As mountains go, the Jabal Arqā was not a high range. Jabel Al-Yniha, the highest mountain, was a mere 2,408 feet. But an extra foot could cause a crash. Nonetheless, the air fleet did not go to an altitude beyond the 2,408-foot mark. The choppers didn't have to. The hills of Section 16 were 400 feet at the highest point. Accordingly, the twelve choppers did climb sky, so that when they leveled off, the three lower SH-3 gunships were at an altitude of 500 feet—this rise only ten minutes before the choppers reached the invisible line that was the southeast edge of Section 16.

The minutes raced by and all twelve of the birds were soon over the Jabal Arqā. In actuality, they were flying over the lower foothills of the actual mountains that were, in spite of their lack of height, jagged and forbidding, as though they were ill-omened tombstones in a disguised necropolis of hate.

Farther in, to the northeast, where the hills actually became mountains and rose to almost 2,000 feet, there would be patches of snow this time of year. During the summer months these peaks would sizzle in the heat, although the desert wind would blow furiously and the area would be cooler than on the plains.

Now, patches of various browns and grays and blacks—and some green—flashed underneath the helicopters. The men looking out the windows and the gunners to port and starboard could see gullies and small, steep valleys, rock overhangs and precipices. If the men had been on the ground, they would have seen that many of the passes and defiles were often so narrow that overshadowing rock blocked out all but a thin strip of sky. On the slopes of the foothills, and even higher, were pine, juniper, some hollyhock, wild olives, and walnuts. Up to the thousand-foot level—miles farther in—one could also find birch and dwarf oak.

The pilot of the command Boeing-Vertol announced through the intercom, "The Tongue of the Devil is in sight. Four miles dead ahead."

Colonel Auda bin Bahadu yelled at the Death Merchant to make himself heard. "If Allah is willing, we might get in, find the scrolls, and get out again without any trouble from either the Jordanians or the Israelis."

"Don't count on it, colonel," Camellion said—*I have yet to see His Majesty, the Cosmic Lord of Death, pass up a banquet.*

It was not necessary, but he automatically checked his

127

weapons—two .44 "Alaskan" Auto Mags in belt holsters and two M81 BP MatchMaster[1] autoloaders in Bianchi Model X-15 shoulder holsters. In his lap was a 9mm Interdynamic KG-9 semiautomatic machine pistol.[2]

Mahmoud Khaiil had not lied, and there had always been the possibility that he had, in spite of Roy Anderson throwing the entire Good Book of Threats at him. Here was the proof that Khalil had told the truth, at least about the Tongue of the Devil. There it was, the tall, thick finger of granite rock, its sides filled with the marks of erosion, the lower portion leaning slightly to the west, the upper portion to the north, the odd-angled spire appearing as if it were poised and waiting, trying to make up its mind which way to topple.

Five hundred feet north of the Tongue were the enormous house-sized boulders, the bare granite as shiny as a saint's halo and as smooth and bare as a baby's bottom.

The low hills were where they should be, to the left of the plain that stretched out in a curve to the northwest, their sides and uneven summits cloaked with sage grass, thistles, hollyhock, scattered dwarf oaks, wild rhubarb, and hogweed.

The Boeing-Vertols and the Sikorskys started to go down, the three lower gunships going in first, toward the north end of the flat section of land.

The fighters of Operation Clover had arrived.

The Death Merchant looked over the hills and the plain as the command Boeing-Vertol started down. The scenery was not pleasant to his eye.

Estheticaliy corrupting, environmentally degrading, and a definite danger to one's mental and physical health. . . .

[1]This MatchMaster is built by Safari Arms for shooters wanting a six-inch barrel for a long sight radius and extra weight. However, the weapon has the same fast cycle time of the standard five-inch slide.

[2]Manufactured in Sweden, the KG-9 incorporates features of the Schmeisser, the U.S. M-3 Greasegun, and the Carl-Gustav SMG. The weapon weighs sixty-seven ounces when fully loaded with thirty-two rounds. Length: just over one foot, including the five-inch barrel.

CHAPTER TEN

Life is full of little surprises. A trite saying, burdened with age. But very true. Even Robert Follmer, who placed Arabs on the third rung of the fifty-rung ladder of racial "purity," had to admit that the Saudis of the Father Holy War commando were very fast and efficient in leaving the Boeing-Vertol choppers that had set down a few hundred feet southwest of the first three SH-3 gunships that had landed. Two other gunships landed a hundred feet south of the troop carriers while the third moved in a wide half-mile circle, scouting the area.

During the previous three days, the commandos had practiced scores of times at the base in Saudi Arabia, and now that practice paid off. Each man knew exactly what to do and went about doing it.

Carrying listening equipment in three large suitcaselike boxes, seven commandos hurried up the east side of one of the hills to the west. Reaching the top, they worked very quickly. They opened the cases and began setting up the parabolic microphone, which had a thirty-seven-inch dish that would revolve slowly and cover all points of the compass. Powered by twenty cadmium batteries, the parabolic microphone had virtually a flat response from 250Hz to 72,000Hz. The output impedance of the electronic was at 400 to 760 ohms. Effective range fourteen miles.

Other commandos set up six Browning .50 caliber HMBs on Tadlum antiaircraft mounts, placing the machine guns at strategic locations, but not around the three rocket launchers of the Bronco Weapons System. The BWS launchers had been set up not far from the bottom of one of the hills to the west, each launcher containing ten Bronco surface-to-air missiles and ten Rattler surface-to-surface missiles.

A map in his hand, the Death Merchant, the other Westerners around him, searched the area for familiar landmarks, signs that by now were commonplace to him and the other men—at least on the maps. The Tongue of the Devil was where it should be, looking even more monstrous and frightening than it had from the air. Viewed from ground level, the giant pillar of twisted rock stood like some grim sentinel. The men sensed that the Tongue was their bitter enemy. The Jabal Arqā was their enemy. They were intruders. The mountains hated them for the invasion of privacy and wanted them out.

"We don't have any problems," Harlon Moore said confidently. "All the landmarks check out." A long-faced, quick-moving man, Moore was to Camellion's left, his hands resting on the butts of the two 9mm Sile-Benelli B76 DA auto-pistols in open leather holsters buckled around the waist of his fatigues, recognizable as being Jordanian because only Jordan used fatigues whose camouflage was identical to the Angolan pattern.

"That's the trouble," remarked the Death Merchant, folding the map. "All of this has been too easy. He turned and looked at Mahmoud Khalil, who was more nervous than a black widow husband on his honeymoon and who was being "guarded" by Kelly Dillard and Terry Macke. Both men had only contempt for the double-dealing Arab. As "racial authority" Follmer had put it, *Khalil is a self-made man, but the job is only 1 percent completed.*

"Very well, me bucko," Camellion joked. "I trust you feel right at home in these dreary mountains? What do you remember of that night? I realize it was dark, but I checked back and there was a full, bright moon when you and Ghassan Nazzal drove in."

Khalil's fox face underwent a series of small contortions before he said nervously, "I remember well. We drove in from the north."

He turned and pointed toward the Tongue of the Devil. "To the left, sahibs. There is an opening, a tiny pass, between some of the hills, not too distant from the boulder hills. We came through that pass and moved south to"—he turned and looked south, then studied the long slope of scree and tumbled rocks to the east—"there. Yes, sahibs. About there." He pointed again, indicating an area several hundred feet south of the troop-carrying Boeing-Vertols. "As I have said so many times during these past long weeks, I did not know about the trail above the slope. As I have repeated over and over to Sahib Anderson, it was Nazzal who knew about the trail and the cave. In the past he had used the cave when he was a smuggler, to store cakes of hashish and sometimes uncut diamonds and other valuable merchandise."

The Death Merchant and the others glanced toward Colonel Auda bin Bahadu, who was coming toward them. The Father

130

Holy War commando chief was accompanied by Sergeant Major Amin Rameh, who was also one of the mullahs.

"Everything is in order; the men are in position," Bahadu said, upon reaching the group. His smile, meant to be ingratiating and designed to inspire a relaxing confidence, was a failure. And unnecessary! The Death Merchant, the CIA men, and Terry Macke had confidence to spare. Faith in ability went with the job. Father Gatdula and Father Norton had faith in God. It went with their chosen profession.

"Then the men with the Viper and the Stinger missiles and the recoilless rifles are spread out up yonder on the hills?" asked Camellion. "I want a clear view of the large plain and of the two passes, the one to the north and the one to the south. But it's the large plain west of the hills that's important. The Jordanians or the Israelis could put choppers down there."

"We don't have a priority on logic, Camellion," cut in Wesley Ritter, stroking his mustache. "The Jordies and the Israelis also have maps of these mountains. More likely than not, they'd try to sit down here."

"I'm counting on it," Camellion drawled, a sly smile crossing his mouth. "If they tried to put down here, we'd knock 'em out of the sky with the Broncos and the Rattlers. The boys with the Stingers could even join in, since the Stingers are surface-to-air missiles."

"It's all academic at this point." Kelly Dillard rubbed a big hand across his mouth. "The thing to do now is to have this worthy fellow"—he jerked a thumb toward a chalk-faced Mahmoud Khalil—"lead us to the scrolls. We can then get the hell out of here. We've been lucky so far, but sooner or later Murphy's Law[1] will take over."

"Kelly's right, of course," Terry Macke said gravely, his eyes boring into the Death Merchant. "The objective is the scrolls."

"The Scrolls are only half the objective." Camellions voice was low, steady, and patient. "The other half is to get ourselves and the scrolls back to Saudi Arabia. We can't walk. And we're more important than any damned scrolls. That means our transportation is the first order of the day. As they would say in Hippy Dippy Holler, 'It jist ain't raht that we'uns shud git plumb ful of holes by ignorin' our own safety.' "

Harlon Moore, dropping his cigarette on the ground, moved closer to the Death Merchant. "Being captured in these Jordie

[1]Namely, "If anything can go wrong, it will."

fatigues wouldn't exactly endear us to the Jordanians—and the Israelis wouldn't be taking prisoners."

Dark anger flashed over Colonel Auda Bin Bahadu's eyes and his voice was loud and penetrating. "Enough of this nonsense about being taken prisoner. We of the *Abu Jihad Falaj'i* have no intention of being taken prisoner by either the Jews or the Jordanians. We would die first." His fierce black eyes pounced on the Death Merchant. "And I ain't a whistlin' Dixie either, Camellion! Ya dig me, Jack?"

The men laughed, including Camellion. Even the two Jesuit priests smiled. American slang coming out of the mouth of the Saudi Arabian was ridiculous.

"Yeah, Mac. I dig," Camellion replied jocularly. He was suddenly serious. "For the record, we'd all die before we'd permit ourselves to be captured. That's always been understood. We just don't talk about it, just as we haven't mentioned the important day that will be tomorrow—for the Christians anyhow."

Robert Follmer's eyes brightened. "Say, that's right—"

"Yes, the *Nasrani* Christmas," said Colonel Bahadu. "And how the Israelis capitalize on the birth of Joshua-bar-Joseph,[2] the Nazarene born in Bethlehem. The world and its gods—a comedy made for fools, gentlemen!"

"Well, are we going out and trim a Christmas tree or get on with this show?" Dillard said scathingly, as if on sudden impulse.

"Colonel, how about communication between the men? They do understand?" said Camellion, who adjusted the heavy gun belt around his waist. "We can't have any confusion if and when trouble starts."

"Walkie-talkie, net method," Bahadu said. He took off his sunglasses. "There won't be any slipups." His eyes swung to Dillard. The CIA expert stared right back at him. "And, Mr. Dillard, you shouldn't worry about my 'sand crabs.' They will do their job. Major al-Staiyum and Captain Majid were trained at Fort Bragg, and so was I."

"Gee, golly, gosh! I guess that means I can throw away my prayer book!" intoned Dillard with mock seriousness.

"I'll get back with the men," Colonel Bahadu said stiffly.

The pilot of the Sikorsky gunship that had scouted the area reported by radio—tuned to the Repco RPX UHF/VHM FM

---

[2]The Jewish name of Jesus Christ. Later, Joshua was called *Jesus* by the Romans and *Christos* by the Greeks. Hence—*Jesus Christ.* Christ's mother, Mary, was Miriam-bas-Jochan.

walkie-talkies that all the men carried—that there was no sign of life in the vicinity, and the Death Merchant made the decision. Ritter, Follmer, and the two Jesuit priests would go with Mahmoud Khalil; they would be accompanied by ten Saudi commandos and Colonel Bahadu. The small party would go to the cave, obtain the Judas Scrolls, and return to the helicopter. The entire force would then depart for Saudi Arabia. On the way to the cave, Ritter and Folmer would make periodic reports to the Death Merchant on a walkie-talkie.

Camellion stood with the three other men and watched the party start for the east slope, his face thoughtful as Harlon Moore remarked, "So now we wait and hope that we can get out without firing a single shot."

"It's possible," Dillard commented, always sounding cheerful. "I have been in on black operations that went smoothly from beginning to end."

Terry Macke hooked his hands around the sling strap of the Velmet M82 "Bullpup" assault rifle[3] slung over his right shoulder, stared at the bleak mountains in the distance, then steadily observed the forlorn hills in the immediate vicinity.

"I assume that if the down-home folks of Hippy Dippy Holler saw this place, they'd say, 'This is mighty pore country, with the land plumb wore out.' "

Kelly Dillard made a noise with his mouth.

"That's jist fahn, an I reckon yore right!" joked Harlon Moore.

With Macke, Moore glanced at the Death Merchant, expecting Camellion to laugh. Or at least smile. Damn it! Macke had made a joke. Hell, some humor was needed in this depressing atmosphere.

Richard Camellion didn't laugh. He didn't smile. He did continue to let his eye walk from the east slope to the boulders, then to the mountains, much farther north of the boulders, where there was only naked rock. The clouds were thick in this region of Jordan, but a tiny patch of them had parted and sunlight was steaming through the gap and splashing over the face of the brown black granite. In the sunlight the cliffs flashed with many colors—reddish, yellow, grayish green, blue and black, due to

---

[3] A brand-new weapon in caliber 5.56mm-X-45mm. There will also be a civilian model, but in semiautomatic fire only. The Velmet M82 weighs 3.92 kg with a full thirty-round magazine. The barrel is sixteen and a half inches long. A very compact and smoothly operating weapon.

the actinolite, barite, and various other minerals running through the rocks like seams of coal; and then the thick clouds came together and the sunlight was but memory. The flickering colors vanished and the cliffs were once more brown with mingled black from the thick chalcedony that ran in streaks through the granite.

The Death Merchant studied the sky. The clouds were tumbling in a maelstrom of indecision. They had thickened and darkened within the last ten minutes.

Camellion recalled the message he had received from Grojean. Top priority, the message had been radioed from Amman to the Company Station at the U.S. Embassy in Riyadh, and from there to Camellion at the commando base. Camellion had not even bothered to decode it.

To hell with Grojean! I've had it with this business! There's not going to be a next mission—not for this lad. It cuts into . . . mah huntin' and fishin' tahm. Besahds, I'm gettin' tirhd of gettin' the short end of the stick. . . .

Very suddenly he felt the cold, insidious evil of the Jabal Arqā, of these ancient mountains sick with spiritual putrescence. He could hear in his mind the shouted blasphemies in sixty different dialects from men who, over the long crawl of centuries, had fought and killed each other for possession of this barren real estate. Within their silent sobs and shouts, 10 million ghosts gave off a stench far more terrible than all the sins that humanity could commit, all the bitter maledictions thunderously denounced by holy men who lived in ape ignorance.

These mountains were actually crypts; and nothing, not even the breath of God Almighty could erase the blood that had flowed over the rocks and down through titanic arcades. Shapes of Hell howled and laughed and strode monstrously within the valleys, flitted across the face of the cliffs, and danced in mockery on the high peaks. The Cosmic Lord of Death had reigned supreme here, and nothing faintly holy would ever dare approach his kingdom. He still reigned within the mighty rocks and still held unhallowed rites with minions of the doomed, with incubi and succubi. There they were, all gathered in hideous abomination—Moloch and Beelzebub, swollen toads and ten-headed Moon calves—all singing the ghastly glories of eternal damnation.

The Death Merchant turned and looked at the slope to the east Follmer and Ritter and the others were nowhere in sight. They had found the skinny trail and were behind the rocks.

So far so good. Maybe our luck is holding.

134

Camellion's Repco RPX buzzed two longs and two shorts, his personal signal from Ritter and Follmer. He pulled the walkie-talkie from its metal case on his belt and switched it on. Dillard, Moore, and Macke crowded around him.

Camellion held the set close to his face. "Go ahead—over."

"Khalil knows the way." Ritter's voice floated out of the transceiver. "So far there have been no problems—over."

"How about Norton and Gatdula? Any problems with them? —over."

"No, but why do you ask? What problems could they cause—over."

"Never mind; it's not that important—over."

"Anything else—go ahead."

"Negative. Just do the job as quickly as you can. Find the damned scrolls and get back here. I have a funny feeling—out."

Dillard gave Camellion a smile that revealed a mouth full of teeth.

"Come clean, Camellion," he said, his voice fraternal, like his savage grin. "What do you suspect those holy joes of—trying to sabotage our getting the scrolls?"

Sniffing the air, Camellion winked at Dillard. "You're too suspicious. Those two couldn't sabotage this mission if they tried and worked double time at it."

"They're only excess baggage," Dillard said, his manner indicating he was positive he was right. "Yeah, yeah, I know. They're here to decipher a few words and to make sure the script is written in Aramaic."

Camellion sniffed the air again. It was thick with the smell of earth and rock, and with the sweetness of honeysuckle growing close by.

Terry Macke's high forehead became a field of puzzlement lines as he said in a slow, serious tone, "I'm more concerned why the Saudis agreed to help us. You know, there's little we could do if Colonel Bahadu and his commandos wanted to keep the scrolls."

"Forget it!" Harlon Moore said. "The Saudis don't give too hoops in Hell about the scrolls. They're secure in their own 'Allah is great' faith. The Israelis—that's another matter. The only thing we don't have to worry about are the Russians. There's no way they can mount an attack, not in this region. It would take a Soviet airborne group all the way from mama Russia to do the job."

"We've been through it before—why the Saudis are lending a hand," Camellion said to Macke. "We can only speculate. It's true that the Saudis have always kept a low profile in the Middle East. But you must remember that the Saudis were deeply angered and humiliated at the Fez conference. The Saudis were voted down in favor of Hussein's plan to side with Iraq. The Saudis want to get even with 'bad boy' Hussein.''

"It has to go deeper than that," said Macke. He got down on his haunches. "We know that Colonel Bahadu either lied or is ignorant of the true facts when he said that King H. was only blowing hot wind about his leading a force against Iran.''

"That's right," added Dillard. "Our own intelligence indicates that Hussein is dead serious. He's taking a terrible risk; yet he means what he says.''

The Death Merchant, now down on one knee, nodded slowly, reflectively. "You've answered your own question," he said to Macke. "King Hussein is using Arab history in calling for a 'holy war' against Iran—ancient Persia, the age-old enemy of the Arabs. What worries the Saudi Arabians is that Hussein wants the Gulf States to join him. Figure it out for yourselves. Oman and the other Gulf States are on Saudi Arabia's southern and southeastern borders. In short, ancient history and modern humiliations are combining to create a new and dangerous factor in the Middle East. We could have a Middle East war—among the Arabs—regardless of what the Israelis may or may not do.''

The Death Merchant's Repco RPX buzzed one long signal— the "net" signal for all the men of the force. Such a signal could mean only one thing—trouble with a capital *T*. The Death Merchant and the others pulled their walkie-talkies from their cases and switched on the sets, Dillard muttering, "Oh shit!''

"Camellion here. Go ahead.''

"This is Major Muhammad al-Staiyun. I'm with the commandos at the 'Big Ear' sound system.'' Major Staiyun's voice, coming out of the transceivers, was colored with controlled concern. "We have picked up the sound of aircraft approaching from the west. Distance at last reading: 13.6 miles, or 20.9 kilometers.''

The walkie-talkies emitted two short buzzes, then a short and a long sound. Both Captain Majid and Colonel Bahadu wished to speak.

First come first served. "Camellion here, Captain Majid.''

"The men with the shoulder-fired missiles and the men at the Broncos are ready," Captain Majid said without any nervousness in his voice. "If they come, we can't miss.''

"Good enough, captain. Colonel, you heard?''

"Affirmative," answered Auda bin Bahadu, his voice tinny as

it came through the two-inch speaker of the Repco RPX. "We're not quite halfway to the cave, according to Khalil. Give me your estimation of the situation."

"Give me yours, colonel."

"Whether we go on to the cave or turn back, there isn't any way we can help the rest of you." Bahadu spoke rapidly. "There's a possibility that all of you down there may die. I maintain that we here continue and get the Judas Scrolls. We can always burn the scrolls, if worse comes to worse. The Jews will never get them. We would then die attacking the Israeli dogs—or the Jordanians."

Whispered Harlon Moore, "Freud would have a field day with him. He has a death wish!"

"My opinoin exactly, colonel," Camellion said precisely, admiring the raw courage of the Father Holy War commando chief. He added with grim irony, "If it comes to that, you'll have damn little time in which to do it, my friend."

"But time enough—out."

The Death Merchant and the other men. switched off their transceivers, Terry Macke saying, "We should get up on the hills where we can see the action."

"You're right," sighed Camellion. Allah and Jehovah may have been napping—

But the Cosmic Lord of Death never sleeps. . . .

CHAPTER ELEVEN

Life is also full of big surprises! Waiting on top of a hill with Major Muhammad al-Staiyun and Sergeant-Major Mullah Rashid l'Halsa, the Death Merchant and the three other Americans first heard the approaching aircraft—a low, steady sound coming from the west, like a train that was coming up fast.

"They're not choppers," Terry Macke said gravely, his head cocked to one side. "I'm certain. They're either props or turbo deals."

"Impossible!" said Kelly Dillard with surprising emphasis. "That would mean transports and paratroopers. The Israelis aren't stupid. They know we'd knock paratroopers out of the sky the way a hunter kills ducks with a shotgun." He turned quickly to Camellion for confirmation. "Don't you agree?"

"Anything is possible. Wait and see what comes," Camellion replied with malicious innocence, his face lit with sardonic amusement.

They waited. They saw. First there were three dots in the distance, the noise of the aircraft growing louder, then still louder. Still, Camellion and the others could only see the noses of the planes, even through binoculars. The big transports then started to turn to the north and everyone saw what they were.

"My God!" gasped Harlon Moore. "Lockheed Galaxies! I don't believe it. I just don't believe it!"

"You had damn well better!" barked Dillard. "You're not looking at a mirage. Those big bastards are swinging around so that they can come in from the north and land on the plain."

"Lockheed C-5A Galaxies!" Major al-Staiyun spit out the words. "Made in America. More of your aid and tender concern for the Israeli devils!"

In spite of the unexpected turn of events, which spelled big BIG trouble, the Death Merchant wanted to laugh out loud—at himself!

At least when I make a mistake, it's a whopper! Well, Dillard said it—the Israelis aren't stupid. I was! I underestimated their

138

daring. We prepared for helicopters and they show up with some of the largest transports in the world! How about that!

Classified as a strategic transport, a Lockheed C-5A Galaxy has four 41,000 lb. thrust General Electric TF39-1 two-shaft turbofans. Wingspan: 222ft. 8½in. Length: 247ft. 10in. Height: 65ft 1½in.

The big transport could carry 125,000 pounds of cargo.

The unobstructed interior has a section 19ft. wide and 13ft. 6in. high, not including the upper deck. Freight is normally carried in containers or on thirty-six standard Type 463L pallets. Two M-60 battle tanks can be driven on board and there is room for three packaged CH-47 Chinook heavy helicopters.

It was the cargo inside the three Galaxies that bothered Camellion and the rest of the force watching the huge planes starting to lose altitude. There would be at least one heavy tank, an armored car or two, and armored personnel carriers.

The Death Merchant's mouth twisted into a bitter, fatalistic smile. *Those clever Israelis! I congratulate you!*

The Mossad had outfoxed and outguessed the CIA—*CIA, hell! They second-guessed me!* They had estimated correctly where the Americans would land. The Israelis also knew that to attack the tiny area east of the small hills and south of the Tongue of the Devil would have been suicide if they attacked from the air. *And so they have come to die in Galaxies.* Privately, Camellion also congratulated the technicians at the Yotvata tracking station. *They had to be good to have coordinated our position with such accuracy.*

Through binoculars they watched the three C-5A Galaxy transports come in for a landing, the pilots coming in one behind the other and a bit to the left of each other. The pilots did a good job, the five-column landing gears—eight wheels to a column—touching, then grabbing the pebbly surface of the plain. The big airplanes rolled 500 feet and slowly came to a halt, the noise of the turbofans dying in silence.

"I estimate they're six to eight klicks due west of us," Terry Macke said. "That's just dandy!" Carefully he tried to get a clearer focus from his Nikon 8X30 IF armored binoculars.

"Four to five miles is too far for accuracy with our missiles," said Harlon Moore through clenched teeth, the rubber cups of his Armored Swift binocs pressed tightly around his eyes. "We'll have to be good—and lucky—when they come up here after us."

"The Sikorsky gunships might do the job," offered Dillard. "With all the firepower they have—"

"No good," Camellion said calmly. "Look at the top of the hulls. See what appears to be needle points?"

Even with the magnification from the binoculars, the three silver and blue Galaxy transports looked small, tiny like toys. Yet even through the haze, Camellion and his people could see that the upper fuselage of each Galaxy had been modified to accommodate an opening for missiles.

A short and a long buzz came from Camellion's Repco RPX. The Death Merchant lowered the binoculars on the strap around his neck, pulled out the transceiver, and switched it on.

Colonel Bahadu's anxious voice came out of the set. The small party had seen the Galaxy transports in the sky, but had not been able to see them land, hills and boulders obstructing their view.

"What's their type and position?" asked Colonel Bahadu, his tone troubled.

"They're American-built Galaxy transports," answered Camellion, "and let's not have any cute remarks about U.S. aid. We estimate they're eight kilometers from us, at maximum. We'll wait until the armor gets close to us, then open fire. If they get through the north and the south passages between these hills, we'll be as wide open as a barn door in a high wind. How close are you to the cave?—over."

There was a very short silence before Colonel Bahadu answered. What he said made the Death Merchant want to strangle him.

"We can't risk that tactic, Camellion. They'll have armored stuff. Their guns will outdistance our missiles—even more range with a tank gun. I'll order three of the gunships to attack."

"Negative! Negative!" Camellion said angrily into the transceiver. "We can see—"

"Not with my pilots he won't!" Macke gave a cynical snort, his eyes flashing. "Risk is one thing, suicide another."

"We can see the tips of surface-to-air missiles protruding from the upper hulls of the Galaxies," Camellion pointed out to the commando boss. "The gunships wouldn't have one chance in fifty. With luck they might get one transport, but it's the Israelis we want to neutralize, not the machinery of the air. And you should know colonel, that Macke is not going to permit any of the Vinnell pilots to toss away their lives in any grand gesture of crazy bravery."

"Very well, I'll use the two *Abu Jihad Falaj'i* pilots," Bahadu said bluntly. "Those transports must be destroyed."

"Colonel, let me remind you that you and I agreed—" The Death Merchant shut off the transceiver. Colonel Bahadu had deliberately terminated the conversation.

Terry Macke looked disbelievingly at Camellion, whose expression was ferocious. "He's going to get his two pilots smeared," Macke said sourly. "Those transports don't mean a goddamn thing. It's the armor in them that matters."

Camellion's cold eyes raked Major Muhammad al-Staiyun, who was ill at east and whose expression indicated he was having serious doubts of his own over Bahadu's hasty decision to send two gun choppers against the three Israeli cargo planes.

"Apparently your boss doesn't realize we might need those two gunships on the return flight," Camellion snapped. "I think one of the mullahs should teach Bahadu the meaning of discipline."

"I do not make decisions, Sahib Camellion." Major al-Staiyun defended himself. "I only follow orders." He didn't sound convincing when he added, "Those transports should be destroyed. The gunships might destroy the Israeli armor before the Jews can move the vehicles from the aircrafts."

Macke snapped, "Not a chance. Those pilots are going to their deaths—and you know it. We all do."

"There isn't anything we can do about it," Camellion said contemptuously. "I can't tell the Father Holy War commandos what to do."

Muhammad al-Staiyun turned his head, avoiding Camellion's hellish stare, in contrast to Sergeant Major Mullah Amin Rameh, who glared furiously at the Death Merchant.

"They're taking out the armor," growled Kelly Dillard, who had never lowered his binoculars. Neither had Moore, who added, "And men coming out too."

Camellion and Macke lay down prone on the rough ground and resumed their survey of the enemy. Israeli commandos, in jungle pattern camo fatigues, were moving down the ramp of one Galaxy. In the rear of another transport-cargo plane, two Israeli built Muza armored cars were going down the ramp. Behind them came more commandos and a South African–built Ratel armored personnel carrier. Fifteen men, plus the driver, could be transported in a Ratel APC—twenty if crammed in.

There was a quick intake of breath from Kelly Dillard. "Look what's coming out of the third big bastard. When we get back, I'm going to get a job in a sex harassment clinic or else in a factory that makes toupees for babies!"

"*If* we get back," intoned Harlon Moore.

The Death Merchant didn't like it either, but there wasn't anything he could do about the big British Conqueror rolling down the ramp of the third Galaxy, its 120mm gun lowered and parallel to the turret. Behind the clanking monster came an

Israeli RBY four-wheel-drive recon vehicle pulling a three-wheeled chassis on which was mounted twin 20mm AA guns. Behind the AA assembly came two more Ratel APCs.

The Conqueror came to a stop thirty-five feet east of the enormous tail of one Galaxy and the gunner began to raise the long, ominous barrel while commandos from the RBY uncoupled the AA guns.

There was a total of ten vehicles—one Conqueror, two RBY vehicles, two armored cars, and five Ratels—and perhaps 175 Israeli commandos carrying either Uzi SMGs or Galil assault rifles.

To the east of the hills the air was full of racket as the GE T58 turboshaft engines of the two Sikorsky gunships roared into life. The blades began to rotate faster and faster. Within seconds the pilots lifted the birds from the ground.

Camellion reared up, got to both knees, and looked from left to right. The hilltops offered no protection. In some places the "dips" between the hills were as much as twenty feet in the center of the two slopes, where the two inclines came together. In other places, the summits ran together.

The Saudi commandos were scattered about on top of the hills, some lying flat, others crouched down behind large rocks. Other than Colt CAR submachine guns and Beretta autoloaders, many of the commandos carried Viper, Stinger, and Tiger missiles.[1] All three types were one-man shoulder-fired from a sealed disposable tube that acted as the missile's shipping and handling container. All three used an advanced infrared guidance system that enabled the gunner to attack the target from almost any angle. The Stinger was a surface-to-air missile. The Viper was antiarmor and antipersonnel. So was the SS-B24 Tiger, although it could be used with some accuracy against low-flying aircraft. But the main weapon against the heavily armored Conqueror would be the M-67 90mm recoilless rifle—also a shoulder-fired weapon.

The Death Merchant jerked his head to Major al-Staiyun. "Major, get on the walkie-talkie and tell your men up here to move to the bottom on these hills. All Hell is going to break loose up here shortly."

Muhammad al-Staiyun pulled the binoculars from his face and gave the Death Merchant a stubborn look. "Sahib Camellion, you can see what is happening out there on the plain, can you

---

[1]The *Stinger* replaced the *Redeye* missile, the *Viper* the *LAW* missile.

not? When the armor of the Jew curs gets within range, we can fire from up here. This is not a time to retreat!''

Oh merciful God! Save me from idiots!

Harlon Moore, lying flat on his stomach, rolled over, raised up on an elbow, and looked around at Camellion. "He's right," he said, puzzled. "The Israelis have formed two columns down there—the tank and four vehicles to our right, the two armored cars and two personnel carriers to the left. We know what they intend to do—attack the north and the south passes. We can blow them apart easily from up here."

Before Camellion could speak, Terry Macke jumped in, his heavy voice angry, "There's some excuse for you, Moore. You're not a military man." His eyes shot to Major Muhammad al-Staiyun. "But you're supposed to be trained in tactics. Camellion wants the men off the hills, major, because when those armored cars and the tank get within range, they're going to churn the dirt and rocks up here with shells. And they've got the range. Now if you don't want your men slaughtered every which way but Sunday, you'll have them move their butts, but fast."

"Now!" Camellion's voice was sharp.

With a desperate look in his ink black eyes, Major al-Staiyun reached for the transceiver on his belt.

The two Sikorsky gunships had lifted off, one swinging to the northwest, the other to the northeast, both zooming over the line of hills at an altitude of 161 feet. Five miles away, the Israelis didn't seem concerned. They didn't scatter and run for cover. Instead, commandos were getting into the armored personnel carriers, which by now had started their engines.

"They can't fit in those APCs," remarked Kelly Dillard. "Those poor bastards who are going to have to walk behind the carriers and the other vehicles are sure going to have tired feet by the time they get here."

"They won't even notice," Camellion said in a matter-of-fact tone. "The Israeli is one tough soldier."[2] *That's what worries.*

[2]In Israel, all eighteen-year-olds spend three years in uniform—longer if they join certain branches or qualify to become officers. They must serve in the reserves until they are fifty-five. Furthermore, 99 percent of the eighteen-year-olds who receive call-up notices present themselves immediately. In contrast, only 12 percent of American eighteen-year-olds required to register for a possible draft have done so. Nor do the Israelis offer "bonuses" to get men to join ground combat forces!

me! If the Israeli commandos ever reach our side of the hills, they'll go through the sand crabs like hot water hosed through tissue paper. Camellion, you damn fool! You've boxed yourself in on this one.

"The gunships are going in to attack," said Terry Macke evenly. "Those poor jerks don't have chance one."

One SH-3 Sea King came in from the north, the second gunship from the northwest, the former at 200 feet, the latter slightly lower. Both Saudi pilots intended to shoot off a dozen 2.75-in. HE rockets, then follow up with GAU-8 Avenger 30mm fire.

Neither gunship got close enough to the Galaxy transports to even begin the attack!

The Sikorsky coming from the northwest was still 1,219 meters from its target, the center Galaxy, when three XBX Saber air-to-air missiles shot up from the top hull of one transport and streaked toward the doomed Sikorsky, whose pilot had pulled-in-pitch and had swung to port in an effort to avoid the deadly missiles.

Two Sabers streaked from the top of another Galaxy and, as fast as twin bolts of lightning, headed for the gunship that, coming from the north, was 1,410 meters away. In only 8.3 seconds the laser sights of the gunships would have locked in on the targets and the gunners could have fired. The Sabers, traveling at supersonic speed, were too fast. Moving with such speed that the eye could not follow them, the five missiles made contact with the two Sikorsky gunships. The SH-3 to the north and the three XBX Sabers that struck it exploded into a ball of red orange fire a hundred feet in diameter. Another second and the other Sikorsky helicopter—plus the 320 pounds of explosives in the two missiles—exploded with a mighty, thunderous roar and became a cloud of flame and blown-apart bodies and 100,000 pieces of chopper wreckage that rained down over a wide area.

"So much for the Keystone Kops helicopter attack!" Harlon Moore said petulantly, taking another look around the hilltop. Most of the commandos had reached the bottom of the hills, as had Major Muhammad al-Staiyun and Sergeant Major Amin Rameh, both of whom were ordering the men to stay close to the hills.

Terry Macke said peremptorily, "We'd better get down there and make sure both passes are covered. We can't trust those nightgowned Allah lovers to do the job right."

A short buzz and a long buzz came from the Death Merchant's walkie-talkie. The caller was Colonel Auda bin Bahadu, who wanted to know if the two Sikorsky gunships had succeeded in their attack against the Galaxy cargo planes.

"Colonel, I told you the attack wouldn't work, and it didn't," the Death Merchant said calmly. The pilots didn't count. In Black Operations there were no men; there were only casualties, numbers, statistics, body counts; and although he had hated to lose the two gunships, he took great pleasure in informing Colonel Bahadu of the one-sided battle. "The Israelis knocked the two birds out of the sky with missiles before the pilots could get off a single rocket. The Israelis have formed two columns of armor and are getting ready to move toward us. Over."

"Those damned Jews must be stopped at the passes!" Bahadu's choked voice, coming from the transceiver, rose to almost a panic. "If they get the chance, they'll blow our transportation all over these mountains. You know that."

"How close are you to the cave with the scrolls?" Camellion nodded when Harlon Moore touched him on the elbow, pointed west, and said, "The armor's moving. We've got to get off this hill." Nodding again, Camellion also noticed that Kelly Dillard and Terry Macke had cocked their heads to one side, as if listening.

"We've reached the cave and are going to go inside," Bahadu said nervously, "and listen—I'm going to order Major al-Staiyun and Captain Majid to follow your orders to the letter." He added magnanimously, "I am turning over the full command to you."

"Oh shucks, colonel! You're too generous!" mocked the Death Merchant. "But it will still be on your record that you ordered the two choppers to attack—out."

Camellion was shoving the Repco RPX into its case when he realized why Macke and Dillard had cocked their heads. Now he heard the very faint sound from the west, a sound that all the while grew louder.

Israeli fighter jets!

"Jets!" yelled Dillard and jumped to his feet. So did Macke and Moore.

"Let's get off this hill!" shouted Camellion. Turning, he started to move down the hillside.

The Death Merchant, the two CIA men, and Macke, the ex-Green Beret officer, were sliding and half falling down the side of the hill as the two Israeli Kfir fighters banked to the south, then roared north and screamed in for the attack, their intention being to rake the small plain from south to north, one fighter a thousand meters behind the other.

The pilot of the first Kfir jet fired two R-F30 air-to-surface

145

missiles at the same time that thirty Father Holy War commandos aimed and let loose thirty Stingers and ten Bronco missiles flashed upward faster than the twinkling of an eye.

It seemed that the entire gray sky shattered itself in one monstrous explosion, all the explosions merging into each other, including the two R-F30 missiles from the first Kfir fighter jet. Both missiles were right on target: one of the big Boeing-Vertol 113 troop carriers exploded into burning, unrecognizable junk, one rotor flying thirty feet into the air and coming down between two other Boeing-Vertol 113 helicopters.

The two Kfirs simply vanished in fire, smoke, and crashing concussion, their instant destruction bringing a wild cry of victory from the Saudi commandos, who began waving their Colt-CAR SMGs in the air.

Flat on his back on the hillside, Macke gasped in pleased surprise.

"I don't believe it! They actually shot 'em down!"

Dillard, picking himself up, snickered, "They aimed, missed, and the missile hit by accident." He glanced at the Death Merchant, who was checking his equipment and seeing if he had dropped anything when he had thrown himself to the earth and rocks of the hillside. "Camellion, did I ever tell you what you get when you cross a Cuban with a Haitian?"

BLLAMMMMMMMM! The first 120mm shell from the gun on the Conqueror tank struck a hilltop and exploded, the blast throwing up half a ton of rocks and dirt.

"Well, it's started," said Terry Macke. "It's a good thing the choppers are parked far apart from each other."

BERRROOOMMMMM! Another explosion on a hill, this one from a 76mm shell fired from the turret gun in one of the Muza armored cars. In rapid succession, shells began bursting on the hills. First there was the telltale "er-rupt" as the shell sailed over, from the guns to the hills, followed by a terrific explosion.

Moore pushed his helmet down firmly on his head. "This isn't our day," he said with a nervous little laugh. "I feel like that last white native-born American running from Dade County[3] carrying the American flag."

Camellion was about to tell Macke and Moore to check on the

---

[3]In Florida. Dade County has the highest murder rate in the United States, all due to the "poor refugees," the Cubans and the Haitians, the former deeply into drug selling, the latter murderous savages lacking in both conscience and morals.

commandos watching the north pass when he saw Captain Falih Bin Majid and two of the commandos running toward him.

"Here comes Captain Marvel!" muttered Dillard.

Bin Majid and the two commandos were out of breath by the time they reached the Death Merchant and his tiny group.

"That was good work, captain." Camellion congratulated the commando officer. "If those planes hadn't been knocked out of the sky, they would have destroyed every one of our choppers."

"I said we couldn't miss." Captain Majid squared his shoulders confidently. "But one Boeing-Vertol was destroyed—but I suppose not all of us will be going back. My concern and the concern of Major al-Staiyun is the two passes. We know it is also your main concern, Sahib Camellion." He paused, cleared his throat, and said stiffly, "Colonel Bahadu has instructed me and Major al-Staiyun to follow your orders. He is too busy at the cave for command."

One of the Saudi commandos jabbered in Arabic to Captain Majid, who frowned and responded sharply, rattling off a reply in Arabic. The other *Abu Jihad Falaji'i* regular looked fearfully at the top of the hill on which a shell had just exploded.

Putting on his West German Siburg sunglasses, the Death Merchant shouted to make himself heard above the bursting of more shells. Automatically he ducked with the other men as small rocks and dirt, tossed up by an exploding shell, fell around him. "Concentrate half the missile men and half the recoilless rifles at both ends of the south pass and the north pass. There will be no retreat until I give the word; and tell that to Major al-Staiyun."

"We are Moslems. We will not retreat before the Jew infidels!" Majid said arrogantly, drawing himself erect. "It—"

"You'll retreat when I tell you to!" roared the Death Merchant, his words a verbal wire whip that stung Majid with the force of fire. "We're not fighting in a mosque. This is war! The Prophet Muhammad himself has written, 'A wise man knows the value of retreat, so that Allah will permit him to strike again at the heart of the Infidel.' Are you not a true follower of the Prophet, Captain Majid?"

Majid's face underwent a series of indecisive contortions and very quickly he nodded. To have done otherwise would be an admission that he was not a True Believer.

"I'll make sure the men are in position at the mouth of the passes," he said. "I'll take the south pass. Major—"

"Both of you will take command of the south pass," Camellion interrupted. "I and the other Americans will take charge of the north pass. Who is in command of the north pass at the present time?"

"Sergeant Major Mullah Fuad l'Sidkim," Captain Majid said significantly. He looked embarrassed and shifted his weight from his left to his right foot. "But, Sahib Camellion—a mullah will not take orders from a Christian. It is unthinkable!"

Merriment twinkled in Camellion's blue eyes. "What makes you think I'm a *Nasrani?*"

Majid shrugged. "Sahib Camellion, all Westerners are *Nasranis* to a mullah. And Mullah Fuad l'Sidkim speaks very little English. Either I or Major Staiyun must go with you."

The Death Merchant was not going to argue over a custom that was ancient before the Vikings (actually the Chinese) discovered "America."

"So be it, Sahib Hajj Falih Bin Majid," he confirmed. "Go in person to Major Muhammad al-Staiyun and transmit my orders. Tell him not to fire at the armor until his men have a clear aim and"—he grinned—"can't possibly miss—and no retreat, not until I order him to do so on the walkie-talkie. We'll wait for you here."

Captain Majid nodded his understanding and hurried off with the two commandos.

The Death Merchant and the other men ducked again when an exploding shell, far above on a hill to their right, showered them with rocks and dirt, several tiny rocks striking Terry Macke's S.E.D. helmet.

Harlon Moore's eyes followed Majid and two commandos who were running south toward Major Muhammad al-Staiyun. "I wonder why all the blanket wrappers think all Westerners are Christians? That's dumb."

"For the same reason the Arabs think that all Israelis are Jews," Camellion said, supplying the answer. "It's that iron-bound dogmatism that defeats the Arab purpose. In this respect they have a lot in common with the Central and the South Americans. If a Latin isn't praying, he's trying to kill you or one of his countrymen, or else he's wanting to be the head honcho in a 'revolution of the people.' "

Terry Macke, glancing up at the darkening sky, knew why the Death Merchant wanted to command the defense of the north passage between the hills: the Conqueror tank was at the head of the short armored column that would attack the north pass. What troubled Macke was how they were going to maintain their positions long enough to even get a shot at the damned Conqueror

Having the same pessimistic thoughts, Kelly Dillard looked a the Death Merchant and said accusingly, "Look, Camellion. How are we going to hold long enough to get within range with the Viper and Tiger missiles? How are we going to get clear shots. I'm not talking about the actual range of the missiles. Why that hundred and twenty mil gun is going to explode every rock in sight!"

"Oh, fate is going to have to be kind to us," Camellion said confidently. He grinned broadly. "That plus a little surprise I have in mind for the Israelis."

The eyes of the three men widened with interest.

"Such as?" Terry Macke was skeptical.

"Wait until we get there and I'll show you how we're going to beat the hell out of 'God's Chosen People.' "

Not quite 250 feet wide and 400 feet long, the passage to the north, was bounded on both sides by rocky hills, the south side of the hill to the north a solid mass of columnar-structured rock that was 101 feet high.

The pass was not a straight-as-a-die passage. It was only 100 feet wide at the east end and maybe 150 feet wide at the west mouth, which faced the large plain on which the Galaxy transports had landed. The widest section of the pass was in its center.

On either side of the passage were numerous grooved boulders of smooth granite and sandpaper-surface sandstone—all in a tumbled mass, without any order. More boulders, mixed with slanting slabs of Precambrian fossiliferous slate, were on each side at the end of the east opening.

It was behind these boulders, past the east mouth, that the Saudi commandos waited with their Viper and Stinger missiles. Five Father Holy War fighters had M-67 90mm recoilless rifles. None were afraid. If anything, the Saudi commandos were over-confident, more than anxious to prove their superiority over the hated Israelis. The Jews might think they were chosen by Jehovah, but the Saudi Arabians were positive that they were the favorite people of Allah! ◀━━

With Terry Macke and Captain Falih Bin Majid, Camellion had crept and crawled among the rocks until he and the other two men were only forty feet east of the western mouth and on the left side of the pass.

Camellion stared through his 8 X 30 Bushnell binocs. To his right, leaning over the same boulder as he, Macke and Captain Falih Bin Majid anxiously watched through binoculars the approach of the two Israeli columns. At the head of one column were the two armored cars; this column was headed at full speed for the south pass. The other column, led by the Conqueror tank, was moving directly toward the north pass. Even as the tank and the armored cars drew closer, the 120mm gun of the Conqueror and the 76mm guns of the Muza armored cars roared. Puffs of smoke, then "er-rupts" followed by shells exploding on hilltops. The Israelis were going to make sure that none of the enemy remained on the hills to fire down on them.

The Death Merchant and the two other men were quick to notice that not a single shell exploded against the sides of the hills within either the south or the north passage. They knew why: the Israelis wanted the passes to remain clear. They didn't want their fast rush inward to be slowed by cluttered rock.

Stepping back, Terry Macke lowered his binoculars and stared thoughtfully at Camellion. "All right, what's this surprise of yours? Whatever it is, it had better be good. The tank, the RYB, and the Ratel APCs are only several kilometers away."

Captain Falih Bin Majid moved behind Camellion and Macke. "Will this—this surprise—as you call it, also work at the south pass? What good will it do us to block the Jews here if they are free to flow through the south pass?"

"It will work on both passes," said Camellion with a touch of annoyance. He turned and pointed upward at the north side of the high hill. "Do you know what a geologist would say about the side of this hill?

"This isn't any time for guessing games!" Macke said curtly.

"See how the black rock moves upward, like square posts side by side? The rock is basalt. A geologist would say this hillside is dominated by basalt columns. They're defined by joints that formed during the cooling of a lava flow. All that black rock, about twenty feet wide in the center of the columns, is a vertical 'basaltic dike' intruding into the granite."

"How do you know these things?" Captain Majid's eyes narrowed suspiciously. "How can you be so certain?"

Camellion got to one knee and looked up at Captain Majid, who, with Macke, also got down to one knee.

"Oh, I acquire all kinds of useless knowledge that I eventually put to use. As for the south pass, it's even more narrow than this one, and both its sides are dominated by basalt columns."

"Damn it!" Macke protested vehemently in impatience. "What are you getting at, Camellion?"

"I'm saying that if we direct fifteen or twenty Viper and Tiger missiles at the basalt columns in both passes, we'll bring down tons of rock," Camellion explained. "Not enough to cover the enemy vehicles, but it will surely slow them long enough for the men to use their missiles. In that minute or three we'll be able to knock out most of the armor.''

Captain Majid's eyes flickered thoughtfully over the Death Merchant. ▰▰▰▰▰

"Your plan might work; it is certainly worth a try.''

"It had damn well better work!'' Macke said gruffly. He put the heel of his right palm on top of the flap-holster containing a 9mm Sig-Sauer autoloader. "It's the only one we have.''

"Let's get back and place the men in the right position,'' Camellion said, then quickly to Captain Majid, "Once we position the men on this end, you can get on the walkie-talkie and explain to Major al-Staiyun what we want him to do. Tell him to have twenty of his men aim their one-shot missiles at the basalt columns on the south hillside of his pass. Tell him the men are to fire as one when the two armored cars are directly beneath the columns.''

"Come on, let's get out of here,'' urged Macke. "We don't have all day and that damned tank is getting closer.''

At the east mouth of the north side pass there were hundreds of wedged-shaped rocks that could protect hundreds of men, but not against 120mm shells. As a protective measure, the British Conqueror[4] would surely shell these rocks at the first opportunity.

A hundred feet east and slightly north of these rocks were more granite and sandstone boulders, all piled together as though dumped from a giant's bag. Many of the boulders had very rough, uneven surfaces that showed the elongation of pebbles resulting from pressure. Two hundred and fifty million years ago, the Jabal Arqā had been a part of a volcanic range; 50 million years later, the mountains had been part of a vast lake; then the present Jabal Arqā had pushed their way upward, forming a new chain.

The Death Merchant had Captain Majid and Sergeant-Major Mullah Fuad l'Sidkim order eleven of the commandos to get behind those rocks with their Viper and Stinger missiles. With these men went Fuad l'Sidkim. He would keep his Repco RPX on. When Captain Majid ordered him to fire, all eleven would

---

[4]Israel army equipment is an interesting collection of intentional and fortuitous acquisitions, much of it of Western manufacture. Main battle tanks are British Centurions. The Israelis also have a lot of U.S. and South African equipment.

sent their missiles at the Conqueror—but only if the first part of the plan worked.

Camellion explained in detail to his men and to Captain Majid what he had in mind. On the south side of the mouth of the north pass were more rocks, another mishmash of boulders playing partners with slabs of gray black slate and rounded masses of gneissic rocks known as roches moutonnées, these boulders curving around ungracefully to the south. Camellion had Majid send twenty-one men behind the rocks where the masses of granite ended, toward the south. In such a position, the commandos could still see the basalt columns on the south side of the north hill. At the same time, the Saudis would be immune to the shells from the 120mm cannon on the Conqueror. Once in the pass, the tank crew would not be able to see them.

"Sahib Majid, better get on your walkie-talkie and tell Major al-Staiyun what we're doing and give him his orders," Camellion said. "Tell him that basically he's to use the same tactic. The rocks at the south pass are spread out like they are here."

"At once, Sahib Camellion," Majid said promptly and reached for the Repco RPX on his belt.

Harlon Moore directed his words at the Death Merchant. "Where are we going to be when the Israelis come in and the fireworks start?"

Kelly Dillard intoned—looking around to make sure none of the Saudis were within hearing range; and Captain Majid had moved ten feet away while speaking to Major al-Staiyun over the walkie-talkie—"Personally, I don't trust these Saudis to do the job. I'd feel a lot better if we could get off some missiles on our own or some ninety mil shells at that damn tank. I'm sure you feel the same way."

Terry Macke and Harlon Moore agreed with quick nods, Macke observing with a slow, meditative smile, "If I'm going to get snuffed on this damn plain, I want to die with the knowledge that I did something to prevent said death."

He and Dillard and Moore didn't get an argument from the Death Merchant, who wouldn't have trusted God to defend him.

"We'll take positions behind the rocks, where they start to wind south," Camellion said, "say, about forty feet from the actual mouth of the pass. That way we can get off the first shot after the basalt comes down, while the Israelis think we're going to blow up the entire pass."

Moore leaned forward, his expression one of alacrity. "Hold on, Camellion. That 120 mil gun can shell those rocks—or have you forgotten?"

·"But not enough to do us any damage," Camellion pointed out. "Up that close the width of all the boulders is almost forty feet. Even armor-piercing shells can't whack through that much granite; and they're not going to lob shells in among the rocks. After all, they haven't been tossing shells over the hills. First of all, they don't know where the choppers are. Secondly, they don't have all that many shells to waste. The Israelis know we came in choppers, but they figure they can demolish the choppers once they're inside, once they're through the pass."

"I still don't like it," Macke said, his tone stubborn. "It's a risk."

"It's a risk just being here," Dillard said with a little laugh. "And if that tank gets through the pass—or any of the armored cars through either pass—what chance will we have?"

"Watch what you say," warned Moore. "Here comes Majid."

Hurrying back to the group, Captain Majid reported that Major Muhammad al-Staiyun understood the orders and was putting his men into the necessary positions. Majid finished with, "All the men here are in position, Sahib Camellion. Is there anything else?"

"We're going up close, about forty feet from the mouth," Camellion said. "Get us a recoilless rifle and four shells. You remain with the men that will fire at the north hillside, and keep your walkie-talkie on. When I say 'FIRE!' you have the men fire. Remember—but never mind. I'll make sure you fire at the right time and with the right group." Camellion glanced at the three other Americans. "Two of you guys go with him to carry the shells."

"I'll go," offered Macke.

"So will I," volunteered Moore.

Watching the three men hurry off, Camellion said, "I'll bite, Kelly. What do you get when you cross a Cuban with a Haitian?"

Dillard grinned broadly. "A car thief who doesn't know how to drive. . . ."

CHAPTER TWELVE

The thunder of the distant cannon shots rumbled in Abraham Siem's ears. Wearing the black shoulder boards with markings that designated he was a *Rav-Seren* ("major") in the Tenth Armored Division, he turned nervously to the heavyset man dressed in khaki shirt and pants and wearing a black beret.[1] Like Siem, he had a gold tank badge on each tab of his collar, and his black shoulder boards and markings identified him as a *Rav-Aluf*, or "general."

"With the two jets shot down, we've lost our chances for a quick victory," Siem offered, wondering how General Sharon could remain so calm as the two men stood by the huge open doors of one of the Galaxy cargo planes. "And we don't know what kind of equipment the Saudis and their American friends have."

"Oh come now, Abraham! We know what they have," mused General Aharon Sharon, who liked his aide of four years, even if he was a *hartsvaitik*[2] with his constant worrying. "We know they came in helicopters. The most they can have is surface-to-air missiles. Without armor, they're helpless. Once our armor gets inside the area beyond those small hills, they'll slaughter the damned Arabs and those American CIA cutthroats, you'll see."

A strong man, sixty-two years old and brimming with robust good health, General Sharon stood with his hands clasped behind his back. He and a part of his Vulture Commando Group G. had illegally invaded Jordan and were without air support; yet there he stood, as calmly as though he were reviewing troops on parade in Tel Aviv.

Abraham Siem exhaled cigarette smoke and said in low, formal tones, "For our sake, I hope we can complete the operation

---

[1] Officers and enlisted men wear khaki shirts and trousers, and berets colored according to the arm of service—paratroopers: Red; armor: black; others: khaki.

[2] "Heartache."

154

before the Jordanians arrive. If we are still here when they attack . . ."

General Sharon glanced in irritation at Siem, with whom he was becoming annoyed. "Quit being such a pessimist. You know as well as I do that the Jordanian pilots are ill trained and their tactics a joke." He moved a hand in a sweeping gesture. "Look around, man! See the weapons at our disposal. We are a small nation, but we are mighty—and we have God on our side. The Temple will never fall again, Abraham—*never again*."

Siem didn't reply as he let his eyes walk around the area. The commandos who were not racing across the plain had set up a dozen AA missile launchers filled with four-foot-long surface-to-air "Hammerhead" missiles. In case of ground attack—not very likely in this part of Jordan—other commandos had ringed the airplanes with six 10.5cm IG42 recoilless guns that had a range of 7,950 yards. Tanks and armored cars, tank destroyers and other armor would never get within range of the aircraft.

Nevertheless, Siem was deeply troubled. To risk all these men over rumors of scrolls—no matter how valuable—was ridiculous. But it was more than the scrolls. It was power! Authority was the real prize. Siem felt ashamed and traitorous.

General Sharon was not as concerned about the attack on the Saudis and the few Americans as he was about the situation in Israel. Particularly tricky were Yigel Bar-Levinsky and Isser Ben Zur. Like two snakes in the palace of Solomon they were! Those two power-crazy *chazzers*[3] had to go, and go they would, along with Begin. Bar-Levinsky and Ben Zur thought they were being clever. The truth of the matter is that they had made a fatal mistake in their anxiety to enlist aid in their effort to topple Begin. That mistake was enlisting the aid of Colonel Eli Lodtz, the chief of military intelligence. General Sharon smiled to himself. This strike would topple Begin, and it would topple General Bar-Levinsky and Isser Ben Zur, although they weren't aware of it. What those two didn't know was that David Mashom and five other members of the Knesset were firmly on the side of Lodtz and Sharon.

A commando ran up to General Sharon and Major Siem and saluted smartly, a triumphant grin on his tanned face.

"Sir, I have a report from *Segen* Kottmann and *Samal-Rishon* Wyman," the man said. "They are about to attack the passes."

General Sharon turned to Major Siem, grinning from ear to ear.

[3] "Pigs"—Hebrew.

155

"As the Americans would say, 'It is all over but the shouting!' "

The action that the attacking Israelis would take was predictable. The two Muza armored cars, the RYB, and the three Ratel armored troop carriers raced for the west entrance of the south pass, the two armored cars side by side, their 76mm guns booming. To the north, the Conqueror tank closed in on the west entrance of the north pass, commandos crouching crablike behind the three Ratel APCs, just as commandos were behind the two APCs in the south column.

The "er-rupts" of shells came fast and furious, followed by thunderous *BERRROMMMSSSS* as the 120mm gun of the Conqueror tossed shell after shell, of the high-explosive-incendiary (HEI) type at the hilltops of the north and south hills on each side of the north pass.

Just before the Conqueror tank entered the west mouth of the pass, First Lieutenant Benyamin Kottmann ordered the gunner to lower the long barrel of the 120mm gun and to start firing at both sides of the gulch, at the very bottom of the north and the south hills that embraced the gully.

At the mouth of the south end pass the two Muza armored cars began using the same tactic, Staff Sergeant Haim Wyman ordered the two gunners to fire at the rocks on both sides of the scission.

The racket of bursting shells was tremendous. It was as if on some platform in the sky fifty thousand carriers were tipping loads of pointed steel bricks that burst on the ground, all with devastating ear-splitting roars, with sounds that were always slightly different, not only in magnitude but also in quality. It was not a continuous roar. It was not a noise. It was a symphony that one felt in his ears more than he heard it. One got the impression that the air was full of vast and agonized passion now and then bursting with sighs and groans, then into shrill screaming and pitiful whimpering, all the while shuddering beneath a rain of terrible blows and torn by whips straight from Hell. Worse than the physical effect, even for the Death Merchant, was the effect on the nerves, a special feeling of total helplessness, an enervating feeling of vulnerability.

Only forty-one feet from the mouth of the pass, Richard Camellion crouched behind a rounded granite roche moutonnée, his head barely above the smooth rock. Watching the approaching Conqueror, he thought of Captain Falih Bin Majid's words "Against the shelling, we are helpless. It is like striking out against empty air, or trying to see your image in a shattered mirror.''

The British Conqueror tank entered the west mouth of the small gorge and stopped; the RYB recon car behind it came to a halt, and so did the two Ratel APCs. The tank then started again, along with the RYB, while the two armored personnel carriers remained motionless. Its road wheels grinding, its wide tracks clanking, the Conqueror—it vaguely reminded Camellion of a World War II German Panzerkampfwagen VI Ausf E, or Tiger-1 tank—started to move slowly through the pass, going straight down the slot.

BERRRROOOOMMMMM! The 120mm gun roared, smoke rolling from the barrel's muzzle brake. A bigger crash of an explosion when the shell struck and blew off on the north side, toward the east end of the pass, crushed rock, dirt, and some vegetation flying up and outward.

The dark green metal monster rumbled forward at 20 mph, its turret turning to the tank's right, the gunner preparing to shell the south side of the mouth. Instinctively, Camellion dropped down and, although he had regulation GI ear plugs in his ears, pressed his hands firmly against his ears, opened his mouth, and began breathing deeply, in and out.

BERRRROOOOMMMMM! Surprise! The gunner hadn't aimed at the bottom of the hill on the south side of the wide cut. He had sighted in on the front boulders on the chain of rocks the Death Merchant was using, the earth-shaking crash—only fifty feet from Camellion—sending up hundreds of pounds of rocks, some chunks the size of footballs, others smaller than pebbles.

Smelling the bitter odor of double-base-ball-nitrocellulose ball propellant and main-base-charge nitroglycerine, Camellion heard chunks of granite and gravel falling around him, dozens of small pieces hitting his shoulders and helmet and clanking off the steel tube of the M-67 recoilless rifle. More pebbles fell onto the Repco RPX transceiver that Camellion had put on the ground against the side of the boulder and onto the three 90mm shells that Moore, Dillard, and Macke had carried to Camellion's position.

The next 120mm explosion was to the Death Merchant's right. The gunner of the Conqueror was aiming at the wedge-shaped rocks east of the mouth and north of Camellion, who reared halfway up, looked over the boulder, and had a good feeling in spite of his precarious position. The Conqueror was almost 200 feet inside the gully, halfway in. Right behind it was the reconnaissance vehicle. The three armored personnel carriers were just entering the west end of the arroyo, moving at less than 30 mph and were several hundred feet west of the recon car and the Conqueror.

A look of pure viciousness on his face, the Death Merchant picked up the transceiver and shouted into the mouthpiece, "Majid, fire at the basalt columns on the north hillside—FIRE NOW!"

Camellion heard Majid shout a loud word in Arabic, then knew it was "FIRE" as fourteen Tiger and seven Viper missiles whooshed from their firing tubes, streaked toward the hillside, and struck the basalt columnar structured rock—fifty feet up and 125 feet north of the tank and the recon vehicle.

The explosions of the missiles—all one gigantic wall of sound and pressure—was as though the universe had blown itself out of existence. All at once there was a fireball, a hundred feet in diameter, with bright red streamers, the savage concussion actually rocking the RYB slightly. One had only several moments to see tons of basalt torn loose and very briefly suspended before it flew outward and started to fall to the ground—chunks and pieces as large as a small car, slabs four and five feet thick and twenty feet long, jagged masses that ranged from table-size to particles smaller than a grain of sand. With a grinding, abrasive sound that grew louder until it was almost a roar, a hundred tons of rock, over a sixty-foot-wide area, started sliding down the face of the hill.

Conscious of his heart pounding in his chest, the Death Merchant saw the Conqueror speed up and swerve to his left, then quickly to the right—as if the tank commander were trying to make up his mind. Camellion was almost certain that there was one thing the tank commander wouldn't do. He wouldn't order a retreat for any of the vehicles. He wouldn't have to, because while the hundreds of rocks had rolled close to the tank and the scout car, none had seriously impeded the progress of the vehicles. There was still another reason why the Israelis would not retreat. They were daredevils, crazy brave because they had to be, becaused they had learned to be—or Israel would have been swallowed alive by the Arab nations. It was tragic that the past successes of the Israelis had led them into developing a superiority complex which had turned them into the Nazis of the Middle East, sadists who pulled the trigger far too often and too readily. Only recently, while Camellion had been in Saudi Arabia, the Israelis had shot down a sixteen-year-old Arab girl on the West Bank. She had been shouting Palestinian freedom slogans at the "brave" soldiers. On the day that final preparations were being made for the operation into Jordan, the Israelis had "fired into the air" and had "accidentally" killed a seventeen-year-old Arab David who had been throwing rocks at the mighty Israeli Goliaths. Hearing the news on the radio had prompted the cynical Kelly Dillard to comment, "It's obvious why it was an accident. The boy was flying through the air."

The Conqueror and the scout car kept coming, and so did the three Ratel APCs, Israeli soldiers running in a crouch behind them. The Death Merchant strained his eyes, doing his best to keep track of the five vehicles almost hidden by the clouds of gray dust rising from the rocks and filling the long gully.

BLAMMMMMM! The 120mm gun fired again at the wedge-shaped rocks to the north of Camellion, the exploding armor-piercing shell making crushed rock out of a three-ton boulder. Camellion had to give the Israelis credit—*They intend to make this a fight to the finish. That's fine with me. I'll finish it for them!*

Lieutenant Benyamin Kottmann, the twenty-six-year-old commander of the Conqueror, knew from experience that his only chance was speed. He had to hit the Saudi commandos before they hit him and the vehicles that made up the rest of the small armored column. He gave the order for full speed forward. At 45 mph the armored fortress charged ahead.

Now! Right now! The Death Merchant yelled into the Repco RPX, "Captain Majid—FIRE! Have the other group hit that tank with every missile they have! Tell those men they'll have to ignore the machine gun firing from the front hull. There isn't any other way."

"At once!" Captain Majid sounded excited.

Like a big rock placed between two millstones to interfere with the grinding, it was the 20mm GX-410 machine gun of the Conqueror that three fourths wrecked the carefully thought-out plan. Meir Yariv, the machine gunner, was wisely raking every forward boulder in sight, the nickel-plated solid-steel-core projectiles glancing off the hard granite and sandstone with frenzied screaming. Ignoring the rain of death stabbing into the boulders all around them, Sergeant Major Mullah Fuad l'Sidkim and the eleven Father Holy War commandos reared up to fire their missiles at the charging Conqueror, now only 127 feet to the southwest of them.

Instantly, just as most of the men fired, 20mm GX-410 machine gun slugs ripped into five of the commandos, including Mullah Fuad l'Sidkim. A holy man he was, but Allah didn't prevent a big 20mm projectile from opening up his chest the way a blast from a shotgun shatters a watermelon. Unconscious before he had time to know he was dying, l'Sidkim was pulling the trigger of his Viper when the 20mm steel sliced into him and knocked him back on his heels. Next to him, Essat Quamiyin gave a loud cry of agony also. He, too, had been pulling the trigger as a 20mm projectile struck him in the right shoulder, tore off his arm, and spun him to the right.

Seven missiles seemed to streak directly toward the Conqueror—four Vipers and three Tigers. Nine including Quamiyins and l'Sidkim's runaway Viper and Tiger. These two missiles shot upward at a steep angle, not even coming close to the tank. L'Sidkim's Tiger struck the top of the hill and exploded, Quamiyin's missed the summit and shot toward the sky.

Six other missiles—four Vipers and two Tigers—also missed the Conqueror, two streaking over the tank, three shooting by to the left, one to the right, the one to the right missing by only a foot. All six shot down the length of the pass, two Vipers very narrowly missing one of the Ratel APCs.

The seventh missile, an antitank Viper, struck the left mud guard of the Conqueror and exploded with a brief bright red flash and a crashing roar, the savage explosion tearing off the track idling wheel, the front road wheel, two sprockets, the suspension bar, and seven feet of wide track. As torn and ripped pieces of metal struck the rocks, the front of the large tank turned sharply to the left and the monster came to a halt. The single Viper missile had dealt a crippling blow to the Conqueror. All it could do now was use its right track and spin to the left, constantly in a circle. Equally as useless were Meir Yariv and Simon Rabinowitz. Rabinowitz, in the driver's compartment, had been only five feet six inches from the exploding Viper and the tremendous concussion had killed him, the pressure rupturing his brain. He sagged in the metal bucket seat, blood dripping slowly from his nose, mouth, and ears, his lap soaked in sticky crimson. The same concussion had partially demolished Meir Yariv, the codriver, machine gunner, and radio operator. Although still alive, he was in a state of shock and unable to think clearly. Only Lieutenant Kottmann and Jossele Shtarkes, the gunner operating the 120mm cannon, were able to function with any kind of precision.

Indeed! This is not one of my better days! Watching from the side of a boulder, the Death Merchant was still wanting to strangle—very slowly—every sand crab in Araby-land when he received his second shock. The RYB recon vehicle that had been twenty feet in back of the Conqueror backed up. The driver shifted, gave gas to the engine, and shot the recon car around the right side of the crippled tank.

A low-profile vehicle, an RBY has four-wheel drive, a long, sloping front, and can carry six men in addition to the driver. Ordinarily an RBY is not enclosed, the occupants exposed to the weather—and gunfire. Not so with this particular Israeli-built rec car. Its top was enclosed in a body of armor plate filled with firing ports. The barrel of a Bren light machine gun protruded from a slot in the right side, its muzzle spitting .303 projectiles. Another Mark-3 Bren was firing furiously from an open port in the right front, next to the driver; still a third Bren was roaring through an opening in the left side, the three streams of slugs knocking off chips from every boulder in sight.

The Death Merchant knew instantly that there wasn't any countermeasures the Saudi commandos could take against the car, at least for the moment. All they could do was stay down— *If they have any sense. Damn! Fudge and double damn! This is worse than sitting down in snake vomit!*

Another fact burned in Camellion's mind: he had very little time, only minutes, to reverse the situation. Spread out in a row, the three Ratel armored personnel carriers were coming through the pass at a fast pace, and soon their light machine guns would be throwing projectiles faster than popcorn popping out of a popper. Furthermore, the turret and the 120mm gun of the partially wrecked Conqueror were in action, the turret turning to the left, the 120mm gun raising, preparing to get off a round at the seven Saudis who had wrecked the big British tank.

Yeah! And tuna fish is up 60 percent! Holy mackerel! He shoved a 90mm shell into the M-67 bazookalike recoilless rifle, raised the weapon to his shoulder, and began to sight in on the RYB. He could easily have sent the shell at the Conqueror, but far better that some commandos get whacked out by a 120mm round than for the recon vehicle to blast its way to the helicopters. Besides, Camellion was certain that the *Abu Jihad* commandos who had whacked out the Conqueror wouldn't be stupid enough to remain in the same positions. And it wasn't that the RBY wouldn't be destroyed. Sooner or later one of the commandos would get lucky—*More likely Dillard or Moore or Macke!* —and destroy the scout car with a Viper or Tiger. But it might be later, after the recon vehicle had exploded the Boeing-Vertols.

A split second before Camellion pulled the trigger, there was a terrific explosion to the south—Vipers and Tigers. The basalt columns to the south were coming down. If Major Muhammad

Al-Staiyun and his group failed to stop the two Muza armored cars in the south pass . . .

Oh well—what on earth would a man do with himself if something did not stand in his way?

Catching the right center of the Israeli RYB in his sights, Camellion pulled the trigger, feeling the tube of the recoilless rifle vibrate ever so slightly as the 90mm shell went on its way.

BLAMMMMMMMM! Just starting to turn south, the Israeli scout car vanished in a thick sheet of yellow and red flames. For the barest slice of a second, Camellion could see a part of the upper armored housing, a Bren LMG, and two corpses tumbling upward and other twisted debris flying in other directions; and then there was only burning rubble, the loudly crackling fire heavily colored with black oily smoke, the harsh wind scattering the stink of burning metal and rubber, plastic and cloth, leather and flesh, the roaring fire consuming to the tune of exploding LMG cartridges, all bang-bang-bang-banging like a string of large firecrackers.

The 120mm gun on the Conqueror roared, the shell exploding in the chain of rocks in which the Saudi tank killers were hidden. Another brain-shaking blast and more chunks of rocks soaring into the air.

Camellion quickly shoved another shell into the M-67 recoilless rifle, raised the tube, glanced toward the three Ratels, saw that they were much closer, and started to sight in on the Conqueror, whose turret was turning to the south. The tank commander had guessed the truth of the situation, that the main body of the commandos on this side was in the curving chain of gray-black granite and gneissic rocks curving to the south and was going to do something about it. He never got the chance. The Death Merchant pulled the trigger of the recoilless rifle.

The 90mm armor-piercing shell struck the right side of the turret toward the front, close to the multibarreled smoke-bomb discharger, and exploded, the transient fire and smoke a changing ball of churning destruction before it dissipated to reveal a gaping hole in the turret, the shell having gone all the way through before exploding with the second charge.

Camellion stared at the tank. The explosion had torn open the hatch of the Commander's cupola and smoke was pouring through the rounded opening. Blue/gray/white smoke also spiraled from the ventilator in front of the turret and from the driver's vision slit. Camellion was confident that nothing could be alive inside the tank. Nothing was. Lieutenant Benyamin Kottmann and Jossele Shtarkes had been splattered all over the interior of the vehicle, which was as dead as they were—and as dead as Meir Yariv, the machine gunner.

Time for the Ratel armored personnel carriers. The Death Merchant was shoving the last 90mm shell into the recoilless rifle when he heard one of the Viper missiles explode on the south side of the mouth of the pass.

Before he put the weapon over his right shoulder, Camellion looked over the top of the boulder sheltering him. The Viper had missed its target. He was just in time to see two of the Ratel armored personnel carriers, and the Israeli commandos running behind them, swing to the south side of the gorge; within a few moments they were out of his line of vision.

There wasn't anything for him to do but to fall back to the others and wait until the enemy attacked. He was putting down the recoilless rifle when Terry Macke, a 9mm Sig-Sauer auto-pistol in each hand, came from around a roche moutonnée and duck-waddled toward him.

"What the devil are you trying to prove?" demanded Macke. "You've already logged more miles up here than a cross-country trucker on No-Doz. Better pack your laundry and get the hell out of here." He frowned when he saw Camellion reach into a Ghurka shoulder bag and pull out a two-pound block of RDX and a remote-control detonator. "What are you doing?"

"A surprise for the Israeli commandos." Camellion pushed the prongs of the detonator through the heavy brown oiled paper into the waxlike composition of the high explosive.

"Good idea," agreed Macke. "I have another surprise for them." He pulled a V-40 Mini grenade, which had a 100 percent kill capability within three meters and could be thrown twice the distance of a regular frag grenade.

"Hold it, buddy," Camellion warned, looking up from his work. "All you'll do is warn them we're here and make them cautious."

"I suppose you're right," Macke said and dropped the Mini grenade back into its cotton duck shoulder bag. "But I'd rather throw a dozen at them, just for the hell of it. In my book, the Israelis are a bunch of bastards, all the way from Boston to Bangkok and back again."

"Don't let emotion interfere with the job," Camellion said. He put the last stone over the bar of RDX. "The Israelis are neither good nor bad. They're only 'the Other Side.' That's the trouble with most people: they won't admit their faults." He reared halfway up and grinned at Macke. "I would—if I had any."

"Your modesty overwhelms me," Macke said with false solemnity. "No matter how anything turns out, there's always some joker who knew it would. Come on, let's blow."

The first crack of thunder came when they were working their way back to the other men, the first raindrops falling on their helmets and shoulders as they crawled around a fifteen-foot slab of slate harboring Moore, Dillard, three commandos, and Captain Majid, the latter of whom was trying to contact Major al-Staiyun on the walkie-talkie.

"Good shooting with the RYB and the tank," Dillard said, and quickly added, "We can't raise Major al-Staiyun. Either he's dead or too busy to report."

Harlon Moore cut in, his voice and eyes worried. "From the sound of the gunfire to the south, something's happening. Camellion, any word from Colonel Bahadu or Bob or Wes?"

"Negative. I'm not worried about them," replied the Death Merchant. "They're not in any danger up there"—he chuckled—"unless there's a time bomb in the scrolls. Assuming the scrolls are there in the first place! How are the commandos on this end spread out?"

"Five of the commandos in the tank group bought it," Moore said. "The other seven managed to race over to us just before you got here. "With us, we have thirty-six men at this end of the plain."

The Death Merchant nodded slowly, "We're going to have to stop them right here. There'll be eighty or more Israelis headed our way shortly—and we still don't know what's happened south of here. As I see it, each man is going to have to fight the battles of three men."

Kelly Dillard snorted and shook his head. "You're wanting the impossible, Camellion. We can't walk on water. We can't control the weather or feed a mob of people on three cheeseburgers."

"I believe it was fishes," Moore smirked.

"What's the difference. We can't do it any more than we can stop the Israelis!"

Macke jumped in, "I had Majid send five of the men down the plain half a mile. They're positioned in the rocks at the foot of the hills. They're there to protect the choppers."

"That's just dandy," sighed Camellion. "That means we have thirty-one men to defend this end."

Camellion and three other Americans jerked around toward Captain Majid when they heard a voice pour out of the walkie-talkie. The words were in Arabic. The voice did not belong to

164

Major Muhammad al-Staiyun. The voice, high and nervous, jabbered on in Arabic. Captain Falih Bin Majid jabbered back, then turned off the Repco RPX and said to the men, his tone as worried as his solemn black eye, "That was Mullah Amin Rameh. Allah has both blessed and cursed us. Major al-Staiyun and his group destroyed one of the armored cars and one of the armored personnel carriers. All the Jew-dogs inside the carrier and the soldiers clustered around it and the armored car were either killed or severely wounded. Major al-Staiyun and five of the men were killed by an exploding shell from the second armored car. Mullah Amin Rameh has taken charge and he and his group are retreating toward us." Majid's voice rose in fear. "The armored car is headed this way. It will destroy the helicopters if it is not stopped. May Allah help us!"

"So far Allah's been out of it; we've had to help ourselves," the Death Merchant declared coldly. He swung to Kelly Dillard and Harlon Moore. "You two grab ninety mil shells and come with me. If the five commandos don't whack out that car, we had damn well better."

Stooping, he picked up the M-67 recoilless rifle, saying to Terry Mack, "You and Majid and the men who are here will have to do your best until we get back."

"I'd say, if we get back," muttered Dillard, lighting a cigarette.

Camellion carried the recoilless rifle. Dillard and Moore each had his hands wrapped around the straps of a shell carrier. All three moved quickly among the rocks, moved south through the rain, which had settled down to a steady heavy drizzle; yet already they were half soaked and could feel the wetness on their backs and chests.

By the time they reached a position 470 feet south of where Captain Majid and the commandos were waiting for the Israelis—a giant granite boulder surrounded by eolian sand and loess—they had a clear view of the plain. The Israeli-built Muza armored car was already halfway up the area, moving straight north at almost 50 mph. Yet it was still too far south, still out of range of the M-67 recoilless rifle.

In contrast, the five Boeing-Vertols and the smoking wreckage that had that had been the sixth Boeing-Vertol were well within range of the 76mm gun in the turret of the armored car. There was only one thing that prevented the crew of the armored car from having a perfectly clear view of the five big Boeing-Vertols that rested a hundred feet from each other—the haze and smoke and one of the Sikorsky gunships that sat a hundred feet south of the large troop-carrying choppers. There had been three SH-3s. The single one that sat there now had been the chopper that had scouted the area after the force had arrived; the two others had attacked the Israel Galaxy transports and had been destroyed. They lay scattered all over the larger plain.

A shell in the recoilless rifle, the Death Merchant watched and waited with Moore and Dillard, his feeling being that he should have his head tripled-checked for even being here in Jordan. He certainly wasn't doing the job for the security of the "American people," who, in general, were too lazy and complacent to comprehend the terrible danger from the Soviet Union. For that matter, the President of the United States and the other unrealistic fools in Washington were even more ostrich-headed, considering that they had more facts. As far back as 1975 the National Estimates Board[4] absolutely refused to believe that the Soviet Union would seek parity—to become as powerful as the United States. Not until later did the boob brains of the NEB reluctantly admit that the Soviets had meant what they had said—*And Washington still believes that the Soviet approach to the issue is the same as ours. They won't believe the truth because it's more convenient and more comfortable to believe the myth that we are invincible. Chicken crap!*

The gunner in the Muza armored car got off the first 76mm round, which exploded thirty feet south of the lone gunship. The driver then brought the vehicle to a stop so that the gunner could range in without having to compensate for the vehicle's forward movement.

BLAMMMMMMM! The second 76mm shell exploded the single Sikorsky into useless rubble that only the flames would enjoy.

"Well goddman it! Are we going to just squat here like three mushrooms in the rain?" Moore said angrily, turning to the Death Merchant, who was putting the recoilless rifle to his shoulder.

"Untwist your balls, old buddy," Camellion snapped, irritated. "I'll try, but the range is still too great for any kind of certainty."

BLAMMMMMMMMM! The third shell from the armored car struck one of the Boeing-Vertol eggbeaters. A lot of fire and

---

[4]A federal interagency intelligence group consisting of the CIA and similar agencies that prepare the National Intelligence Estimates—NTIs—for the President and Executive branch, giving the consensus of the intelligence community on international concerns.

pieces of aircraft taking off in all directions. It was that fast, that final.

Camellion didn't get a chance to even complete his sighting in on the armored car, much less pull the trigger of the M-67. The five Saudi commandos, hidden in the rocks at the bottom of the hills to the west, fired off three Vipers and two Tiger missiles. One Tiger and two Vipers missed. One Tiger and one Viper did not. There was an enormous blast of sound, a rolling ball of fire, and the armored car exploded, its side shooting outward, the turret and the 76mm gun flying twenty feet into the air. One of the eight big wheels rolled to the east, another to the south. Then there was only smoking junk, and bloody and burning, stinking pieces of frying flesh.

"I guess Follmer would call that 'frying a kike!'" Dillard smirkled. "I don't think he likes Jews any more than he's fond of blacks and Mexicans."

The Death Merchant was all business. Rain dripping from his face, he put down the recoilless rifle and pulled the walkie-talkie from its case but did not switch it on. "We must make sure that Mullah Amin Rameh and his group do not link up with Captain Majid. Rameh and his men must check the Israelis that came through the south pass, or we'll have to flap our arms and pretend we're birdies in order to get back to Arabia. I'm going to contact Majid and have him order Amin Rameh to hold the last man."

Kelly Dillard's face grew dark. "I told you only a little while ago that you're expecting the impossible. We've only four troop choppers and three gunships left. I say we call Operation Clover and leave this damned land while we can. This situation is impossible."

"He's right, Camellion," agreed Moore calmly. "We've had it—or soon will."

"There aren't any impossible situations," Camellion said coldly. "There are only men who have grown hopeless about them."

Moore shrugged. A professional career officer[5] in the Central Intelligence Agency, he felt it was beneath him to argue with a mercenary like Richard Camellion, even if one part of his mind did insist that the tall, lean Texan was far far more than a mere trigger.

It was far different with Kelly Dillard, who, although, he, too,

[5]There are no officers as such in the CIA. Employees are under a rating system. For example, a G-4 rating is the equivalent of a colonel in the Soviet KGB.

was a career "Government employee," considered the Death Merchant's words an insult, one he wasn't about to take.

"Don't talk like a philosophical fool," Dillard said viciously, rage in his eyes. "You know that these Saudis are no match for Israeli commandos, not unless we whittle down the odds by a good 50 percent." His tone became a sneer. "If you don't have any ideas, 'genius,' we're as good as dead."

Camellion surprised Dillard and Moore by smiling. "I've got a lot of ideas. Why do you think I had each man bring seven blocks of RDX with him, plus remote-control detonators?"

The eyes of Moore and Dillard flared with intense interest.

"How?" asked Dillard.

"Listen to what I tell Captain Majid." The Death Merchant switched on the walkie-talkie, it suddenly occurring to him that not a single shot was being fired from the north.

WHY?

CHAPTER THIRTEEN

Neither Captain Falih Bin Majid nor Sergeant Major Mullah Amin Rameh were enthused over the Death Merchant's plan, which, according to Camellion, would give them the edge over the Israelis. Neither were Harlon Moore and Kelly Dillard. Only Terry Macke, the ex-Green Beret officer, saw the possibilities. The plan was to attach a V-40 Mini grenade to a two-pound block of RDX and throw the double explosive package at the Israelis ahead of them.

Still crouched behind the large slab of slate, Captain Majid again said, "I cannot understand why the Jew-dogs have not attacked. They have to be in the rocks directly ahead of us. It wouldn't make sense for them to maintain a hold position to the south side of the mouth of the pass." He blinked in confusion. "Or would it?"

"It wouldn't," Camellion replied, his eyes inflating. "They're playing it extra cautious." He glanced up and down the rocks where commandos were tying Mini grenades to brown-paper-wrapped blocks of RDX. In moments, the commandos would be ready.

Sitting flat on his backside, Dillard gave Camellion a long look. "We can't all throw at the same time. The concussion would be too deafening. It would bounce back on us."

"He's right," Terry Macke said seriously. "I suggest one by one. Sixty feet is about as far as those grenades and RDX will travel."

"That's how I intend to do it," Camellion answered Macke, then turned to Captain Majid. "Get on the walkie-talkie and tell Amin Rameh that—"

An explosion far to the south cut him off. It was followed by another and still another explosion—scores, in fact.

Camellion sucked in his breath. "It seem that Rameh already had the idea. Good for him." He pointed a finger at a sharp-featured Saudi next to Captain Majid. "What is his name?" Camellion asked Majid.

"I speak English," the man said with a thick accent. "I am Khodr Kaddourch, Sahib Camellion."

"Khodr Kaddourch, go north. Go to the last man in the line and tell him to throw his Mini grenade and bar of RDX. Tell him that after he throws his explosive package, he is to order the man next to him to throw."

Regarding the Death Merchant with cool appraisal, Kaddourch turned to Captain Majid for confirmation.

Majid nodded. "Do as he says," he ordered the man, who rose to go.

"One more thing, Khodr Kaddourch," said Camellion. "As you come back to the south, tell the men that after all the grenades and RDX are thrown, they will hear a loud pistol shot from this end. As soon as they hear that shot, they are to attack. They are not to throw grenades. We'll take care of grenades forward from this end. Do you understand all of it, Khodr Kaddourch?"

Kaddourch's eyes widened in disbelief. Attack? This man from the West must be mad! But weren't all Westerners a little crazy?

"Attack?" Captain Majid's mouth fell open and he drew back in astonishment. "Sahib Camellion! What are you saying? Our position is precarious enough without our making it worse."

"Hot damn!" murmured Kelly Dillard. "There's nothing like committing suicide the hard way."

Camellion's eyes remain fixed on Majid. "Yes, I know" (*what you're thinking too*), he said. "Allah set definite limits on man's wisdom, but placed no limits on his stupidity—and that isn't fair, is it? But can you"—he swung his eyes around the grim faces "—can any of you suggest a better plan? Or would you rather just sit here in the rain and wait?"

Surprisingly, Camellion got support from Kelly Dillard, who, wiping his face with a handkerchief, said in a frank, somewhat excited tone, "It could work to our advantage. The Israelis have one trait in common with the Russians. They think they're superior to everyone else. They're 'God's Chosen.' The Israelis are always at a psychological disadvantage whenever they are forced to defend themselves against a counterattack."

"I agree," said Terry Macke. "During the Yom Kippur War of 1973 the Egyptian army first made hash of the Israelis, who couldn't even conceive of such an attack."

The Death Merchant's eyes jumped to Captain Majid. "Tell Kaddourch to get going, captain."

* * *

170

The first V-40 Mini grenade and block of RDX,[1] thrown by Nitzan Gabush to the northwest, exploded seventeen minutes later. Man by man the Saudis tossed their explosive packages to the west. With each terrific explosion that pounded at the minds and the sanity of the Death Merchant and "his" force, dirt and crushed rock flew upward like sharpnel; and now and then there were short, high-pitched screams of agony, proving that the Death Merchant had been correct. The Israeli commandos were in the boulders and slabs to the west; they had been creeping in very slowly. Now their strategy was wrecked. All the survivors could do was retreat. At the beginning, Camellion's one big worry was that the Israelis would attack, and that the attack would be preceded by a constant volley of grenades, in which case *We would have had no choice but to retreat. All we could have done was take off in the choppers, swing to the east, pick up Colonel Bahadu and the others, and hightail it back to Saudi Arabia.*

Not using grenades had been the fatal mistake of the Israelis. Their supercaution—not wanting their positions revealed—had been their undoing.

Finally came the turns of the men around Camellion. Captain Majid threw his explosive package. Kelly Dillard then pulled the pin from the Mini grenade attached to the block of RDX in his hand and tossed it as far as he could, the explosions making the ground shake. Then it was Moore's turn. After Terry Macke tossed his block, Camellion took out the remote-control detonator, switched it on, and exploded the block of RDX he had covered with rocks.

More thunder from the west; yet the rain had slackened off to a mere sprinkle. The men couldn't have cared less; to a man they were soaked to the skin. But so were the Israelis.

The Death Merchant pulled an Alaskan Auto Mag from its belt holster, switched off the safety, pointed the stainless-steel weapon toward the sky, and pulled the trigger, the blast of the .44 mag cartridge sounding almost as loud as one of the V-40 grenades.

"Let's do it," the Death Merchant said. He shoved the Auto Mag into its holster and cocked his KG-9 machine pistol.

"This is for the birds," sighed Harlon Moore.

The attack was under way.

* * *

[1] "Cyclonite," one of the world's most powerful explosives. In fact, RDX is the most powerful of all military explosives.

In a very crooked line that stretched out for 278 feet, the Saudi Arabian commandos began to advance, each man his own protector, each man his own best friend. Dart ahead, weapon ready to fire. Race to the side of a boulder, pause, look around, wait a moment or two, then do it all over again—all the while smelling fresh rain mixed with burned RDX and burnt material from the still smoking Conqueror and RYB. There was also a pleasant smell, as if there might be a restaurant out in the middle of this Jordanian wilderness, a restaurant that specialized in roasted pork.

Every now and then, either Camellion or Captain Majid or one of the other men would toss a Mini grenade ahead, making sure the forward section was clear of the enemy. There were no shrieks of pain, an indication that the Israeli commandos still alive were in rapid retreat.

It was starling to discover that the closest enemy commandos had been only eighty feet to the west. In only ten minutes, the Death Merchant and Majid, Dillard and Moore and three commandos came across the first Israeli casualties—three corpses, twisted in positions of agony and extreme horror. Young men in their twenties: now fresh dead men, the desert-pattern fatigues of all three torn and bloody, ripped by fragments of exploded rock. One fresh cold cut lacked an arm; it had been pulled off at the shoulder, from which protruded twisted tendons and piece of shiny white scapula. Another corpse was missing a leg—ripped off at the knee.

The tops and sides of boulders were splattered with blood that seemed alive as the raindrops struck. The force of this particular RDX blast was evidenced by a 500-pound boulder than had been split in half. Apparently there had been a commando close to the boulder where the RDX block had detonated. There was a small crater—five feet in diameter and three feet deep in the center—to one side of the boulder and hundreds of bits of uniform and chunks of flesh blood-gore plastered to the sides of nearby rocks, all of it looking as if it had been "shot" into the rocks. Part of a head (minus the helmet)—the left side of the skull, no lower jaw—lay sideways on one sandstone rock, the single eye open and staring sideways.

The Death Merchant and his group, as well as the rest of the force, pushed on, coming across more battered and bloody corpses as they neared the south side of the wide mouth of the pass. All this time they could hear weapons firing to the south, the snarling of Uzis and Galils and of Colt-CAR SMGs, the rapid firing of the automatic weapons occasionally punctuated by shots from

9mm Berettas carried by the Saudis, or the heavier booms of Eagle .357 mag auto-pistols carried by the Israelis.[2]

Camellion and force knew they were closing in on the Israeli commandos when they heard gunfire from the center of the line—the chattering of several Uzis and the loud whine of 9mm projectiles popping from hard granite rocks. The Israeli rear guards were standing firm, doing their best to halt the advancing Saudis, their tactic geared to give the other Israelis a chance to reach the three armored personnel carriers. The snarling Uzis were instantly answered by three CAR-15 SMGs.

"It seems the 'Chosen People' are getting stiff-necked," sneered Kelly Dillard, who was crouched close to the edge of a large chunk of sandstone that was almost square. Holding his Bushmaster SMG, he carefully stuck out his head and instantly jerked it back, in time to avoid a blast of 7.62 X 51mm projectiles fired by an Israeli using a Galil assault rifle. If Dillard hadn't ducked, the dozen solid-point projectiles would have literally blown his head off, and part of his neck and left shoulder as well. As it was, the slugs stabbed into the edge of the rock, throwing off a cloud of dust and rock chips before zinging off into space.

"I'm going to cram rotten pork in that son of a bitch's mouth!" snarled Dillard in rage, wiping rock dust (turned to gray mud by the rain) from his face.

Khodr Kaddourch touched Dillard on the arm. "Sahib, how many fired at you and what is their position in respect to us?" he asked slyly, a V-40 Mini grenade in his right hand.

"Only one that I could see," Dillard said. "He's about forty feet directly ahead and ten feet to our left."

"Feet?" Kaddourch was puzzled.

"Thirteen meters ahead and three meters to my left."

Kaddourch nodded. "As soon as you hear the explosion, fire, sahib," he said. He mentally calculated the distance, pulled the pin from the Mini grenade, and tossed the little bomb. Five seconds later it roared into life—and so did several screams, a half an instant later.

[2]Produced by IMI, Israeli Military Industries, the Eagle is a large, semiauto, gas-operated single-action autoloader. Overall length is 10½ in.; height 5½; width 1¹⁄₁₆ in. Parkerized black finish, adjustable trigger-pull; all machine parts. Fires .357 mag shell only. Magnum Research—2825 Anthony Lane South, Minneapolis, MN 55418—is the sole U.S. distributor for the Eagle, which retails for $590.00 and will be available in the United States during the late summer of 1982.

Leaning around the edge of the rock, Dillard was in time to see an Israeli stagger to his feet, part of his fatigues hanging in shreds, his face blackened by smoke from the blast. Dillard's Bushmaster chattered briefly, the slugs ripping out the man's stomach and part of his spine. Dead, he fell as loose and lifeless as an egg yoke.

The Death Merchant and the Saudi commandos, whose morale had soared a hundred percent, quickly closed in on the Israelis, who now had only a slight numerical superiority, since they had lost twenty-three men in the Mini-grenade-RDX explosions. Another twelve Israelis had been wasted trying to slow the Saudi counterattack.

Their attack plan in total disarray, the Israelis, now under the command of *Samal* ("Sergeant") Gideon Alal Padon, rushed wildly toward the south side of the pass, their one ambition to get to the three Ratel armored personnel carriers parked by the side of the gorge. Once more the Israelis were in for a shock—and the Death Merchant and the other three Americans were in for a pleasant surprise.

Corporal Said Dajoni, Sergeant-Corporal Nitzan Gabush, and two other Saudi Father Holy War fighters had proved that even "sand crabs" could use logic. The four, at the north end of the line, had done so by making a preposterous dash to some of the basalt that had tumbled from the side of the north hill—half a dozen steamer-trunk-size rocks that were 350 feet northeast of the three Ratels.

Instantly, the four Saudis began sending streams of Colt CAR-15 projectiles at the forward group of Israelis trying to reach the APCs, the 5.56mm projectiles killing four Israelis in only two seconds. For good measure, the four Saudis raked the three troop-carriers with hydraulically swaged slugs, the metal rain falling all over the vehicles like hail.

Said Dajoni and the three other Saudis were in all their Islamic glory. Striking a blow against Allah's most hated enemy, they wanted nothing more than to get their hands around the throats of Israelis, their lust for blood already at the boiling point. Like African blacks, Arabs are prone to become utterly bloodthirsty and sadistic during battle and to revert to instincts far lower than those in so-called animals.[3] Controlled by such insanity, a

[3]With the exception of animals such as the leopard, the wolverine, the mink, the weasel, etc., the vast majority of animals kill only for food or for protection. Not Man. It is ironic that this silly creature, while having the egotism to proclaim that he is "made in the image of God," is the most murderous animal on this planet.

Arab, or a black, will commit any murderous act. No atrocity is too cruel.

Cut off from their only salvation, the APCs, the Israeli commandos were frantic. Yet all they could do was get down among the rocks at the south corner of the cut and bitterly regret the serious mistake that had been made. That mistake was the way the drivers had parked the three Ratels. Wanting speed and never for a moment dreaming that they would have to retreat, the drivers had *backed* the vehicles against the south wall, so that the *front* end of the APCs faced north. The entry hatch, other than the hatch over the driver's compartment, was on the right side of each vehicle, facing east. There wasn't any way on God's bloody earth that the Israelis could get inside the three personnel carriers—without geting ripped to pieces by slugs from the four elated Saudi commandos.

With savage cries of joy and of victory, and firing short bursts from their automatic weapons, the "Father Holy War" fighters closed in on the Israelis, moving in a large semicircle that very quickly closed at both ends. Within minutes, the two forces had intermingled, the men of both sides eyeball to eyeball, most of them unable to fire their automatic weapons because of the proximity of the rocks: the danger from ricochets was too great, too dangerous. Furthermore, in the confusion there was also the very real danger that one could hit a friend if he aimed at an enemy and missed.

With loud shouts of hate, with curses in both Hebrew and Arabic, the Saudis and the Israelis sought to send each other to their respective god in hand-to-hand combat—the most vicious kind of battle. The Israelis, with the gut feeling that they had lost, were determined to take as many of the Saudis with them into death as they could. The men of the *Abu Jihad Falaj'i* were determined to live and kill every Israeli in sight, although they, too, were more than willing to die. To die fighting the enemies of Allah meant instant paradise.[4]

The Death Merchant paused long enough behind a large boulder to divest himself of bulky grenade, explosives, and ammo bags. Dillard, Moore, Macke, Captain Majid, and several commandos did likewise.

Camellion made only one comment as he placed the shoulder

---

[4]The early Christians were equally as fanatical in their search for martyrdom. This too meant "instant salvation," instant Heaven. This is no surprise to anyone who has studied history. All religions have always advanced on the innocent blood of victims.

175

bags against the side of a rock, "I hope none of our guys lobs any RDX into the armored carriers. We're going to need them."

Macke was instantly alert. So were Moore, Captain Majid and two of the Saudis who understood English.

"Uh huh. Like why?" Dillard was immediately suspicious his eyes narrowing to slits. He reminded Camellion of a little boy at a carnival peep show—he doesn't understand it, but he has to look.

"I'll tell you later—if we're alive. If we're dead, it won' matter." Camellion smiled. "Let's go out and do it. Just preten the Israelis are American liberals or Washington politicians. The rest will be easy."

"I think you're right." Dillard grinned back. "They're the worst kind of lying trash."

Yeah, even worse than Rance Galloway and the "Creature-it Thing" he's married to!

An Auto Mag in each hand, the Death Merchant stepped from the side of the boulder, Terry Macke darting to his left and Dillard ahead of Macke. The other men charged into hell from the other side of the large sandstone rock.

Israeli commandos were as thick as ticks on a neglected hound dog. Two of the "Lord's Chosen" drew up short and started to swing their weapons toward Camellion, Nahman Schumacher armed with an Uzi SMG and Noah Hydermann using an Eagl mag auto-pistol. The two might as well have tried to shoot th wind.

"*For genunterhait!*" smirked Camellion in Hebrew,[5] raise both AMPs, and fired, the big booms a litany of pure death tha touched the two Israelis. A dynamite .44 slug stabbed Schu macher in the stomach, doubling him over and taking a foot c his intestine with it as it flew out of the hole in his back an ripped into the side of Uri Landri, who had just had his throat cu by one of the Saudi commandos. Blood spurted all over Ramahi Than'lli and his *bi'rang*,[6] who jumped back and, gripped b bloodlust, yelled, "*Al hamd u lillah!*" ("Praise be to Allah" Than'lli should have kept his body in motion and saved hi praise for later. He paid with his life for breaking the rule. A Israeli commando shot him in the left temple with an Eagle mag the .357 slug blowing Than'lli's skull into five parts.

---

[5] "Bon voyage." "Travel in good health."

[6] An Arabian knife. It has a brass inlaid handle and a thirteen-inc double-edged curved blade. If used properly, it can decapitate victim.

Noah Hydermann didn't fare any better than Schumacher. A .44 Alaskan projectile slammed him in the chest and knocked him all the way back against Shimon Nacher, who was doing his best to bury his eight-inch commando blade in a Saudi's stomach and doing a poor job of it.

Well, hell! The Alaskan Auto Mags—which were really big-game handguns—did have a drawback: they were not close-in combat weapons. The .44 cartridges were so powerful that they could drive bullets all the way through an enemy target and then take out a friend. Accordingly, Camellion dropped the big pistols into his cartridge belt holsters and reached for the twin M-81 BP MatchMasters resting in shoulder holsters. He never got the chance to pull the pistols.

A brawny arm snaked in from his right and went around his neck. Another Israeli—mean-eyed and two hundred pounds of hate—came at him from the right, a knife in his hand.

Playtime was over! The Death Merchant realized he had about two seconds of life left if the man behind him had a knife in his left hand and intended to tickle his kidney with it.

Incredibly fast, Camellion arched his back and executed a right rear foot stomp, the grooved heel of his Special Forces mountain boot smashing down like a pile driver on the right instep of Saul Drabbkin, who howled in agony as the bone snapped.

Almost all in the same motion, the Death Merchant, who had reached up to Drabbkin's arm with both hands, grabbed the commando's wrist, twisted the arm inward, carefully judged the distance between him and Ephraim Markek—the commando rushing at him from the right—and let fly a deadly right-legged *Tae Kwon Do Hyung Chungdan Ap Chagi* middle front snap kick that made the astonished Markek think that he had run into an invisible steel wall. Then he wasn't thinking anything, but was sliding down a long black vortex of unconsciousness. The Death Merchant's right foot had almost buried itself in Markek's celiac olexus,[7] tearing loose the diaphragm and giving the thoracic ganglia and the left portion of the liver a shock from which they—and Markek—would never recover.

Saul Drabbkin, in spite of the agony in his broken right foot, did his very best to use his commando dagger, intending to bury the blade around the third cervical vertebra in the back of Camellion's neck. Again, the Israeli commando was too slow.[8]

---

[7] The same as the solar plexus.

[8] A lot of speed is built around experience.

He gasped loudly and almost yelled when the Death Merchant twisted his right arm toward him, the inward motion making him automatically raise up on his good left foot and move back from the Death Merchant. During that split second, Camellion pulled Drabbkin's arm outward and dropped slightly, jerking his head from under the arm. Quickly then he stepped to his left, spun, jerked forcefully on Drabbkin's forearm, pulled the man off balance, and delivered a left-legged *Mawashi geri* roundhouse kick to the right side of the commando's head. Drabbkin was finished, demolished. The Death Merchant's savage kick had broken his lower jaw, knocked out seven teeth, and reptured his eardrum. Unconsciousness grabbed him and he sagged faster than a sand castle caught in a tidal wave.

Camellion didn't have time to be satisfied with his quick kill. He jumped back as an Israeli commando, who had ducked back to avoid the swish of a *bi'rang*, slipped on the slick, wet surface of a rock and fell backward—right into the Death Merchant's arms.

Instantly, Camellion had David Mapalm in a naked choke hold and neckbreak.[9] Camellion quickly whipped his left forearm across and under the desperate man's chin, jerking his arm in and up, exerting tremendous pressure against the larynx. At the same time, the Death Merchant drove his right forearm hard against the back of Mapalm's neck, keeping his right elbow a bit higher than his left forearm, this motion enabling his left hand—now that his left forearm had completed its encirclement of Mapalm's throat—to lock snugly in the crook of his right arm at the elbow.

The Israeli—he wasn't more than twenty-two years old—knew he was in a death lock, but he couldn't react fast enough. The Death Merchant, his arms locked like a vise around Mapalm's neck, leaned forward as he stepped back and snapped Mapalm's neck over his left forearm by applying pressure with his right arm and right hand on the back of the man's head.

Four more Israelis came at the Death Merchant—two from the front, one from behind, and one to his right. *My work is cut out for me!* ___

Swift and brutal death was the only rule, one that Kelly Dillard knew well. He had applied that rule all over the world. He used the last three rounds in his Bushmaster SMG to scatter an Israeli's skull all over space and time; then, with the commandos

[9]The same as a Commando neck-break hold.

coming at him, he tricked them by pretending to use the weapon as a club.

Predictably, Eliahu Lantz and Walter Ornstein grabbed Dillard by both wrists, pulled the empty Bushmaster from his hand, and started to stretch his arms while Herman Weiss, a third Israeli, prepared to open up his belly from north to south with a commando knife.

Dillard had a lot of surprises in store for the three young Israelis who, while strong and his junior by thirteen years, didn't have all his know-how and expertise. A 5th Dan in *Tang Soo Do*,[10] Dillard used a high battering ram right-legged snap kick that flattened Weiss's stomach almost to the thickness of a dozen postage stamps, the blow so violent and crushing that the inferior vena cava, the main blood vessel in the lower part of the body, was crushed. Shock soared up. Weiss went down, the world growing dim in his mind.

Lantz and Ornstein weren't all that safe! Surprised at the speed with which Kelly had taken out Weiss, the short but broad Dillard ducked a right sword-ridge hand tossed by Lantz, leaned slightly to his right, jerked up on his right arm, and, when the arm reached the vicinity of his mouth, leaned down farther and bit Lantz savagely on the hand. The Israeli yelled in pain and surprise and tried to grab Dillard's right arm with his left hand. Far too slow was he. Dillard jerked back on his right arm, spun to his left, dodged a three-finger *Nukite* stab attack by Ornstein, and lashed out with a right-legged round rear-kick aimed at Lantz, his foot connecting solidly with the man's groin. It was as simple as that. Consumed with shock and agony, Lantz began going down, the pain so intense he did not even have the strength to groan.

A now scared-stiff Ornstein, still hanging onto Dillard's left wrist with his left hand, attempted a right *Haishu* open backhand and a *Sokuto* edge-of-the-foot slam against Dillard, who sneered, "Fruitcake! You have raisin's for eyes. Time you bake 'em!" Kelly blocked the *Haishu* with his shoulder and wrecked the *Sokuto* with a knee block. Ornstein didn't have time for another attempt. As quick as half-slow lightning, Dillard used a piercing two-finger strike, the tips of his fingers stabbing into the eyes of

---

[10]*"The way of the knife hand,"* a Korean martial art very similar to *Tae Kwon Do*. It is based on the ancient Korean fighting arts of *t'ang su* and *subak*. Primarily kicking techniques—thirty basic kicks and variations that must be mastered before the student proceeds to hand techniques.

Ornstein, a fingernail slicing through the iris and lens of the commando's right eye and right on through the ciliary processes so that the egg white of the vitreous body would run. A high-pitched scream jumped from Ornstein's mouth and automatically, in reflex, he released his hold on the arm of Dillard, who polished him off with a left-handed stab to the throat and a right-handed chop to the left side of the neck. Ornstein had no choice but to start choking to death as Dillard let fly a right legged high spin kick—and missed! He missed because *Turai-Rishon* Amos Burg jumped back to avoid the deadly kick. But in jumping back, Lance Corporal Burg put himself in a position that left him wide open to Harlon Moore, who knew as much about *Tang Soo Do* as an African Bushman knows about differential, infinitesimal, and integral calculus. In contrast, Moore was an Einstein in *Bersilat*.[11] He jumped high and sideways, executing a perfect leg strangle, his legs going around the neck of the surprised Burg, who went crashing sideways to the ground as Moore went down, breaking his own fall with his left hand and left shoulder. The stunned Israeli never had a chance to formulate any kind of counterattack—not that there was any. His legs tight around Burg's neck, Moore reared up on his hip, taking half of Burg with him. He brought his legs back down, twisted his body slightly as he did so. Burg's left temple cracked loudly against a tiny pinnacle-shaped rock. He went limp, as dead as he could get.

RULE NUMBER TWO. In close combat, never deliberately let yourself get on the ground in a horizonal position. By so doing, you lose 80 percent of your defensive capacity. For ignorning this rule, Moore almost paid with his life. Adkim Bar-Jochims rushed in toward Moore, his empty Galil assault rifle raised, He would have smashed in the top of Moore's head if Terry Macke hadn't spotted the Israeli and—just in time—thrown a Furley custom-made dagger whose blade caught Bar-Jochims in the right rear side of the neck, the thin thirteen-inch blade going all the way through his throat, so that the bloody steel protruded from the left front side of the neck of the com-

---

[11]A Malayan martial arts technique. *Ber* means "to do." *Silat* means "fighting." Bersilat is derived from Indonesian *Pentjak-Silat*, which it resembles in many ways. Like *Pentjak-Silat*, *Bersilat* emphasizes open-hand and kicking techniques, as well as the use of certain weapons. However, the present emphasis of Bersilat is on pure sport. The dance ritual is called *pulat*. Secret combat techniques are known as *buah*.

mando, who began to jerk as though he had the worst case of shivers in his life—and to gurgle, a flood of blood bubbling from his half-open mouth.

Terry Macke didn't see Bar-Jochims fall. All at once he had his hands full with two other Israelis coming at him, one with a commando knife upraised, the other man holding a commando knife down and in a position for a sideways slash.

Ethan Vito Beraldi, the only Italian Jew with the Israeli commandos and the man holding his knife in position for a sideways slash, didn't get very far. What he did get was a *bi'rang* buried in his back, the Arabian knife thrown by Nitzan Gabush, who them went down and died and felt the breath of Death when Moshe Rovitz grabbed him around the throat and shoved a knife into the right side of his back. Rovitz next turned his attention to another Saudi commando being attacked by three other Israelis.

"Ussil mul'id ul um'ja h lillah!"[12] shouted Captain Falih Bin Majid, who had a *bi'rang* in his left hand and a 9mm Beretta auto-pistol in his right hand. He had only two rounds left in the Beretta and now he used them, pulling the trigger, the weapon roaring, although its crack was soon lost in the racket of screams and shouts of the other men. Two of the commandos attacked him, cried out, and threw up their arms when stuck by the 9mm hollow points. Moshiv Shuberinski, the third Israeli, who was the only man among the enemy who had worried all his life about his stuttering and who was rushing at Majid with a commando knife, screamed when he felt a sudden sting in his right wrist and saw his very own hand—his fingers still wrapped around the handle of the knife—go flying off into space. Shuberinski had thought he would stab Majid in the stomach. What he hadn't expected was the swiftness of the Saudi Father Holy War officer and his expert use of the *bi'rang*. Shuberinski had thrust his arm and hand inward for the stab he thought would end the life of Majid. Jumping back slightly, Majid had promptly brought down the heavy blade of the *bi'rang* and cut off Shuberinski's right hand. Only for a flashing second was the horrified Israeli able to witness the gush of blood pumping from his right wrist. He then felt the hidious pain—but again only for a moment—as Captain Majid slid the bloody blade of the *bi'rang* into his stomach and ripped upward. Never again would Shuberinski have to worry about his stuttering. H-H-He w-a-sss de-de-de-de-dead and si-si-si-si-sink-inggg into e-eter-nity.

Richard Camellion, however, was very much alive and having

[12]"May you die when touched by the holy breath of Allah."

181

the best exercise of the day. He aimed a *Yoko Geri* ball-of-the-foot spin kick at Sergeant Gideon Alal Padon, the closest Israeli rushing him from the front. Missed! Seeing the foot and leg coming, Padon jumped back very quickly.

The Death Merchant, now engaged in the unexpected, leaped back, spun to his right, and used an expertly delivered *Yoko geri kekomi* side-thrust kick that landed precisely where he wanted it to go, in the center of the chest of Lev Gochen, who had been approaching from the rear. A loud wail came from Gochen and he fell back, shaking from the pain of his broken sternum.

As quick as he was, Camellion, however, wasn't fast enough to avoid Simon Luvirol, the commando to his right—and Padon and Josef Gann, the two Israelis who had started to rush him from the front, were coming in very fast, Gann's right hand snuggled into a pair of brass knuckles with spikes.

Luvirol, who also knew karate, tried a left handed *Seiken* forefist aimed for Camellion's throat and a right-handed *Seiryu toh* palm edge hand targeted for the left side of Camellion's throat. The Death Merchant blocked both with a *Gyaku shuto* reverse chop and a *Shuto uke* block. Very quickly then, he grabbed Luvirol's right wrist with his left hand, executed a *Fumikomi* front snap kick on Luvirol's right instep, and, simultaneously, jerked on the commando's right arm, pulling the man roughtly toward him. Luvirol's defense fell apart. The Death Merchant quickly let him have a terrific *Hiji* elbow strike in the throat, his elbow making apple butter out of Luvirol's Adam's apple.

An expert, in thanatology, Camellion was no longer concerned about the gasping, gagging, choking Luvirol as he spun and concurrently used a double-handed *Gedan barai* to stop the leg of Gideon Alal Padon, who was trying to ace him out with a *Mawashi geri* roundhouse kick, and let fly a *Mae geri kekomi* that caught Josef Gann (who was also a secret Mossad agent) in the solar plexus, the vicious slam paralyzing Gann's central nervous system and almost making his eyes pop out of his head.

Padon was not as easy to terminate. Camellion barely managed to block a right *Shuto* knife hand aimed at his left temple and a *Yon bon nukite* four-finger spear thrust directed at his lower chest. He countered with a *Tsuma-saki* tip-of-toes kick, aimed at the testicles, combined with a right *Herabasami* inside-ridge-hand feint that was coupled with a left *Yubi basami* knuckle-fingertip strike that wanted the center of Padon's throat. Padon wasn't fooled. He made Camellion fail by using a *Sukui uke* scooping block. He then twisted and tried a right *Ushiro kekomi geri* rear thrust kick. Fatal mistake! Camellion stepped aside, snarled, *"Geharget zolstu veren!"* [13] grabbed Padon's right ankle, and twisted as hard as he could to the left, Padon yelling in pain and anger as Camellion flipped him over and he fell heavily on his stomach, the fall knocking the wind out of him. He didn't have the time or the strength to jerk away. And he was in agony from his twisted leg, the pain shooting through his hip.

The Death Merchant released the leg, kicked Padon savagely in the left side of the rib cage, the slam breaking four ribs and bringing another howl of pain from the Israeli commando.

Victory! Camellion jumped high and came down on Padon's back, the heel of his left foot smashing into the Israeli's neck, his right foot slamming into the small of the back. There was a sound like two sticks being snapped. Padon shuddered and lay still.

Camellion jumped again—all over—when he heard the loud roaring of a Colt CAR-15 submachine gun. Stepping off the corpse of Padon, he turned and—*I'll be double damned!*

Sixty feet away, to the south, stood Colonel Auda bin Bahadu and five commandos. Smoke was still curling from the muzzle of the SMG that Bahadu was holding. He had just blown up an Israeli who had stabbed Khodr Kaddourch in the right side of the neck. Both the Israeli and Kaddourch went down in a wide spray of blood.

Another CAR-15 roared angrily to the northeast. In desperation, three Israeli commandos had tried to reach the first Ratel armored personnel carrier in line. Said Dajoni had gleefully cut them down with CAR-15 5.56mm projectiles.

Nitzan Gabush and two other Saudis had left the rocks to join in the battle. Dajoni had remained behind, convinced that some of the Israelis would try to reach the armored vehicles. He had been right.

Now, for the glory of Allah, he would make certain that the three APCs would never leave this spot in the dreary Jabal Arqā. Shoving a full magazine into the hot CAR-15, he jumped up from behind the rack and began running in a zigzag toward the Israeli vehicles.

Feeling tired but elated, the Death Merchant looked around the area. Death lay heavily over the ancient, rain-wet rocks. The rain had stopped entirely. Over it all was a hideousness beyond all articulate description, a feeling compounded of the wild ecstasy

[13]"Drop dead." Literally—"You should be killed."

of nightmare and the summation of the fiendish combined with the demonic and the apocalyptic.

We've won—at least in the north pass. So far . . .

Silence, a strange on-edge quietness broken only by the sinister sigh of the constant wind, the mute, insane laughter of the Cosmic Lord of Death, and the various sounds made by the Saudi commandos reloading their weapons and searching the bodies of the Israelis. There was more.

Camellion's eyes grew hard. Fifty feet to his right, Ophin Yassin, one of the *Abu Jihad Falaj'i,* was lopping off the head of the still conscious but helpless Josef Gann. Yassin's *bi'rang* flashed, and there was a sound like a watermelon being cut in two. Another Saudi commando was cutting the throat of Lev Gochen. All through the boulders the Saudis were going about their grim work, killing any Israeli with life in him.

Camellion saw with satisfaction that the three other Americans were alive. Terry Macke, the front of his fatigues soaked with blood, was lighting a cigarette with a trembling hand. Harlon Moore, sitting on a rock, was wiping his face. He glanced up at Kelly Dillard, who, stepping over corpses, walked over to the Death Merchant, who was pulling out his walkie-talkie.

Starting to reload one of his ASP .44 Special revolvers, Dillard said harshly, "I never thought I'd spend the day before Christmas like this—in Jordan." He laughed, amusement in his eyes. "Are we going to look for the big star in the east?"

"We're not going to sing 'Silent Night' either," Camellion said.

A loud explosion from just inside the pass, from the south side, prevented him from turning on the Repco RPX.

One of the armored personnel carriers had exploded!

CHAPTER FOURTEEN

You can't have egg in your beer every day of the week. In fact, there will be days when you can't even have the beer. The Death Merchant had not had time to contact Sergeant Major Mullah Amin Rameh and, through Captain Majid, order him not to destroy the two Ratel APCs in the south pass, nor time to give the same order to the Saudis at the north gorge.

As Nitzan Gabush blew up the three Ratels to the north—by running by them and tossing RDX blocks, triggered by V-40 Mini grenades, through their firing ports—Amin Rameh and his men began blowing up the two Ratels to the south.

Very quickly the air shuddered with explosions.

"Look at it this way, Camellion. It proves we've won," Kelly Dillard said jovially. "Anyhow, why were the APCs so important?" His eyes raked Colonel Bahadu, Mullah Rashid l'Halsa, and the four other Saudi commandos who, by then, had reached him and the Death Merchant.

Colonel Auda bin Bahadu was ecstatic. "Gentlemen, we have the scrolls," he said happily. "Everything went as planned and we didn't have any difficulty whatsoever."

Camellion didn't show the elation he felt. "You're sure? You're positive they are the Judas Scrolls?"

"Of course," Bahadu said evenly. "Your two experts from the CIA, Norton and Gatdula, are confident that what we uncovered in the cave is the prize."

Dillard asked, "Where are they and the others now—and the scrolls?"

"Waiting by the helicopters," Bahadu said. "We came for the scrolls. We have them; and we've won a great victory over a crack Israeli unit. What else is left but to go home? I see you've been busy down here. Tch, tch, tch. The men we've lost. Most regrettable. The price of victory, and it's victory that matters."

Fool! Death is always the only victory!

Bahadu's attention turned to Dillard. "What were you saying

about the Ratel troop carriers?'' His eyes swung back to the Death Merchant. "To save the APCs was your idea? Why?''

Backbone of a jellyfish!

Without even looking at Bahadu, Camellion sat down and adjusted the gun belt around his waist; the Alaskans were heavy.

"I was going to use three of the Ratels to attack the Israeli Galaxies," Camellion said, as if speaking were an effort. He suddenly was alive with a new vitality, jabbing a forefinger at a perplexed Colonel Auda bin Bahadu. "Don't rattle and roar what a dumb plan it might be! I don't like leaving an enemy intact in the field. One of the commanders of the columns could have made a radio report. But it's not likely that one of them had time to radio back and say 'We're getting our butts beaten.' We could have faked it. We could have gone back in those cars and blown the hell out of those planes before the Israelis realized how they'd been suckered.''

Colone Bahadu drew himself erect. "Attack the Galaxies?'' He couldn't keep the awe out of his voice. "I admit that you are very clever, Sahib Camellion. But—why attack the Israelis' aircraft? We have what we came for. Let us not stretch the mercy of Allah and demand that He perform miracles. We should return at once to my country.'' His voice lowered and became hard, his tone sharp. "In your American English, let's not play at being heroes!''

"Camellion, he's right," said Terry Macke, who, with Harlon Moore, had walked up to the group. In the distance, Captain Majid, his right arm bloody, was telling the commandos to regroup. "We have the scrolls. Let's get out while we can.''

"We don't know when the Jordanians will put in an appearance," Kelly Dillard said quietly.

At the moment, the Death Merchant would like to have killed all of them because they were interfering with what he would like to do. *But you can't destroy the Galaxies. The armored personnel carriers are destroyed. We can't pretend to be Israeli and fake a retreat.* He caught up within himself, within his own mental processes, and realized he was listening to the impulse of violence, not to the rationality of common sense.

He stood up, adjusted his gun belt and the bottom of his fatigues over his Special Forces mountain boots. "You're right colonel. We have the scrolls. Let's get to the choppers and lift off. I'll contact Mullah Amin—''

"I'll contact him," Colonel Bahadu cut in quickly. "He i under my command.''

"Be my guest," Camellion said smugly, his hand movin

from the Repco RPX on his belt. His eyes caught Dillard's, and he knew that Kelly was thinking the same thing: that Bahadu was only too anxious to be a commander when there was smooth sailing, but more than willing to relinquish his command when the seas were rough.

The news from Mullah Amin Rameh was both good and bad. The good was that there wasn't a single Israeli commando alive. The bad was that only Rameh and five other Saudis were alive.

Through the black smoke, which the wind was whipping around from the burning Ratel APCs, the commandos moved toward the four Boeing-Vertols and the three Sikorsky gunships. It was ironic that two of the Boeings would be flown back empty to Saudi Arabia. Three-fourths of the members of the Abu Jihad Falaj'i had been killed and two of the troop-carrying choppers would easily carry the survivors.

The men had regrouped but had not boarded the helicopters. There was one more thing to do before lift-off—at the insistence of the Death Merchant. To scout the Israelis and to make sure the skies were free of the Jordanians. Accordingly, Camellion and Colonel Bahadu sent three men to the top of one hill to the west to monitor the "Big Ear" and to see what the Israelis were doing.

"We can't be too cautious," the Death Merchant said. He stood in front of one of the big Boeing-Vertols, his eyes on another wrecked troop carrier than had been destroyed. In one hand he held his Repco RPX, its Channel 14 open. "Should we be caught flat-footed, they'd blow us all over the sky. The last thing we'll do is take down the six Brownings from their Tadlums and dismantle the Bronco launchers."

"You are correct," Colonel Bahadu conceded politely. "However, I am convinced that we don't have to concern ourselves with the Jordanians. I don't think they want any part of the Israelis—or us."

His eyes on Father Norton and Father Gatdula, the Death Merchant did not reply. He felt sorry for the two Jesuits, both of whom appeared tired and worried.

"You could be very wrong, colonel," warned Terry Macke. "The Jordies are fiercely nationalistic. This is their land, their soil. Our being on their soil might make a lot of difference."

A half a minute later, the "Big Ear" proved that Colonel Bahadu and Harlon Moore, who was also convinced that the Jordanians would keep their heads in the sands, were wrong.

The anxious voice of Wayne Gasty, one of the American

pilots, came from the Repco RPX in the Death Merchant's hand. "Aircraft coming in fast from the northeast. An entire fleet from the sound of it."

Like Samson taking charge in the Temple of Dagan, Camellion barked into the transceiver, "Get the hell out of there—fast. Leave the ear." His eyes glowing with fury, Camellion swung to Colonel Bahadu and Captain Majid, whose faces mirrored fear and indecision.

Dillard ground his cigarette underneath his right heel. "Well, that tears it!" he growled. "If this keeps up, we're still going to have to fly kites home."

"Get the men away from the choppers and to the rocks in the foothills," Camellion snapped to Bahadu and Majid, "and tell the men on the Brownings and the Bronco system to get set."

He looked over at another Boeing-Vertol, to the port side of which stood the two Jesuits, a group of Saudis, and Robert Follmer and Wesley Ritter. At the feet of Ritter and Follmer was an aluminum chest the size of a footlocker. Inside the bulletproof chest were the precious Judas Scrolls.

"Jordie planes are on the way," Camellion yelled. "All of you get those scrolls to the rocks and stay down."

Without any hesitation, Ritter and Follmer picked up the chest and, with the Saudis and the two Jesuits, began to run toward the rocks to the west. Half a dozen Saudi commandos still had Stinger and Tiger missiles, and Captain Majid deployed these men in the rocks to the east, telling them to scatter out in a 150-foot-long line. The six commandos were reaching the granite boulders and Camellion, Harlon Moore, and another group of men were coming to a line of rocks to the east when the sound of the Jordanian planes became very clear—helicopters.

Everywhere men were running for rocks and looking nervously at the gray sky that was now loud with the flup-flup-flup-flup of helicopter rotor blades.

The Death Merchant crawled between two large sandstone boulders, then got on his hands and knees and moved underneath a large "lip" of granite already protecting Moore, the two Jesuits, and Mullah Amin Rameh.

The Repco RPX on the Death Merchant's belt buzzed. The caller was Wayne Gasty. "Camellion, I thought you'd want to—"

"Get off that hill, you idiot!" Camellion roared. "The Jordi planes will machine-gun and rocket the hills. The smoke coming from the destroyed Ratels will guide them in. If the Bronco

Rattlers don't get them, we'll be thumbing all the way back to Arabia.''

"I thought you'd want to know that the Galaxy transports are getting ready to take off," Gasty said. "And don't worry about me. I'll be off by the time the Jordie planes get here. Frank's watching through binocs. Looks like ten to twelve MI-24s.[1] OK. We have to get going. They're less than five miles away. Luck, you guys.''

The Soviet Hind As (named for Mihail Mil, the Soviet aircraft designer) may have been piloted by Jordanian pilots, but those pilots seemed to know what they were doing. American or Israeli pilots could not have done better. Five of the Hinds veered off to attack the four Boeing-Vertols and the three Sikorsky gunships, the latter three of which Colonel Auda bin Bahadu had ordered to defend the area. ("The only intelligent order he's given so far," Kelly Dillard had remarked.)

The five other Jordanian gunships went to the southwest to attack the three Israeli Galaxy transport aircraft.

With two TV2-117A free-turbine turboshaft engines, the Hind A was a formidable opponent. Besides two 12.7mm guns aimed and fired from the nose, there was also a 120mm electric cannon in a pod under the nose, plus a stubby wing on both port and starboard. Each wing had rails for four wire-guided antitank missiles, as well as for four other stores. In this case the four wire-guided missiles were West German Hellfires. The other four were American Maverick AGM 65 self-homing TV, laser-guided tactical air-to-surface missiles.

From a range of 4.6 miles, five of the Hinds released their long-range Mavericks, which whooshed from the Soviet-built choppers and streaked toward the Israeli Galaxy transports. The Mavericks were a third of the way to the Israeli planes by the time a very worried General Aharon Sharon ordered the XBX Saber missiles fired from the top bay of two of the transports.

It was a formula for mutual annihilation.

One Galaxy had risen to the extent that the pilot was taking in the landing gear. The other two giant airplanes were still gathering speed for the takeoff. The three big planes couldn't have chosen a worse time to take off.

Watching from a rear window in one of the Galaxies still on the ground, Major Abraham Siem screamed in horror, "The enemy missiles are coming straight at us! We—''

[1] Soviet MIL-24 versions with the NATO names of Hind A and Hind B.

It was the last words he ever uttered. Ten Mavericks hit the three Galaxy transports and a combined charge of 2,900 pounds of high explosives detonated. There was a tremendous crash of noise and fireballs exploded all over the three Lockheed C-5A Galaxy cargo ships, intense red and orange fire that seemed to have a special life all its own. When the smoke and fire halfway cleared, the Galaxies no longer existed. There was only a skyful of parts and pieces trailing fire, either scattered on the ground or dripping from the low sky.

BLAAAAMMMMMMMMMMMMMMMMMMMMMM! One tremendous explosion and five bright balls of flame, and the five Hinds became blazing wreckage that instantly headed earthward—none of which did the Death Merchant and his whittled-down force any good. The five other Hinds few southwest, banked, turned, and came back straight north, starting to make the sweep down the long, narrow plain. The three SH-3 gunships roared south to meet the Jordanian choppers.

The Jordanian pilots now made a mistake as far as killing the four Boeing-Vertols on the ground. Three of the Hinds occupied themselves with the three attacking Sikorskys. The two other Hinds began the run, their pilots feeling it would be a simple matter to destroy the enemy helicopters on the ground.

The SH-3 farthest to the east began hosing the air with its GAU-8 Avenger seven-barreled electric 30mm cannon at the same time it shot off four of its 2.75-inch HE rockets at one of the Hinds. The pilots of the three Hinds, attacking the Sikorskys, intended to make short work of the three Saudi Arabian gunships. Each Hind fired two Hellfire missiles each, the Jordanian confident that within seconds all three SH-3s would be blazing wreckage.

Almost in the same second, the three Sikorskys fired four 2.75-inch HE rockets each.

Faster than the HE missiles, the laser-guided Hellfires caught two of the Sikorskys, exploded with thunderous roars, and blew the Saudi gunships all over the sky, much of the burning wreckage narrowly missing the two other Hinds as they screamed down to attack the plain. One Hind raked the chain of hilltops with its 20mm electric cannon in the nose pod, almost 3,000 rounds per minute pouring from the muzzles of the seven barrels, small rocks exploding as the hurricane of steel projectiles chopped into the summits.

WHOOOSHHHHHH-WHOOOOSSSHHHHHH. The second Hind went to work on the large Boeing-Vertol choppers, firing off two deadly Maverick missiles. On target! There were two crashing explosions, brief flashes of fire, and the two Boeing-Vertols ceased to exist. for practical purposes, so did a third Boeing-Vertol. A three-bladed rotor from one destroyed bird sailed through the air and came down hard on one of the blades of the tail rotor of another Boeing-Vertol, the impact blending the blade so that its end tip was only a few feet from the ground.

There were other casualties. Some of the wreckage from one exploded chopper flew west and came down heavily in the middle of some boulders in which the two Jesuits, Wesley Ritter, Robert Follmer, and four Saudis had sought refuge underneath a kind of ledge. With the men were the precious scrolls. There was a loud crash, the wreckage rolling off the slanted edge, some of it crashing down on the exposed right leg of Father Norton. Norton screamed in agony, the pain shooting into his right hip and coursing throughout his body, making him wonder if this was how Christ had suffered on the cross. Quickly the other men began to tug and pull at the hot, smoking metal that had been a part of a GE T58 turboshaft engine.

"His leg's smashed to a pulp," Wes Ritter said in a low voice.

"Hurry up, all of you," said Bob Follmer, slipping on a pair of gloves. "We must work fast or he'll bleed to death."

The third Sikorsky—now the only Saudi gunship—was not struck by any of the Hellfires fired by the Hinds. It wasn't because of a million-in-one freak accident. Some of the hundreds of projectiles from its GAU-8 cannon struck three Hellfire missiles and exploded them, the tremendous concussion rocking not only the Sikorsky but also the three Jordanian Hinds, whose pilots were revving up to escape the HE rockets fired by the three Sikorskys, two of which had been destroyed. The Hinds could have escaped the HEAT rockets fired by the two SH-3s to the north—and did. They couldn't escape both the missiles from the two destroyed SH-3s and the HE rockets from the Sikorsky whose cannon was still firing. One Hind almost did, the pilot working the collective and throttle desperately, doing his best to lt the rotor. He failed. An HE missile struck the tail rotor and xploded at the same time another HE rocket slammed into the ort side of another Hind and turned the chopper and its three-an crew into memories.

The third Hind B tried to shoot off more Hellfires but failed. he finger of the frantic gunner was only an inch from the button hen scores of 30mm projectiles from the Sikorsky's GAU-8 nopped into the cockpit section. The instrument panel exploded.

Pilot, copilot, and gunner died with their flying clothes bloody and pieces of their helmets and skulls scattered all over the wrecked control section. More 30mm projectiles had ripped into the engines. The Hind exploded, the burning debris showering over the sky like ten thousand meteors.

The Hind that had swept the hilltops with cannon fire was pulling up, the pilot preparing to roar to the north for the swing-around. He was manipulating the cyclic controls to correct the dissymmetry of lift when the Saudis with the four Stinger and the two Tiger missiles fired their shoulder tubes and the three commandos at the Bronco launchers fired a dozen surface-to-air Rattler missiles.

Incredibly, every single missile missed the Hind. Five came close, zipped on by, and kept right on going toward the ugly mountains to the north. Two then struck the Das'ayid'a Shaitan, the Tongue of the Devil, causing the tall, sinister-looking pinnacle to shake and quiver.

It was the last remaining Sikorsky that brought down the Hind. The gunner shot off three HE rockets, two of which caught the Soviet-manufactured helicopter as its pilot was beginning to make the run, the three HEs also exploding the two Mavericks just leaving the runners on the stubby wings.

The last Boeing-Vertol had been saved by only a hundredth of a second!

The other Hind "died" quickly. The pilot was banking to the east and, in his anxiety, had increased speed to 214 mph, this high speed affecting the lifting and the propelling characteristics of the rotor, a phenomenon termed "blade stall." He was correcting the condition when the Saudis at the Bronco launchers fired off their last ten Rattlers. Nine struck the Hind as the pilot was righting the big bird and letting out pitch to come down for the run.

BLAMMMMMMMM! Fire! Smoke! Pure destruction and thousands of pieces of debris raining down on the wet, death-soaked ground.

Even the Death Merchant, after crawling out of the shelter of boulders with the other men, found the sight fantastic, yet fascinating. The plain was littered with burning wreckage, as someone had gone to the trouble to light hundreds of small fires. A strange wind had begun blowing, an eerie movement of air that brought with it an uncanny suggestion of faint devil pipes playing an evil and hellish tune.

The small force moved quickly, for now each man knew he

life was ticking on time that was less than borrowed. The plain had become Corpse City, blasphemous with all that was unholy and loathsome. The grim sky, the silent mountains, even the smoky air exuded hate, an intense vindictiveness that was keenly felt by Camellion as he told Colonel bin Bahadu and Captain Falih Bin Majid the facts of survival.

"B-But all of us can't get back in the single Boeing!" cried Colonel Bahadu, making an effort to control himself. "We'll be able to lift off—that's true. Yet the craft will still be overloaded. Should we meet any Jordanian aircraft! . . ."

"We're dead if we stay here." Camellion's sharp voice revealed his contempt. "Tell all your men to get rid of their weapons. Anything that's heavy—grenades, everything."

"But do you think—" began Captain Majid.

"Shut up and listen! Tell your fly-boys to take the T66 heavy machine guns off their port and starboard mounts and to throw out all the ammo belts." He disregarded the curious negative shaking of Colonel Bahadu's head. "Move if you want to live—and move fast."

The Saudi officers hesitated only for a moment; then they turned, moved off, and began shouting orders at the remnants of the *Abu Jihad Falaj'i* while the Death Merchant turned to Kelly Dillard, who had raced over to him.

"How is Norton?" demanded Camellion. He dropped his shoulder bags filled with spare ammo and grenades. He left the .44 AMPS and the M-81 Matchmasters in their holsters. If he died, he didn't intend to go "naked."

"The hypo that Macke gave him put him out," Dillard said absently, wiping his smoke-darkened face. "He's in a bad way. His leg is mashed to jelly. It will have to come off, provided he doesn't croak from shock before we get back, if we get back." He shoved the handkerchief into one of the breast pockets of his fatigues and stared flinty-eyed at Camellion, who was surveying the area. "I have a question. What do we do if Father Gatdula tries to give him the Last Rites? The sand crabs won't take kindly if they find out we've smuggled two Catholic priests—Jesuits at that!—into their precious midst."

The Death Merchant saw that Saudis were tossing out the T66 machine guns and other equipment from the Boeing-Vertol, whose pilot had started the turboshafts. To Camellion and Dillard's left, Terry Macke, Harlon Moore, and Father Victorio Gatdula were carrying the unconscious Father Norton to the chopper."

"There isn't anything we can do about Gatdula," Camellion
193

said doggedly. "If you get the chance, whisper to Gatdula to keep his prayers to himself, or you'll blow his head off."

"Keeping him quiet may not be all that easy," Dillard said. "Gatdula has more religion than sense." He sensed, from the expression on Camellion's face, that something was wrong. "What's the trouble?"

"I see all our people except Wayne Gasty," Camellion said.

"He bought it before he could get off the hill." Dillard stepped closer to Camellion and lowered his voice. "In case the sand crabs give us trouble—in case there isn't room for all of us in the bird or it won't lift off properly—what do you have in mind?"

A slow grin spread over the Death Merchant's face. "In that case we'll pretend that we support the arts and that all the Saudis are musical. We'll kiss 'em—with slugs, then toss them out. Let's go."

The two men started for the helicopter. . . .

CHAPTER FIFTEEN

Three days after Christmas.
The CIA station in the United States Embassy in Ar-Riyad, Saudi Arabia. 1522 hours.

The Death Merchant removed his macaw pink sportcoat, draped it over the back of a chair, sat down at the table, and began deciphering the message, pleased that Courtland Grojean had been tearing out his hair in rage for the past four days and had finally sent a terse message over the radio—*Have Camellion report at all costs.*

The message from Grojean was triple coded, a combination of the Vigenère, Gronsfeld, and polyalphabetical substitution methods. Decryption would not be difficult, only time consuming.

Working with paper, ballpoint pen, and a cipher wheel, Camellion thought of how the chest of Judas Scrolls was now on its way to the United States and of the eerie tale that Father Bernard Norton had told him, six hours before the Jesuit priest had died. Realizing that he was about to "stand before my God," Norton felt that he could no longer keep the secret that had tortured him for nine years.

"The Vatican has known the true story for almost eighteen hundred years," the dying priest had confessed to the Death Merchant, Kelly Dillard, and J. Norris Smedley, the latter of whom was the Chief of Station of the Ar-Riyad station.

Judah-bar-Simon, the man that history knew as Judas Iscariot, was not the arch-traitor the world thought he was.

Judas was just the world's biggest patsy!

However, Judas did believe in the divinity of Jesus Christ and hoped desperately that Christ, after he was arrested, would save himself by performing a miracle. What better way to prove he was the Messiah?

John, the actual brother of Christ, was in agreement with Judas. Working secretly against the rest of the Apostles, Judas and John hoped to make a deal with the Jewish Sanhedrin.

Judas did have powerful connections. Not only was he the son of a wealthy Pharisee Jewish family, but he was also the son of Leah-bas-Ezekial, who was the daughter of Ezekiel-bar-Jacob, whose uncle was a member of the Sanhedrin, the Jewish Supreme Court in Jerusalem.

Judas and John made their plans. Judas then went to the Sanhedrin and offered to betray Jesus if the Sanhedrin would spare the life of the Master.

The members of the Sanhedrin agreed, and although Judas felt they would double-cross him and John, they did keep their word. The Sanhedrin only wanted to humiliate Christ. They didn't want to crucify him and make him a martyr to his cause. Already there were too many "risen gods," and the Sanhedrin didn't want another phony resurrection.

A phony resurrection is exactly what they got! Camellion mused the Death Merchant. *How stupid the Sanhedrin must have felt!*

What happened is that Pontius Pilate, the Roman governor of Judea, hated all Jews. He considered it a vast joke to enter into an agreement with the Sanhedrin and then double-cross them at the last moment.

Pilate sentenced Christ to Death.

Christ was crucified.

The Death Merchant decoded the words: *The situation in the United States is extremely grave. It—*

What Pilate and the Sanhedrin didn't know was that Christ was a master Yogi—learned in India during the so called lost years.

Jesus Christ was crucified but used Yoga to turn off the pain, to lower his heart rate, respiration, and other body functions.

It was Crito, the Syrian mercenary with the Romans, who ruined what could have been a perfect "resurrection."

Crito stabbed Christ in the side with a lance and almost killed him!

Christ was not dead when taken down from the cross and "buried." He was never buried, but almost died from the lance wound in his side. He lived—hidden in the house of Joseph of Arimathea.

Knowing a good thing when they saw it, the followers of Christ faked the "resurrection." All the rest of the myth was added by writers over the centuries, each one feeling free to tell all sorts of lies—". . . for the Glory of God. . . ."

Christ, half mad from his experience, was smuggled to Jordan, where he died at the age of fifty-one.

Judas did not hang himself. With the help of the embarrassed Sanhedrin, a suicide was faked, the corpse, a recently deceased begger. Bitter and alienated, Judas secretly traveled to Jordan, where he lived for several years, leaving when he learned that Christ was in the same area. Judas went to Syria and died there at the age of sixty-four.

The real truth was the most carefully guarded secret of the Vatican, confessed Father Norton. There was even a centuries' old society dedicated to keeping the truth from the world—the Society of the Golden Rose. Any Cardinal of the Church, upon being elected Pope, was immediately told the secret and automatically became the head of the society.

It was the Society of the Golden Rose that, in A.D., 1148 had the Shroud of Turin faked, with a now lost process known as "reverse painting."

On leaving Father Norton's hospital room, Kelly Dillard had remarked sardonically, "I wonder what religious know-it-alls would think if they knew the truth?—not that the Company will ever believe it?"

"They wouldn't believe it," Camellion said simply. "Belief in a god never requires logic, only superstition and a desperateness against the obvious, against oblivion. That kind of madness is called 'faith.' The company could print the truth in banner headlines in every newspaper in the world. The 'faithful' would call it lies, or commie propaganda."

"Or the work of the Devil," added J. N. Smedley laconically. "Old Satan gets more blame than we do."

The Death Merchant paused in his work of decoding. The situation is grave? Well, there were a lot of situations that could be regarded as desperate in the United States. The economy for one.

Most Americans had never heard of Culpepper, Virginia, much less of the federal facility built into the side of a mountain close by. This facility was ERF—the Emergency Relocation Facility, whose main purpose was to allow the Federal Reserve to carry on its functions in the event of nuclear war. How many Americans knew that, in addition to communications network and records storage, Uncle Sam had printed replacement U.S. currency in the supersecret plant?

The $5 bills are blue; $10s are brown; $20s are red.

There were no $1s.

There were other projects afoot in the secret facility, such as the development of a high-speed money counter, one capable of sorting and counting 72,000 bills per minute. At the present time, the entire Federal Reserve System had only 7 machines, which sort and count at the rate of 55,000 per minute. By mid-1983 there would be 110 new machines, an increase of 2,200 percent.

What a joke on the American people! Within a year and a half to two years, the Fed will have the capability to physically replace the entire U.S. currency in circulation in just four days' time.

The Death Merchant brought to mind other bits of evidence that indicated that a vast change was under way in the continental United States. Bank employees in many of the larger banks were already reporting a change in the manner in which new currency was being delivered from the Feds. In the past, new money arrived in sealed, transparent cases, this permitting the stacks of bills to be counted from the outside, without breaking the seal. Recently that changed. The new money cases were opaque and were being stored uncounted. . . .

Camellion did some hard thinking. Although Reagan was the only President in decades to make a real effort to curb fiscal irresponsibility—*The United States may have to reap the karmic effects of past economic sins.*

Or could the grave situation be racial?

The United States was being flooded by an alien invasion from Southeast Asia, India, Burma, Pakistan, Hong Kong, Maylasia, Israel, Puerto Rico, Cuba, and Mexico. U.S. Education Commissioner Ernest Boyer had revealed during the winter of 1982 that only 28 percent of Americans eighteen and younger are Anglo, while 36 percent are black and 41 percent Hispanic. Only 39 percent of Anglo families have children in school, against 61 percent of Hispanic families who have children in public schools. It was only a matter of time before white Americans would be a minority in what was their land. Already the nation's schools were becoming obsolete and the United States was becoming a nation of undereducated citizens. Another fact was clear: if the taxable incomes of the rapidly increasing minority groups did not keep pace with their growth in numbers, the whites would either be taxed to death or the entire system would collapse—*The latter is more likely because the white people are not going to take it. There's a lot of truth in what Bob Follmer says. One can look at the problem in terms of a diminishing upper and middle class having to support a lower class of ignorant, lazy trash. Right now there are more El Salvadorians as illegal aliens in Los Angeles than the total population of San Salvador! But the trash*

198

have a technique—*any person who gives the facts is called a racist. Well, there are a lot of good Mexicans and other Latins—all dead.*

To complicate the overall situation was the hostile attitude of the Mexican government to U.S. policy in Central America. It was already too late for Central America—*The Communists have won in the banana republics.*

Yet Mexico is the ultimate target of Soviet-Cuban encouraged and supported insurgency—*Referred to by Moscow theoreticians as "naturally evolving liberation movements."*

A "People's Democratic Republic of Mexico" would not be to the benefit of the United States, especially since much of the southwestern United States is made up of territory that was originally either Mexican or claimed by Mexico.

The Death Merchant realized that the concept of a Moscow-Cuban-Mexico connection was not popular with either politicians—who would always ignore the danger of communism in preference for votes—liberals—who were too stupid to have a grasp on any situation—and priests, to whom more babies meant more souls and more cash for Mother Church.

All three types of idiots can "pray" when the bombs begin falling!

Who would have thought, twenty years ago, that the Castro victory in Cuba would have such widespread international repercussions? The Bay of Pigs was a humiliating fiasco, while the missiles of Cuba taught Moscow a lesson—the result was a massive naval building program and a rerouting of the communist revolution, with the ultimate objective being changed.

The Death Merchant leaned back, glanced out the window in front of him, and watched the sun growing low in the Saudi sky. His face went hard. Had the United States and its Western allies learned any lessons?

NO—or we would not keep making the same mistakes, over and over, getting into similar crises and then being eternally surprised and shocked when the inevitable result occurs.

Camellion finished decoding the message from Courtland Grojean.

The entire message read:

The situation in the United States is extremely grave. Millions will possibly die on the East Coast; and the Middle West and the West cannot be ignored. Urgent that you report to Station Y in the New City as quickly as possible.

Smiling, the Death Merchant tore the slip of paper into many tiny pieces, got up from the table, went over to the open window, put out his hand, and let the wind catch the pieces.

Well, well, so Grojean was worried. Poor fellow. Millions had died before. Many millions would soon die, for only by Death could Life continue.

Camellion put on his sportcoat and wondered how the Company station would dispose of Mahmoud Khalil, whom Colonel Bahadu had wanted to terminate in the Jabal Arqā. It didn't matter. Khalil was no longer his concern. He had done his job. He had obtained the scrolls written by Judas.

He who has sinned, rebuke him!

He that crosses you—kill him.

The Good Book of Death—Verse One, Chapter One!

The Death Merchant left the room. He would be in New York City within twelve hours. First, he would radio Grojean.

APOCALYPSE USA! was very near. . . .